THE SECRET OF THE SCREEN

Borgo Press Books by S. Fowler Wright

Arresting Delia: An Inspector Cleveland Classic Crime Novel
The Attic Murder: An Inspector Combridge and Mr. Jellipot Classic Crime Novel
The Bell Street Murders: An Inspector Combridge and Mr. Jellipot Classic Crime Novel
Black Widow: A Classic Crime Novel
The Capone Caper: Mr. Jellipot vs. the King of Crime: A Classic Crime Novel
Crime & Co.: An Inspector Cleveland Classic Crime Novel
Dawn: A Novel of Global Warming
Dead by Saturday: An Inspector Cleveland Classic Crime Novel
The End of the Mildew Gang: An Inspector Cauldron Classic Crime Novel (Mildew Gang #3)
Four Callers in Razor Street: An Inspector Combridge and Mr. Jellipot Classic Crime Novel
The Hanging of Constance Hillier: An Inspector Cleveland Classic Crime Novel
The Jordans Murder: An Inspector Combridge and Mr. Jellipot Classic Crime Novel
The King Against Anne Bickerton: A Classic Crime Novel
The Mildew Gang: An Inspector Cauldron Classic Crime Novel (Mildew Gang #1)
Murder in Bethnal Square: An Inspector Combridge and Mr. Jellipot Classic Crime Novel
The Police and the Public
Post-Mortem Evidence: An Inspector Combridge and Mr. Jellipot Classic Crime Novel
The Return of the Mildew Gang: An Inspector Cauldron Classic Crime Novel (Mildew Gang #2)
The Rissole Mystery: An Inspector Combridge and Mr. Jellipot Classic Crime Novel
The Screaming Lake: A Lost Race Novel
The Secret of the Screen: An Inspector Combridge and Mr. Jellipot Classic Crime Novel
Three Witnesses: A Classic Crime Novel
Too Much for Mr. Jellipot: An Inspector Combridge and Mr. Jellipot Classic Crime Novel
The Vengeance of Gwa: A Fantasy of Prehistory
Was Murder Done? A Classic Crime Novel
Who Murdered Reynard? A Classic Crime Novel
The Wills of Jane Kanwhistle: An Inspector Combridge and Mr. Jellipot Classic Crime Novel
With Cause Enough?: An Inspector Combridge and Mr. Jellipot Classic Crime Novel

THE SECRET OF THE SCREEN

An Inspector Combridge and Mr. Jellipot Classic Crime Novel

by

S. Fowler Wright

Writing as "Sydney Fowler"

The Borgo Press
An Imprint of Wildside Press LLC

MMVIII

CONTENTS

CHAPTER I.

IT was in the August of 1929 that Evelyn Merivale had left Saxton Court to avoid a man whom her brother wished her to marry.

It was in February, 1930 that she returned home, having had an interesting experience as chauffeuse-secretary to Lady Barbara Dillington, inherited a sum of £20,000 under the will of Mr. Wilfrid Ralston—this being the residue of his brother's ill-gotten gains, after the provision of an annuity for their mother at Todmorden—and being in possession of a formula of an estimated value of one million pounds.[1]

In addition to these circumstances, she had met the man to avoid whom she had left home, and was inclined to revise her opinion concerning him (but we must not take that too seriously, for a woman may change her mind for a second time just as easily as a first); she had to look forward to the unpleasant ordeal of having some stitches taken out from around the top joint of her little finger; and she was sadly aware that her weight had increased by something over six pounds during her urban experiences, and that her days must now be saddened by the harsh discipline of a healthy appetite, if she were not to allow herself to commence the fatal drift that anchors at last in the port of the heavyweights—anchors and does not leave.

A consideration of these various circumstances inclined her to the opinion that things might have been worse, and she would have endorsed Browning's optimistic dictum as to the state of creation very readily as she ran the two-seater car (which she had bought last week on the credit of her expectations, and a reference from her solicitor, Mr. Jellipot) up the drive and heard the pigeons cooing on the frosty tiles of the stables.

She was a young lady of active habits, very little likely to become the author of a sonnet on mutability or anything else, but even

---

[1] See *The Bell Street Murders*.

she must observe the incessant changes of circumstance which are too gradual to be noticed while we are the centre of their occurrence, but which become disconcertingly prominent when we return from a period of absence, though it be only of a few months…

"Where's Foster?" she asked rather sharply of the strange man who came forward to open the garage doors as her car turned into the yard.

"Foster left, Miss, a few weeks ago. I don't know rightly why. I've been here a week come Monday."

"And what's your name?"

"Mitchell, Miss. Ted Mitchell."

"You don't belong to round here?"

"No, Miss. I've come over from Catesby. I was groom there at the Hall, and got sacked when they sold the stud."

"I see. Well, Ted, I shall want Gwen ready tomorrow as soon as breakfast is over. You'd better bring her round about nine."

"Gwen, Miss?" the man said vaguely.

"Yes. Gwen. The grey filly. I suppose she's—"

"Oh yes, Miss. But we don't call her that. We call her Ailsa. His lordship—"

"Yes. So he would. But she's Gwennow." She went on to the house, entering by a side door, and meeting Kate, the parlour maid, as she made her way to the front hall.

"Good afternoon, Kate," she answered the girl's pleased greeting. "Yes. So am I. Have my trunks come?"

"Yes, Miss, they came this morning. Mary's unpacking them now."

She made her way to the stairs, intending to go to her own room, but did not do so without another interruption. The footman, a lengthy youth burdened with the name of Christopher, barred her way respectfully to announce that his lordship was in the library, and had expressed a wish to see her immediately on her arrival.

"Then he'll have to wait till I come down," she answered, with a smiling quietness of voice which discounted the cool abruptness of her decision.

"Yes, Miss Evelyn, I'll tell him you won't be long."

Christopher had first come as boot-boy eight years ago, shortly before her father's death, when she, who was twenty now, had been of about his own age, and Cyril Merivale, now Lord Britleigh, had been ten years older. He was familiar with his master's alert impatiences, and the quiet independence with which from childhood she had always met them.

But she called him back now to say, "But I thought Lord Britleigh was up in town."

"He came back, Miss Evelyn, about half an hour ago."

"Very well…. What did you say, Chris?"

"There's a telegram for you in the hall, Miss. I thought, you might like to know."

"Very well. Fetch it along."

She wondered who could be communicating with her in such a way almost before she was home. It was only yesterday morning that she had agreed to return. But she was interrupted, as she was tearing open the yellow envelope, by her brother's impatient voice at the library door.

"Christopher, I told you to tell Miss Evelyn…. Oh, that you? Look here, Evelyn, I told him to tell you I wanted a talk as soon as you arrived. And there's someone on the telephone for you now. Someone who won't give his name."

"All right, Cyril. There's no need to fuss," she answered coolly, but in a fresh wonder at the atmosphere of excitement around her. She had thought to come back to the quietness of the country isolation of Saxton in the winter months, where she could forget the incidents of which she had been the centre. Not waiting to open the telegram further, she went on to the telephone.

"It's the police station at Hilton," she said, as she put back the receiver. "Inspector Combridge is coming to see me this evening, and doesn't want me to go out till he arrives, nor to mention whom he is when he calls. He'll be Mr. Smithson. I suppose he didn't mean I was to keep it from you! I wonder why he didn't ring up direct, instead of telling them to do it from Hilton."

"Perhaps he didn't want anyone listening in. They may do it more to the long-distance calls."

"But he must have called the station up from London."

"Then he must have wanted to speak to them, as well as to get the message to you."

"Yes. I wonder why. There must be something fresh to bring him down here. It looks as though I'd better have stayed where I was…."

"Well, there's something else I want to talk to you about. Vantons have refused to ratify your agreement this morning."

"Yes," she said quietly, "I know that."

"But I've only just come from the board meeting. How on earth…?"

She looked down at the now open telegram in her hand. "Mr. Jellipot has sent me the information. He is coming here to see me this evening.... Why did they turn it down?"

"If you come and sit down—"

"If you'll have the patience to wait for about a quarter of an hour."

"Very well. But it's an important matter. Reggie says—"

"You know I came back on your promise that you wouldn't mention his name."

"Yes, that was what he proposed himself. But this is business."

"So was the other with you," she answered, smiling. "Everything is. Anyway, this business has got to wait for half an hour. I'd better change while I'm about it, and then I'll talk till dinner-time, if you want to; and, if it's business, I expect you will."

CHAPTER II.

"I DON'T usually talk about what goes on at a board meeting when I get outside," Lord Britleigh began, when the conversation was resumed half an hour later, "but you've got a right to know, and, anyway, Jellipot was there most of the time, so you'd get it from him.

"To begin with, Blinkwell reported against it. He said it wouldn't work. The pictures don't last on the screen. He had Nichols with him, and Ramsbottom, and Groves, and they all said the same. The picture blurred and faded out in places almost completely."

"But you knew that, and Mr. Jellipot—and, of course, Professor Blinkwell had heard. We all knew that the screen was a fake of Wilfrid's."

"Yes, so we did, most of us, more or less. Though there's no saying how much each believed. But you see that didn't alter the fact. The demonstration *had* failed, and we were entitled to turn you down."

"You needn't talk as though it was me."

"Well, it is now. It's all yours under Ralston's will. And the formula's in your hands. You see, we'd done just what the contract required. There's been a scene acted before the screen, and the start of it photographed, and then it was left alone for a week, and they went back, and the key photographs worked well enough, and they picked it up on the screen but after that it came blurred in places, or almost blank."

"Yes. We knew it would. Have they turned it down finally because of that? Aren't they willing for us to show them how it can work?"

"They might be, or not. They didn't all agree on the board. But the point is that it's off now, and you're free to do what you like. And if it's all that you think, I dare say that Reggie and I—"

"I dare say you could. Did you vote for turning it down?"

"I didn't vote either way. I said that you, being my sister, and it having been left to you, I thought I'd better stand back."

"And you were to have put up a lot of the money if it had come off?"

"Yes. £75,000."

"I see. Cyril, you are clever. What I can't see is why the Professor wanted to turn it down. He knew well enough."

"That's one thing I want to talk to you about. Are you sure he hasn't got the whole thing up his sleeve? Because, if he has, there's only one thing to do, and that's to work through the night and have the papers ready to make an application when the Patent office opens tomorrow morning...of course, he may have done it this afternoon. But I scarcely think he would. He'd prefer it to date from the day after we'd sent the formal letter to Jellipot turning it down, he being in the position he is. It'll look queer enough at the best, but he'll probably say that it's his own improvement, working on Ralston's idea."

"I should think the formula in Wilfrid's handwriting could upset that."

"So it might. I can't say. We should know, one way or other, when the lawyers had finished drawing cheques on us to pay them for finding out. But the first question is, has he got it or not?"

"I don't see how he could. He might hope to find out. But I know that Wilfrid felt sure that no one could. I'm sure he hasn't got anything from me. I won't be rushed, anyway. Wilfrid thought that keeping it secret was better than patenting it till someone was really ready to take it up. I think it ought to be done as he wished. I'm sorry Vantons are turning it down. I should have thought they would have been glad to try it out further."

"I don't think it's any use expecting that."

"You don't want it to be."

"Perhaps not. But I mean what I say, all the same. Nichols wanted to go on, and cut you down in the price if it turned out right. He said a woman thinks a lot of a few thousands. 'Let her see the notes on the table.' That was what he said, before Jellipot came in. And Ramsbottom was inclined to go with him for once, which he doesn't often do. But the chairman—that's Levinstein—put his foot down. He said he'd rather be clear of it, bad or good. It had meant two murders already, and the men who were murdered seemed to be crooks more or less, and those who'd done them in couldn't be any better, and—"

"But the murders weren't anything to do with it. Not Dudley's, anyway."

"Well, he doesn't know that. No one does, except ourselves and as many as are in the secret at Scotland Yard. And, if you come to think, we don't really know why the Professor shot Wilfrid Ralston, whatever we may guess. And of course Levinstein hasn't the least idea it was he."

"Perhaps he thinks it was I, if he thinks it was because of this formula. I'm the one that's got it now, and the benefit of Wilfrid's will too."

"I don't suppose he thinks that. He's too shrewd. But he doesn't know what to think, and so he draws back. That's how he always would act in such a position. And the matter's too big, even for Vantons, unless we are all agreed. We were putting up half the money from the firm's account, and the rest from among ourselves. The real question now...."

The door opened and Christopher appeared to announce that Mr. Smithson had called to see Miss Merivale.

CHAPTER III.

THERE were two guests to dinner that night at Saxton. Inspector Combridge was persuaded to stay without difficulty. He mentioned that he had not come socially prepared, and that his car was waiting to take him back, but that was no more than a formality. When he was occupied professionally he did not care a straw how he was dressed, nor how those might be dressed who sat opposite to him. His mind was concerned with the question of how far he should talk to Miss Merivale in her brother's presence, and what opportunities there would be for a privacy which would not be significant in its exclusion, should he decide in that direction.

Mr. Jellipot was more reluctant to stay. He also was conscious of unsuitability of attire, to which he attached greater importance. He wished to be back at business in the morning, and he depended upon the last train from Hilton for his return, which left at 9:13 P.M.; he wished to see Miss Merivale only, and saw no reason for reticence on that point.

She was his client, and with her brother he had no business at all. It was only when he found that Evelyn had the Inspector already on her hands, and that gentleman, who saw the position, and had his own reasons for the proposal, offered to run him back in his own car, that he reluctantly gave way. They were both too cautious to touch on the subjects that held their minds till the dinner was over and coffee had been served in the lounge. There had been an unwary word from Evelyn during the dinner, when she had addressed the Inspector by that title, which might have meant some gossip in the servants' hall, but he had met the position with an instant adroitness, answering that he should be called an examiner rather than an inspector, and giving an impression that the title which she had been attributing to him was that of an Inspector of Schools.

But though there had, so far, been no direct allusion to the circumstances which had brought them together, the delay had not been fruitless, and these four protagonists of a drama that was behind them and in all their minds, and of another that was before them which they could not guess, were disposed to a larger measure of confidence than would have been the case without that preliminary intercourse.

Inspector Combridge, for one, had made up his mind that what he had to say to Evelyn Merivale might well be said also to her solicitor, and to a brother who, whatever difference might have divided them recently, could still be counted on (he thought) to put his sister's safety before any question of business interests, and her business interests second only to his own. He began immediately that they were freed from the danger of overhearing.

"You'll easily understand, Miss Merivale, that we learn things at Scotland Yard that we can't use, and sometimes in such ways that we can't say how we've learnt them at all, and if I'm rather vague in the warning that I've come down to give you tonight, I don't want you to take it less seriously on that account."

"Perhaps you'd rather speak to me alone? If so—"

"No, I don't think there's any need for that. What I say may be just as well heard by these gentlemen here; it's not much more than reminding you of things that you know already, and asking you to see what they mean.

"You know, because everyone knows, that we've arrested more people over the world in connection with the drug traffic—and more important people—in the last ten days than in the ten years before, and most people think we've been able to pull this off because of the work of the League of Nations, and the credit goes to Geneva, and we're content to let it, but Miss Merivale knows the truth. She knows that it all comes of what happened in an upstairs room at Number Thirty, Bell Street, about a fortnight ago, and that it's happening through information we're receiving from a gentleman we won't name, though I've no doubt you all know who I mean. It's a thing we can't talk about, and there aren't more than three of us at the Yard, except the Commissioner himself, who know all the facts. I don't mean that they don't know at the Home Office—of course they do; and at the Foreign Office, more or less; but what I'm really meaning is this: we can't speak, but Miss Merivale knows what happened that night, and I expect she's told both of you gentlemen, and, if so, you'll understand what I mean without my saying more than I should."

"My client," Mr. Jellipot answered with his usual precision, "has, I have good reason to believe, given me her entire confidence."

"It's one lower than that for me," Lord Britleigh followed, "but I'm not quite in the dark."

"Very well," the Inspector went on, choosing his words slowly, "then you can understand this. When a man's lost a large part of his income—when he made it in criminal ways, and when he gave it up to save himself from jail or the rope—and when he sees a bigger thing than the one he's giving up almost under his hand, he's not likely to stick at a trifle to pull it in. And you'll understand this too, that while a man's giving us information—and going on doing so— that's enabling us to lay the strongest gang of international criminals in the world by the heels, we can't act toward him just as we might like to do, even if we know he's a murderer (though I don't say we could have proved it in court, even if things hadn't been as they are), and we don't want anything to happen that forces us to run him in, nor that makes it look as though we're letting him run loose to do anything he likes. It's not quite an ordinary position. You're not in the dark as to where the danger lies. We all know well enough who shot Wilfrid Ralston, though we may have to guess, more or less, as to just why it was done, and we know that he would have treated Miss Merivale here in the same way. He made that clear enough."

"Yes," Evelyn answered, looking at her damaged finger, "he was quite clear about that."

"Well, he's not likely to have changed; and though he wouldn't do a thing like that quite openly, or send us cards for the stalls, he's quite cunning and bold enough to calculate that we couldn't easily move against him, everything being as it is, unless we had very clear proof. You've got to deal with a man who has wealth, ability, exceptional scientific qualifications, and no scruples at all."

"I have already," Mr. Jellipot remarked, "put this aspect of the position before my client, and it was the main purpose of my hurried visit here to night. I felt—and I have no doubt that you will agree— that the refusal of Vantons, Ltd., to complete the purchase, and the fact that Professor Blinkwell advised them to that effect, produces an acute and urgent position, where there was previously no more than a potential danger. But we may surmise, may we not, that there is some more specific reason for the warning which you have felt it necessary to give?"

"I am sorry," Inspector Combridge answered, "that I cannot be more definite; but I may tell you that when I telephoned that I would be here tonight I was not aware of the result of the board meeting this morning, though it is what I should have anticipated would occur. Would you tell us, Miss Merivale, confidentially, where the

16

formula now is? If it were known that it has been securely deposited—"

"It isn't deposited anywhere," Evelyn answered, "except in my own head. I've argued that over with Mr. Jellipot till we were both tired out. It was Wilfrid's own way, and he wasn't a fool."

"Still," said her brother, "he got shot. You don't want—"

"Not because of that.... You see, I've got the paper that he gave me—it's here in this bag now—and I've made a copy in case it got stolen or lost; but it'd be of no use to anyone without his explanations, which are not written at all."

"You mean," Lord Britleigh asked, "it's a kind of cipher? There aren't many of them that can't be read when there's a million at stake. I've told Miss Merivale, Mr. Jellipot, that the proper thing to do is to get a patent agent working on this through the night, and be ready to lodge the papers when the office opens tomorrow. I wish you could persuade her. She never would listen to me. If we did that, we should know where we are."

"It isn't exactly a cipher, Cyril. It's simpler than that, and a bit cleverer."

"Can I see it?"

"Yes."

She took from her bag a small piece of folded paper, a leaf torn from a pocket-book, on which there was a column of five letters, with a corresponding one of figures beside them.

The three men passed it round in silence.

"Professor Blinkwell had this in his hands for some minutes?" the Inspector asked.

"Yes, he did."

"Long enough for him to have memorized it completely?"

"Yes, I dare say. I couldn't have done it. It wasn't exactly a quiet time. But he may have been feeling differently."

The three men looked at each other doubtfully. It would have been an unusual feat of memory, but the Professor was an exceptional man. If he had remembered it, and had solved the problem, it would explain his attitude at the morning's meeting. It might make Evelyn's personal position more secure in exact proportion to the hazard at which the invention lay.

"You say it isn't a cipher, Evelyn?"

"No, not exactly. There are some things there that don't belong, and some that are in the wrong order; and some ought to be there that aren't. I should think it would be millions to one against anyone getting it all right. Probably lots more than that."

"And the key's only in your own head?"

"Yes. That's the place."

"And if you were to die, this thing, and all that it means, would be lost for ever?"

"I'm feeling quite well, thank you, Cyril."

"I dare say you are; but you've heard the Inspector warn you of the risk—the absolutely needless risk—that you're running. I should have thought, after what you'd been through—"

"Yes. You might. But, you see, it didn't work out like that. It was more like an insurance policy. If I'd had it all down on the sheet I'm not sure that I should be here now, even with Reggie turning up when he did and knocking the Professor flat with his shadow. I never thought bankers had any brains before that. You know, Cyril, while I've got this thing in my head even you might take a little more care to see that I don't go without my tea."

"There is a good deal of force in Miss Merivale's argument," Mr. Jellipot conceded. "The trouble is, as I've put it to her already, that it gets us no further forward. However safe the formula may be where it is now, it can't be turned into anything useful till it's known to those who can handle it."

"I don't want to keep it where it is," Evelyn answered. "I only want to be sure that I shall be making it known in the right way. It seemed simple enough till we'd got Vantons' decision. If they agreed to complete, I'd got to give it to them, and I meant to keep it in the safest way in the meantime. But I don't know what's best to do now, and I'm willing to listen."

"I don't really come into the discussion," the Inspector interposed, "except so far as the question of Miss Merivale's personal safety is at stake. On that issue I am bound to advise her to rid herself of the custody of the secret as promptly as possible, in whatever form, and in such a way that it will be known that she has done so in all interested directions. In the meantime, I can only tell you that they will take such precautions as are possible at the Hilton Station, and that I am always available. I strongly advise, Miss Merivale, that you should not go out alone in the meantime, and that you sleep in a room which is more than usually well secured. It might be advisable to have the grounds watched in the night, but, in that case, you should inform Sergeant Merritt of any patrol which I may be made by your own servants. I can't say more than that, and, if you'll excuse me now, I'll be getting back...or I can wait ten minutes if Mr. Jellipot has anything further that he wants to say to you tonight."

It appeared that Mr. Jellipot had. Mr. Jellipot had come over with the conviction that prompt action should be taken now that Vantons' decision had been given. He did not like being rushed. He was anxious to be back in town, but this was not a matter to be discussed while the Inspector was, so to speak, standing waiting at the door. Besides that, there was his promise to Sir Reginald. That gentleman had rung him up and had been urgent and explicit in the statement of his views on the position. Sir Reginald was an important man. Very important indeed. He could send enough business into Mr. Jellipot's office to keep him occupied for the rest of his life.

While he hesitated in his reply, Lord Britleigh, whose thoughts moved in the same groove, interposed: "I don't think we can spare Mr. Jellipot tonight, Inspector. I'm going to ask him to be kind enough to stay the night with us, and I'll run him up to town in good time tomorrow. You see, Jellipot. I want to come to business terms with Miss Merivale without any delay, and when a man's dealing with his own sister, and in a matter like this—well, you'll probably agree that her legal adviser ought to be somewhere about."

Mr. Jellipot said that he thought perhaps he had better stay.

CHAPTER IV.

"I WANT you to understand, Mr. Jellipot," Lord Britleigh began at once, when the Inspector had taken his leave, "that if this invention is all that it seems, I am willing to see it through, and to find any money that may be needed. If it's any good at all it must be worth a huge sum—a sum hard to estimate at this stage. It is only necessary to put through some preliminary demonstrations, and we might be in a position to get almost anything from the public that we care to ask. Sir Reginald Crowe wants to come in on the ground floor with me, and I've told him he can if you consent."

"So I have understood."

"Well, we reckon we're strong enough together to do all that's necessary; and to protect our own interests if any infringement should be attempted. As to terms, I look on it as a family matter, and I'm not talking to you just as I should if it wasn't my sister's. You must tell me what you think fair, and there mayn't be much difficulty over that. Not if we're both reasonable.

"But there's one thing we've got to face, which may have been rather overlooked, though it was behind a good deal that was said at Vantons' meeting this morning.

"We know that the demonstration proved a partial failure. It showed that Ralston had made a most interesting—indeed, an amazing—discovery, but it failed to show that it has the commercial possibilities that he claimed.

"Well, we know he said he meant it to be a fake, and he gave a good enough reason. We accept that. Personally, I believe it's going to prove all that he claimed. But we've got to face the fact that it isn't proved, and we've got to remember that he was one of the trickiest men that I ever met.

"We don't even know that he told Miss Merivale the truth, and we don't know that, even if his discovery was all that he claimed, that it hasn't gone to the grave with him."

20

"I agree with all that you say," Mr. Jellipot answered. "I have warned Miss Merivale that we may be dealing with something which will lead only to disappointment. But this consideration has led me to a rather different conclusion from that which you appear to have reached.

"I'm not alluding to any terms of purchase or option, to which I suppose you were referring just now. I hope we shall agree on those without undue difficulty, and I should advise Miss Merivale that she could not have her interests in better hands than in Sir Reginald's and yours.

"But when you propose an immediate patent application which involves a public disclosure of the formula as Miss Merivale had it communicated to her, I feel great difficulty in agreeing.

"If it should prove to be defective or incomplete in some adjustable way, we are simply inviting the successful competition of those who will be working upon it within a few hours of it being on the file.

"I see your point about Professor Blinkwell having had the document in his hands for some minutes, but I doubt that he could have memorized it in the time. I doubt very much that he attempted to do so, things being as they were, and it seems to be extremely improbable that it would be of any use to him if he did.

"There is another consideration that falls into the same scale. We've had a plain warning from Inspector Combridge that Miss Merivale is in danger at the present moment. That would be—I won't say impossible—but very much less likely if the Professor had got from her all that he wanted to have."

Lord Britleigh, an alert and impulsively restless man in most of the relations of life, had trained himself to a disciplined self-control, and to keep his judgment cool in the business issues which were for him of an almost sacred character. He said only, "What do you advise?"

"I suggest that the formula—the full correct formula as Miss Merivale believes it to be—should be written down by her, and sealed immediately. No one else need see it at all. It should be placed without delay in a bank strong-room, or in the care of a safe-deposit company. A reporter from one of the press agencies might be invited to be present. We want a publicity which will make it certain that everyone will know that she has relieved herself of its custody.

"Meanwhile, she will privately communicate it also, under suitable guarantees, to Sir Reginald Crowe and yourself, and you will subject the formula to such secret tests or demonstrations as shall be

21

conclusive as to its value and qualities, after which you can continue to use it as a secret process, or (more probably, if Mr. Ralston's opinion was sound) patent it simultaneously throughout the world."

Mr. Jellipot spoke quietly, as one who suggested rather than urged. Lord Britleigh, a good judge of men in such connections, renewed the opinion of his capacity which he had formed in the course of the Vantons, Ltd. negotiations. A good man. Not brilliant, perhaps. Not impressive. But careful, logical, sound. One who kept his head. A very good man.

He considered the proposal in a short silence which was long for him. He adjusted his mind to accept it. He said, "I dare say it's the best way. Anyway, if that's what you advise, I don't suppose I could talk Miss Merivale over. Not before morning.... There'd be one thing to the good. We could prove the date of the sealing, and if it were stolen in any way we might make it awkward for anyone who patented it after that. I don't know what the legal position would be, but it would be a card in our pack.... What do you say, Evelyn?"

Evelyn yawned, "I'll agree to anything that means we can go to bed now."

CHAPTER V.

MR. JELLIPOT, mild of manner and speech, and capable of eating a musty egg rather than dispute its age with his landlady, had been a man of war from his youth up. But he did not fight with his hands, living as he did by a law which was unfriendly to such methods of altercation. He was not used to giving battle on the physical plane, and the energetic precautions taken by Lord Britleigh to guard against a night assault upon his sister's security gave him a feeling of actual nervousness such as he would not have experienced had a client's fortune and reputation (and he valued the fortunes and reputations of his clients almost as his own) been staked upon his instant decision at some unforeseen development in the conduct of a legal action. In the atmosphere of the law courts, which most men hate or fear, he moved with the assurance of familiarity. Even of a High Court Judge he had no actual awe. His deference was the etiquette of routine. But the excitement which Lord Britleigh communicated to the hurrying servants, the clanking of door chains, and the squealing of seldom-used, superfluous bolts gave a sense of reality and imminence to the danger which Inspector Combridge had thought sufficiently serious to occasion his hurried journey to Saxton.... It is astonishing, in a large country house, how many points of insecurity may be discovered, how many people it contains who may be suspect.

Lord Britleigh left nothing to chance. He must see the fastenings of every window. He must question butler and housekeeper as to every servant that the house contained.

As to that, assurances were ready enough. Most of the servants had been there since his parents died eight—ten—years ago. He was generous in expenditure, and had the male lack of supervision which English servants prefer. So long as there was a surface efficiency, and his comforts were not neglected, they could waste almost as they would, and an Englishwoman desires to waste as a Frenchwoman to save. No, they said, there was no one lately engaged, except Ted Mitchell, who slept outside over the garage.

Over the garage? Outside the house? That was so much to the good. When did he come? Only this week? What references did he have? From Catesby, was he? Well, it was not too late to get through. Lord Britleigh must ring up Catesby Hall, getting little satisfaction therefrom. Sir George Rigglesworth was in town. There was no one there who could, or would, say definitely whether a man named Mitchell had been in employment there. It was a large establishment. Many men had been dismissed when the stud had been sold following Lady Rigglesworth's accident. Probably it was right. Anyway, would Lord Britleigh kindly ring up again tomorrow? Lord Britleigh would. Meanwhile, he must take satisfaction from the fact that the only servant of whom he was not sure was sleeping outside. Inside, all are safe enough. Dogs are brought from the kennels to roam through the house during the night, or to sleep on what mat they will. Christopher is to sleep at Miss Merivale's door. Would she like one of the maids in her room? No, she would not. Not even Mary. She is emphatic on that. She wants to go to bed, without all this fuss, which seems rather absurd.

Still, being alone in her room, and securing the window bolts, she is reminded by a careless movement of the state of a finger which is still bandaged. Perhaps she is glad to feel that her room will be watched during the night—both inside and out. She admits that Cyril is thorough, but she does wish that he wouldn't fuss. She can hear him now at the conservatory door, giving orders that the ladders are to be padlocked together.

It is no wonder that Mr. Jellipot, getting into a suit of Lord Britleigh's pyjamas, feels as though he were in a beleaguered castle destined for storm and massacre in the midnight hours.

He is wakened more than once by the sound of footsteps on the gravel path under the window. But there is nothing furtive or aggressive in the ponderous tread of P.C. Gunn, and he goes to sleep reassured, to wake to the fact that there is the faint light of a winter morning without, and that he, at least, has survived the night. Today they will motor up to town, and the dangerous secret will be placed where such things should be. Thinking contentedly of this, he dozes off again, and wakes late (for he had asked not to be called, preferring to avoid the unfamiliar ministrations of the household staff), and comes down late to breakfast to find Lord Britleigh (who had risen almost equally late) in a worse excitement than the night before. Miss Merivale had got up much earlier, and had gone out riding almost as soon as it was light. Not alone, surely? No, the new groom had ridden with her, or had followed her. It was not certain which. It was, he said, an old habit of hers to ride before breakfast. "Even in winter?" Mr. Jellipot asked, in some surprise. Yes, if the weather were fine and mild. But she would not be out for more than half an hour. She ought to have got back ten minutes ago. Confound all women. Meanwhile, it was no use not to have some breakfast themselves. The devilled kidneys, Mr. Jellipot would find, were quite good.

CHAPTER VI.

THERE are three methods of slimming which are reliable in their results, though in reverse proportion to their desirability. The first, which is infallible, is to encourage a quarrelsome temper. The second is to shun food, which is almost equally effectual, if it be done resolutely, and without those distressing lapses which we hope that Nature may be sufficiently good-natured to overlook. The third is to take vigorous exercise.

It is the least certain method of the three, and its effect is, unfortunately, to render us incapable of practising the two which are more so, but it is by far the most pleasant, and it was that upon which Evelyn Merivale had always depended to resist the adipose tendency which she inherited from a somewhat corpulent father. A horse and a tennis racket had been the weapons with which she had fought her foe, with no worse than a drawn battle as yet, though she must envy the unconscious ease with which her brother's restless energy maintained a figure to which he attached less importance than to the market fluctuation of his least investment.

She came down early, to resume the habit of the morning ride which had been broken by her five months' absence in London, and was delayed and annoyed to find that the new groom had saddled an ancient pony in place of the more skittish animal that she had ordered on the previous day.

"I didn't think Ailsa—"

"Gwen, Ted."

"Yes, Miss. I didn't think she'd be very safe to ride this morning. She hasn't been out much lately. She's not one that—"

"Oh yes, she is.... I'm not going to look silly going out on an old pony that I used to ride when I was ten. Besides, I want a good gallop. You'll just saddle my own horse as quick as you can. It's almost time to be back for breakfast now."

The man still hesitated, and she looked at him with more attention than she had done previously. He was obviously a groom. Obviously a man familiar with horses. Few men can live among them without their faces becoming somewhat equine in consequence. It cannot be observed that horses are equally influenced by their human companions. Their faces remain unchanged. If it be deduced that they are of the stronger or more independent character, it seems a reasonable conclusion.

But if Mitchell were an obvious groom, she yet felt that he was not quite an ordinary one. He spoke with respect, but with a tone which implied an equality which it did not assert. He had a control of grammar unusual among his kind, which was the more significant because he spoke without affectation, using the colloquialisms of the stable-yard. A rather small, spare man. One of habitually leisurely movements, as such men are, but looking of a potential activity. Not otherwise conspicuous. Neither young nor old. Neither dark nor light. He might have been a jockey once and have allowed himself an extra stone or two since he had retired from that ascetic occupation.

Now he went reluctantly to obey her order, while she followed him to the stable, where she was annoyed again to find him saddling a powerful, evil-tempered hunter which her brother sometimes rode, but which was never lent to a guest without warning of the reputation which it had acquired.

"What on earth...!" she began. "You don't think I'm going to ride that brute, do you?"

"No, Miss. I thought I'd better come with you."

"Then you thought wrong. Can't you understand that I know how to ride my own horse? If she's a bit fresh, I'll take her up to the downs by Millett's Hill."

The man made no further protest, and she was soon out on the road. The morning was fine, but dull. There was a slight mist. The road was soft and wet, but there was a white frost on the grass. She held Gwen in with difficulty till she had taken the turn to Millett's Hill, and then let her go as she would, confident in the steepness of the ascent which was before them.

Five minutes later, looking back from the height of the downs upon the roofs of Saxton, half-hidden by the pine wood which lay between, and well content with her mastery of a now-disciplined horse, she was annoyed to see that Mitchell was following up the hill. He had been distanced for a time by the mad gallop to which she had loosed the filly on the lower slope, but was now only a short distance behind, though he did not see her as she looked down upon him from where the road bent westward on the level height.

The man's persistence annoyed her. What was it to him? Did he think her a child? The obstinacy which underlay her habitual seren-ity hardened a resolution that he should not interfere in this manner. If she could get over the next two hundred yards before he reached the top of the hill she would be out of sight, and it would be strange if she could not dodge him successfully and be home again while he was still following an empty way. She knew the downs so well, every dip and curve. All that was needed was that first short burst of speed.

There was no difficulty about that. Gwen had been brought to a momentary docility by the steepness of Millett's Hill, but she had by no means exhausted the energy that had been accumulating during the last ten days in the Saxton stables. Finding to her own astonish-ment that her youthful exuberance was suddenly encouraged rather than checked, she raced forward over the open land, and it was only when Evelyn would have turned her left-hand, where the ground fell slightly, to take the homeward path at which she aimed that she real-ized she had roused that which she could no longer rein.

Well, let her have her gallop out. What did it matter on this open land? But suddenly she had realized that the old gravel pit, deep with the excavations of centuries (for gravel is hard to find in the chalk downs), was straight ahead, less than two hundred yards away. At the thought she struggled desperately, if she could not check her, to turn the filly from the peril upon which she ran. But though she pulled at the left-hand rein with all the strength that she might, and beat at the obstinate head, she did no more than rouse her mount to a swifter rush.

But Gwen had been that way before. She knew the gravel pit as well as her mistress, and had no intention of going over the edge just because she felt like a gallop in the cold, keen wind. Had Evelyn understood what was in her horse's mind she might have saved her-self, for she was a good enough rider. But she was occupied in her useless efforts to impose her own will on the rebellious animal. When Gwen swerved round at full gallop on the very edge of the pit she shot her rider into the air, and clear over the edge.

CHAPTER VII.

LORD BRITLEIGH was at the telephone. It was an hour now since Evelyn had ridden out, and he had forgotten the devilled kidneys in a real and rapidly increasing anxiety. He got through to Catesby Hall again, and was answered with better courtesy and fuller knowledge than had been the case on the previous night. Ted Mitchell had been employed there for about three months. Nothing was known against him except that he had not been popular with the other men. Sir George might know more when he returned. He had engaged the man himself. Lord Britleigh was conscious of some carelessness of his own. He should have made enquiry before. He had had the man nearly a week now. But he had applied so opportunely, just as Foster went. Someone had been needed to superintend the stables at once, and he had been very busy at the time. Probably it was all right. But why did Evelyn not return? He rang up the police.

It was an abortive activity, neither Lord Britleigh's worrying, nor the police, making any difference to what had occurred either for good or evil, and we may be better occupied than in observing him further if we transfer our attention to the quiet luxury of the Mayfair flat where Professor Blinkwell is still sitting at his own breakfast-table, though the meal is over.

His niece, Myra, is with him (Mrs. Blinkwell does not get up for breakfast), and they are engaged in a conversation too much of which we may have missed already.

The Professor liked talking to Myra. She was his only confidant. Even he was not always sure how much she understood, or what her thoughts might be, but she always listened with a pose of interest, seldom failed to reply with the right word, and could be trusted not to divulge anything that she heard. She was invariably good-humoured. Absolutely without conscience or honour. Extravagant almost to the point of insanity, even for a woman. Entirely dependent upon the Professor. Entirely confident that he would succeed in anything that he undertook, though there were a hundred against him, and largely competent to carry out anything which he might require of her to assist his plans.

"I don't see," she was saying, in a voice of enquiry rather than criticism, "why you should have let Inspector Combridge get alarmed if you're really doing nothing. It must make it more dangerous later on."

"No, I don't think it will. I think we can provide for that. I wonder whether you've heard the tale of the lion that roars in such a way that the deer don't know from which direction the danger threatens, and so run round till they fall into his jaws. I don't say how far it's true, but it's quite a good plan."

Myra Blinkwell showed no sign of interest in this illustration. She said: "I see they've got Burton now. There won't be many left. Not of those that count. I suppose it means a big loss to us, but I'm glad that that bank business is over."

"Yes," the Professor answered, "there's an end of that. It ought never to have begun. It is such silly subterfuges that cause suspicion and confirm it when enquiry is made. But they would have it their own way." He smiled slightly at his own thoughts. It was certain that he would never be under their direction again. A knife in the ribs, if they ever learnt the truth, was a more likely thing. But the danger was not great, and the jails of Europe are strong. He went on: "You needn't worry about the loss. It's only a stoppage of what I've been picking up, at the worst. I don't lose all that I've got.... I reckon I shall be the richest man in Europe in about three years."

The words were said with a quiet confidence, and Myra knew him too well to doubt that it would be as he said.

"I suppose you're thinking of this screen invention?"

"Well," he answered, "perhaps. But not only of that. Don't you see that the drug traffic must start again, and everyone in it that had any brains cleared out from Tokyo to New York? Don't you see that all the connecting links have been broken away? Those that are left are just running round like a headless fowl."

"You mean you'll be the head of it all when the present trouble dies down?"

"Yes," he said quietly. "I think I may. There are things less likely than that.... I am going to see Simpson today. I want a new overcoat for the spring."

Having finished breakfast, he spent a short time in his private laboratory—which was on the floor above that of the residential flat which he occupied—and then a somewhat longer period with his confidential secretary in an office on the floor below. It was a peculiarity of his business habits that these apartments were entirely separate. His laboratory was in charge of a chemist of international repute and unimpeachable character, but who had never entered office or residence, nor been encouraged to any intimacy with the secretary, whose "confidential" position, while appearing absolute, even to himself, was of a very circumscribed character. He had charge of the Professor's investments and financial operations. He knew his principal as a man of somewhat unusually trustful character, who had made large sums by always following the advice of his business associates, who gave it in gratitude for the brilliance of the Professor's scientific assistance to their common objects. He dealt also with the Professor's correspondence and obligations in connection with the directorships and other offices which he held. He knew his master as a forgetful man who would often overlook his appointments if he were not reminded of them.

Having dealt with the morning's correspondence, or, more accurately, having ascertained that there was nothing with which the secretary could not deal for him, and having left that gentleman dictating rapidly to his stenographer, the Professor took a taxi to Oxford Street and called upon his tailors, Messrs. Burrows and Simpson, to order the overcoat which he would need in the coming spring.

He was received by Mr. Simpson (Mr. Burrows had died of acute alcoholism about three years ago) with the deference due to one of his most affluent customers, and was asked if he would kindly step upstairs to the private fitting-room which Mr. Simpson reserved for those who had the honour of his personal services.

Being alone there, the manners of both men changed. The Professor said briskly: "You'll understand, Mr. Simpson, I've come to order an overcoat. Put the measurements down as they were last year, and cut it to that. I'll call in next week to have it fitted, and you can make any adjustments then. I shall be about ten minutes. Not longer. Don't go down, or let anyone come up, in the meantime."

The Professor knew that he could trust Mr. Simpson, who was indebted to a certain gentleman of his introduction for a sum of £5,000 which it had become suddenly very urgent to find when the premature decease of the generous and careless Burrows had caused enquiry by unsympathetic executors into the partnership accounts. Mr. Simpson paid the quarterly interest on the loan with punctuality. He knew that it could be called in at any time at a month's notice, and would be difficult to find. Perhaps difficult is hardly the word. The matter had never been mentioned between him and the Professor since he had come to his rescue with such opportune liberality.

The Professor ordered his clothes from him, and settled promptly, not questioning the charges made. He bought quite a lot of clothes. He was a man who dressed carefully. When he ordered clothes, he usually came upstairs and passed into a small closet at the back of the fitting-room. The end of this closet was a door. Having closed and locked the one behind him, the Professor inserted a key into this one, and entered an office, the address of which was 17, Bruton Street, and which was occupied by Messrs. Tonbridge and Wilkinson, turf commission agents. If this firm had attracted the notice of the police (which it never did), it might have been observed that it had a considerable correspondence, but no callers. Its business was conducted entirely by post. If the firm preferred to work with its doors locked under these circumstances, there was no law to prevent it. In fact, no one knew.

The doors were locked against the possibility of the Professor's unexpected appearance from a cupboard door, which might have occasioned astonishment to a casual visitor. The four occupants of the double office which constituted the first floor of 17, Bruton Street worked in the constant knowledge that the actual owner of the firm might appear at any moment in that unusual manner. They knew that when he did so, he expected to find an exact order in the arrangement of the correspondence, an accurate summary of all that had occurred since his last visit, which was to be written up at least three times daily or immediately that there should be anything of importance to record, and that it was quite likely he might appear among them only to glance over his report, and to retire in a space of minutes, perhaps without a word of enquiry or recognition to those who served him.

But on this occasion the four men observed his presence without interrupting the game of bridge at which they were occupied. His own desk, where the report should have lain, was bare. A heap of about fifty letters were piled on a side table unopened.

The Professor observed these indications of inactivity without surprise or dissatisfaction. He went straight to the heap of letters and turned them over rapidly.

"James," he said, "you can go over these now, but don't answer *anything*. I don't care what it is, or from whom, I'm not going to get you caught in this trap, any more than I mean to find myself in it. But you needn't lose any more time—no, don't stop the game, there's no hurry—but I want you to start a new index of the men who are still free—that ought to mean those who've got more brains than the rest—and when you've done that you can destroy all the old records; we shan't need them again."

"Do you mean the cash ledgers, sir?" asked Billy Stitson, a slight, pale-eyed man, who had been a bank clerk until it was found that mysterious deficiencies of cash occurred in his vicinity as naturally as a dog barks.

"Yes. *Everything*. After a new index is made."

"What about the current account, sir?"

"What is the balance now?"

"Six hundred and thirty-two pounds, four shillings, and sixpence."

"You can divide that. Let me have the chequebook."

The Professor wrote some figures at the right-hand foot of the cheque. After that, they knew that their four signatures would be sufficient to withdraw the balance. The figures were always different, and they could not discover the cipher, if such it were. They had signed an instruction to the bank, which had been in blank, and which the Professor had afterwards completed. They could not guess that it had not been sent to the bank at all—that the Professor had destroyed it within an hour. He had no intention of being connected with the account in any way, and he knew, in any event, that what they signed they could cancel. But there had been tens of thousands of pounds going through the account of a business of which they were represented as the sole partners. He had calculated accurately that they were not of the kind to agree upon a perilous course. The mystery served its end. They had been like prisoners confined by an open door which they believed to be barred, but which they dare not try.

Now, with the papers announcing fresh arrests every week of the members of the international gang of which they were four among hundreds of subordinate tools, they believed, perhaps rightly, that they owed their safety to the promptness with which the Professor had shut off all communications with other members of the gang; and they supposed that he had secured himself by the exercise of the same measure of astuteness. Now he evidently thought that the storm would soon have spent its force, and that preparations should be made for the time when operations could be resumed...on what basis, or under what superior controls, they were not likely to ask, and it was very certain that he would not say.

CHAPTER VIII.

TO sit on a short and slanting trunk of a thorn that juts out of the side of a cliff about ten feet below the edge is an uncomfortable thing to do; it is particularly so when you are able to look down upon a sandpit bottom thirty feet lower, and it is a discomfort which does not diminish as the hours pass; yet it is not so bad as sitting precariously among the thorny branches that project therefrom.

As the hours passed, Ted Mitchell became an authority upon the first of these experiences, and Evelyn Merivale gained an exceptional competency to expound the second.

It is due to Ted Mitchell's chivalry to observe that he had descended voluntarily to the position he occupied, whereas that of Miss Merivale had been thrust upon her. Whether he would have proved of a sufficient generosity to accept the thornier seat must remain a conjecture only, for the exchange was too perilous to attempt.

When the groom had looked over the edge, and had observed Miss Merivale to be suspended precariously in midair, in an attitude too undignified to be more than vaguely indicated here, it is due to him to observe that he slid down to her rescue without considering the possibilities of recovering his own position. Having bestrode the trunk, he had succeeded, with sufficient difficulty, in assisting her to a comparative safety, but to do more was impossible.

Regaining her mental, almost as soon as her material, balance, Evelyn had endured the discomforts of her position for the first hour in the expectation of a speedy rescue. She remembered with some satisfaction that her absence could not fail to be promptly observed, and to excite an exceptional alarm, for which the formula would be responsible, however little it might have to do with her actual predicament. Search, she concluded, would be swift and thorough. The horses would return to the stable, with an obvious inference. She had a good voice, which she alternated with that of her companion in announcing her location.

But the hours passed, and nothing else did, till the midday sun looked down upon a most uncomfortable pair, the monotony of whose position was only broken by an occasional creaking sound from about the thorn tree roots, or a little scatter of soil from the same place, suggesting that it might be inadvisable to put the strain of movement upon a support which already considered itself sufficiently burdened.

Two circumstances combined to produce this unfortunate interlude. The scene of consternation and bustle at Saxton Hall was all that Evelyn could imagine or desire. The horses had returned in the way that horses are expected to do under such circumstances. The fact that no one had observed the direction in which she had ridden would not have long delayed the exploration of Millett's Hill and of the downs beyond. The trouble was that William Pickthorn had (or was almost sure he had) observed a lady riding upon the London road. Or it might have been a man. And whichever it was would fit the case, and he was quite willing to concede that there might have been another man (or woman) either before or after. Very likely indeed.

Added to this, Lord Britleigh recalled to mind the suspicion that he had already felt regarding the character of Ted Mitchell. Had he not remarked the sinister cast of his countenance to—well, perhaps not aloud, but certainly to himself? The suspicious circumstances of his too-recent, too-careless engagement were very naturally remembered. Lord Britleigh recalled a man with similar eyebrows who was of a very active dishonesty.

Obviously, he had led his mistress into a kidnapping trap upon the London road. A moment's holding of her rein...a rush of men from the hedge...perhaps the threat of a gun, if she should call for help...the waiting car into which she would be so quickly hustled... she might be already at the destination which Professor Blinkwell had prepared for her undoing. At the best, it must mean the surrender of the formula, and the loss of the fortune which he regarded as at least likely to be hidden therein. At the worst—Evelyn could be a very obstinate girl—torture or even death might be the conclusion of this lawless outrage. Best and worst are not the actual words that entered Lord Britleigh's mind. He was a brother, not without natural affection; but a fortune, vague but possibly enormous, cannot be regarded lightly, even in comparison with the well-being of a young woman of the same parentage as oneself. Her death would, of course, be the occasion of sorrow, and (if possible) of vengeance also; but if she should prove to be of so exemplary a fortitude, well—must not there be some satisfaction in a villain's overthrow?

—in a great stake saved? Saved? Are we sure of that? Is not the formula in her head, and there alone? Oh, folly of woman! Most reckless folly that would go riding with such a stake in hand after the warning of the night before!

Folly, also, Lord Britleigh owned, not sparing himself, that had failed to guard her with a bolted door, that had failed to watch Ted Mitchell until he should have established his integrity.... Now, if Evelyn disappeared, or were coerced or outraged in whatever form, it might well be, as Inspector Combridge had so plainly hinted, that the Professor would not appear in it at all, or that the proof would be too weak to justify action by police who were in such difficult relations with him already.

From all these maddening thoughts what conclusion could there be? Cyril Britleigh was a businessman. He was not one to let emotion become a hindrance to action, or its futile substitute.

The London road must be searched, and every crossroad, every byway, every coppice that might shelter a potential crime, every vacant house and barn and hovel for fifty miles along its course, and for twenty on either side! Never before, perhaps, had such activity been roused so swiftly and over so wide an area as was waked that morning, as the news flew by phone and wire, stimulated from Saxton on the one hand by the £1,000 reward which Lord Britleigh offered, with a seeming recklessness of amount, for his sister's rescue, and on the other by the urgency of a Home office that realized the importance of preventing that which might develop into a particularly embarrassing crime.

Such was the position when, at 11:12 A.M., Sir Reginald Crowe's car ran up the long chestnut drive which is the front approach to Saxton Hall (we have not seen it in daylight previously, except from the stable side), and Sir Reginald himself disappeared into the house, and came out again three minutes later, looking grave enough, but with an obvious purpose of his own, as he jumped back into his seat and said curtly, "Millett's Hill, Piper, and let her out," and it was just thirty-three minutes after that that the car returned with two additional and exhausted occupants.

"I knew you were barking under the wrong tree," Sir Reginald said, in simple explanation, as soon as he was assured that Evelyn was receiving the attention that she needed in the comfort of her own room, and Lord Britleigh had given the necessary instructions for calling off the hunt which had been aroused by his misdirected energy, "when I heard that your theory was that Mitchell had led Miss Merivale into a trap—"

"I don't see how you could tell that. The man seems to have done well enough, and I suppose I've got to give him something besides the sack, though he'll get that for sure. I don't see how he could claim the full reward—"

"Meaning the thousand? No, you'll give that to me."

Lord Britleigh gazed at his friend in a moment of astonished silence. He hadn't thought of that. He didn't like the idea at all. But he knew Reggie Crowe well enough to be aware that if he'd made up his mind to have that cash he himself would waste brain tissue in vain to oppose the sacrifice. He actually pulled a chequebook from a drawer at his hand. He wrote rapidly as he said, "Oh, well, if you look at it like that."

The Chairman of the London and Northern Bank said that he certainly did. "It's the right way, isn't it? It'll just come in handy for Evelyn and me when we start furnishing."

"When you...? I thought we'd agreed that that idea shouldn't even be mentioned to her again?"

"Well, I'm not mentioning it to her, am I? I thought she might mention it to me next for a change.... But why have you got your knife into Mitchell so deep that you can't pull it out when you find you're cutting up the wrong carcase?"

"Because of what I learnt not fifteen minutes ago while you were up Millett's Hill. It appears that he's no better than a hired spy. They found out after he left Catesby that he'd been stationed at Catesby Hall by Billington's Agency—you know, the firm that specializes in divorce cases—to watch a guest who often visits there. You can guess what he's doing here."

"So I can. He's been costing me just eight pounds a week to Billington's since he came. I fixed that as soon as I knew that Evelyn might be coming down here, and had him on the spot ready for any help he could give."

"If you'd only told me!"

"Yes, I suppose you can say that. But in these cases the fewer who know, the less chance there is that they'll tell where they shouldn't. Anyway, that's the man. So, you see, I knew that he wouldn't lead her into any trap, and I knew she wouldn't choose the London road. She always rides for the downs. So I saw that, though it might be as bad as anything you could fear, it couldn't be just how you supposed, and I went the right way to find out what it was."

Sir Reginald folded the cheque and pocketed it as he spoke. "You should give a pony to Mitchell. He's earned that, and he'll think he's been well paid. He doesn't think in thousands like you and I."

Mr. Jellipot, during this time, had stood somewhat aside from a drama in which he could take no leading part, but in which he was too directly interested to leave till the curtain fell. The morning engagements at his London office, which had seemed so imperative the night before, received no better attention than the facilities of the telephone would allow, leaving a distracted clerk to instruct counsel as best he could upon the defence of a procedure summons while the essential papers which he required were locked securely in Mr. Jellipot's private safe. But with the knowledge that Miss Merivale was rescued, and had retired for renovation and rest to the peaceful securities of bath and bedroom, the urgency of these matters resumed their routine prominence in his mind, and inclined him to Sir Reginald's side of an argument which followed the pocketing of Lord Britleigh's cheque, and in which both these gentlemen appealed to him for support.

"I tell you, Cyril, Evelyn's shown more sense than any of us in this matter more than once already, and when she says that it's quite safe in her own head it's no more than we ought to see without being told.

"I dare say Blinkwell's rather a slimy snake, and I've no doubt he'd steal it from her if he could, and if he thinks it's as good as we hope it is. But I should think he's got his plate about full enough just now with this trouble with the police, and having gone as near as he has to getting a rope round his own neck. I shouldn't think he puts his collar on now without feeling a bit choked.

"You've all got the idea that he's a kind of superman because he's been part of a big gang, but I've met his sort before in commercial deals, and when you've pricked them and let the conceit out, it's surprising how small they look. I should say he's busy saving his own skin, and finds it a full-time job.... Look at all the nonsense this morning, and that thousand quid that this fussing's cost you now; besides that it might have been Evelyn's life as well if you'd left her much longer there while you were combing the London Road."

"It's always a mistake," Lord Britleigh replied, "to underrate your opponent. Evelyn says she's not really hurt. It couldn't do her much harm to be run up in your car, and we should get the thing done and know we'd left nothing to chance. Inspector Combridge gave us a hint that her life isn't overly safe, and that's more important than feeling a bit fagged."

"Look here, Cyril, we're not going to quarrel. I hope we've both got too much sense for that. But it isn't any fear of Evelyn's life that's making you propose this. It's a fear that we're risking a million-pound invention a bit more than we need.... I don't underrate anybody. I showed that when I hired Mitchell to be ready to look after her if she came down here, and I had a bigger difficulty than you might think getting Foster to give up his job to make way for him. I don't believe in running any risk you can avoid, and when I take a thing up at all I've got rather a habit of seeing it through. But I'm not going to say a word to persuade Evelyn to come to London this afternoon after the morning she's had.... I'll run Jellipot up, and we can talk business on the way, and phone you in the morning, when we've all had time to think things over and quiet down, and then we'll decide what to do."

"And meanwhile, Evelyn's here, and all the responsibility's left on me."

"Oh, no, it's not. She's quite old enough to take care of herself. Besides, you can lock her up in her room if you like and watch the door and windows, and the chimney pot too, if you want to make it a thorough job, and telephone Hilton police station if anything bigger than a sparrow comes within fifty yards.... And, besides that, you've got her solicitor here, and you can take his advice, and I'm not sure that that isn't the best thing we can do! I'll tell you what, Cyril, we'll let Jellipot decide this. He's the right one to speak for her, and if he says he thinks we ought to take her to London this afternoon I won't say a word more."

Lord Britleigh agreed to this, seeing it to be the best bargain he was likely to make, for if Mr. Jellipot were against him also he knew that his own influence over Evelyn (assuming it to exist at all) would be powerless against the united opposition of his two guests.

Mr. Jellipot hesitated in his reply. He had very urgent business awaiting his return to town, which must be neglected further if he were to give his time that afternoon to the semi-public depositing of Miss Merivale's formula, according to the programme on which Lord Britleigh's heart was set. He was anxious to conciliate Sir Reginald Crowe, whose position as Chairman of the London and Northern Bank rendered him of enormous potential importance to a solicitor of good reputation, but only moderately successful practice, and he was honestly doubtful of his client's fitness for the expedition after the physical and mental ordeal through which she had passed. He hesitated in a scrupulous mind as to how far the first two of these considerations might deflect his judgment. But their weight remained, to which was added a doubt as to whether Lord Britleigh, in his anxiety to get the formula deposited somewhere other than in his sister's brain, might not exaggerate the immunity to herself which might result from that course of action.

39

"I doubt," he said cautiously, "whether we shall lose anything by leaving this till tomorrow. As a matter of fact, we have not obtained my client's consent to the course which we are now proposing.

"I gave this matter a good deal of thought during the night, before our minds were disturbed by what seemed to be the evidence of very sudden hostile action, which we now know to have been otherwise occasioned, and I came to the conclusion that nothing but a full and public disclosure of the secret formula could bring any real security to my client.

"This would have to be through the medium of the Patent Office, or otherwise it would involve the abandoning of any monopoly or control of the invention, and its value would be substantially, if not entirely, lost. We agreed last night that it might be a mistake— that is, a commercial mistake—to patent it unless or until we have demonstrated its possibilities to our own satisfaction, and can feel some confidence that the patent for which we shall apply will be sufficient in description and accuracy of detail to give it the full protection which an invention of such importance requires.

"To this extent, it appears to me that my client's financial interests are in opposition to those of her personal safety, and that that position will continue, even though the formula be deposited in other hands, so long as it remains an unprotected secret which she may be supposed to have memorized accurately.

"Feeling this as I do, I feel also that these arguments should be placed before her without haste, and when she is in a condition to consider them coolly, and the decision as to whether there be an immediate application for a provisional patent must be left entirely to her."

As Mr. Jellipot thus formulated his own conclusions for the hearing of others, they became more decisive in his own mind, and his hesitation ceased.

"And that," Lord Britleigh commented, with his usual brisk cheerfulness, "is one in the eye for me, if not two; and I'm not sure that you're wrong. So we'll let Evelyn rest, and order the car."

40

CHAPTER IX.

THERE was a short space of silence as Sir Reginald's limousine glided swiftly forward on to the London road with the silent smoothness guaranteed by the four-figure cheque which had changed hands when it had been purchased a few months before.

Mr. Jellipot, elderly, precise, learned in law, and entirely master of himself, felt that it was for the banker to commence conversation, or to remain in the quietude of his own thoughts. He looked with respect upon a man who had come by a succession of able audacities to a position of wealth and power while he was still young. He knew—all the world knew the tale in one form or another—how he had made a fortune in the Lancashire cotton boom, quarrelled with his bankers, and then obtained control of a majority of their shares, by which means he had become the Chairman of the Board. And in that position he had extended the operations of the bank in a spirit of audacious enterprise, until it had become one of the leading powers in the financial world. Those who discussed the powers of the English banks had ceased to speak of the big five. It was the big six today. And he had not reached this position by following in the footsteps of his predecessors. He had introduced a new spirit to the banking world....

"Jellipot"—Sir Reginald broke the silence with deliberation—"I want you to tell me what this invention is, and I want your honest opinion as to whether it's a genuine proposition. I want you to talk frankly, and you needn't be afraid of damaging your client's interests. You know what my feeling to Miss Merivale is, because you've been informed of why she left home, and the conditions under which she had come back. Perhaps you realize that she is destined to become Lady Crowe rather more clearly than she does herself. But, quite apart from that, we are going to give the thing a thorough try-out, and if it proves a success it won't make any difference what you may have said to me now."

"Well, Sir Reginald, I think you know the facts up to this point about as well as anyone does who's left alive, except perhaps Professor Blinkwell. Of course, I can give you a personal opinion for what it's worth."

"But that's where you make a mistake. I know practically nothing. You must remember that the help I gave the police was in connection with the Professor's drug-dealing activities. I'm not one of the Vanton crowd. All I've heard about this invention is from Lord Britleigh and Miss Merivale, and—just general talk. I never met either of the Ralstons. I want you to explain it just as though you were putting the proposition before me for the first time on Miss Merivale's behalf, and had made up your mind that it would be best to take me into confidence without reservation."

"If I were in that position," Mr. Jellipot answered, "I should have to commence by asking you to adjust your mind to accept the possibility of an invention which sounds enormously improbable—almost as much so as the idea of wireless telegraphy must have been to those who were first approached to support it with the capital which was essential to its demonstration."

"Consider that done."

"Mr. Wilfrid Ralston claimed that he had invented a substance the surface of which retained an impression of everything that was reflected upon it, such impressions not being normally visible—indeed, how could that be when so much would be reflected upon it?—but anyone who first had a picture before his eyes of the commencement of anything which had been previously exposed before it could then watch upon its surface the development of the scenes that followed.

"Subject to two conditions—the cost of production, and the permanence of the records—it is evident that such an invention must be of enormous commercial value. It opens the possibility of the same screen offering a number of different films simultaneously to one audience, and it would make it possible for people who entered at different times each to begin at the commencement of the one in which they were interested."

"It is just that point," Sir Reginald interrupted, "that makes the whole idea sound so fantastically improbable. How could it be possible that a number of people gazing at the same surface at the same time should see different pictures? Do you tell me that one man would see a continuous picture upon the screen, and that another, who had entered a few minutes later, would be seeing an earlier stage of the same picture following the first?"

"I confess," Mr. Jellipot replied, "that the same idea occurred to myself as demonstrating the absurdity of Mr. Ralston's claim when he first consulted me, but on that, as on other points, he was able to give me a simple and convincing answer. Indeed, it was one that warned me against the folly of a too-confident scepticism, by showing me that an equal wonder becomes no more than a commonplace when we are familiarized with it. He pointed out that there is exactly this quality in the reflections of common glass. It is not merely that we can look into a mirror, and see, as it were, round the corner, but that two people, standing in different positions, do, in fact, see different pictures on the same part of the surface; just as a man looking down on a dark stream at night will see the shining reflection of the moon making a line of dancing silver upon the waves, while to another man, standing twenty yards away, the water which is bright to him would be dark and invisible, and that which was dark to the first would be of a shining beauty to the second."

"There is, of course, no exact parallel—"

"No. It is no more than an illustration which warns us to be cautious in scepticism.... Mr. Ralston gave Vantons an option to purchase outright for a million pounds, one of the conditions being that he should demonstrate his invention to the satisfaction of one of their directors, Professor Blinkwell, which he partially did, but with the important qualification that the impressions received by the screen which he erected at his brother's house in Bell Street were not of an enduring character. His own statement, before his death, was that this limitation was deliberate, and arose from the fact that he had less than entire confidence in Professor Blinkwell's good faith, on which point we cannot say that his distrust was without cause.

"As it was, the screen retained a record of the events which took place before it sufficiently long, and fulfilled the conditions under which they could be recovered, sufficiently to enable Miss Merivale to discover the manner of Wilfrid Ralston's death.

"Speaking with the frankness for which you asked, I can say no more than that, and that the formula which he placed in Miss Merivale's hands was explicitly represented by him to be one which, when placed with the apparatus he had constructed in the hands of a sufficiently qualified chemist, would ensure that his invention would not be destroyed by his own death.

"There remain the questions of whether he was misleading Miss Merivale, which I think unlikely, or was deceiving others, and perhaps himself, as to whether the impressions which the surface of his invented substance receives are of a permanent character or will fade away within a short period.

"In the latter case, I suppose—subject to the correction of others who may see possibilities which I have overlooked—the invention may be little more than a very curious toy."

Sir Reginald had not listened to this lucid statement so closely that his mind had been incapable of any separate activity. He was a man of bold and rapid decisions, or he would not have reached the position which he now held. As Mr. Jellipot concluded his statement, he gave his verdict upon it, and the programme of future action on which he had resolved.

"That's quite straight, Jellipot, and quite clear. I agree with you that we shouldn't patent anything at present till we know better what we can do, and how.

"I don't attach so much importance as Lord Britleigh does to this idea of his that the formula should be publicly deposited, but it can't do any harm, and we'll let him have his own way about that.

"Miss Merivale had better come up to town for that tomorrow, and we'll have something about it in the evening papers that Blinkwell won't overlook. I don't think we've really got much cause to worry about him, or at least I shouldn't but for Inspector Combridge's warning, which we can't disregard.

"In any case, it's foolish to run any risk that we can avoid, and she'd better stay quietly at Saxton, and not go out alone till we've got a valid patent, or let all the world know that we've thrown it up.

"The really urgent thing is for us to have a first-rate man that we can trust on the job, and for her to communicate the formula to him, so that he can get to work. I can find the right one for that.

"As to Miss Merivale's interest, you can arrange the terms of sale with Lord Britleigh, and I'll agree. I'm taking a half-share. But I know that you and Britleigh'll fix up a fair deal, and I never waste time.... You look after Miss Merivale's interests and you'll please me. And I dare say you can make a guess that you'll have no cause to regret that.... And here we are, and when Piper's dropped me here he can run you on to your own office."

Sir Reginald extended a hasty hand, and was out of his car and up the steps of the bank before Mr. Jellipot had commenced what would doubtless have been a suitable and assenting answer.

CHAPTER X.

DURING the following week Sir Reginald Crowe had opportunity for congratulating himself both upon the accuracy of his judgment and the soundness of the business programme which he had outlined to Mr. Jellipot.

Evelyn had been motored to London by her brother, with a police car following a hundred yards in the rear, and had returned with the same escort after depositing a copy of the formula, with its solution, in the safe deposit vaults in Porchester Street. She had been unmolested, as he had foretold, and though the precautions which Lord Britleigh adopted for her security may have been in themselves sufficient to guarantee her immunity, they did not alter the fact that no one appeared concerned to disturb it.

They barred doors which no one attempted to force; they patrolled roads and examined ditches which were empty of human life, except the harmless aborigines that the district knew.

And meanwhile, in the laboratory that Sir Reginald had secured from certain customers of his bank (with an overdraft sufficiently serious to ensure a willing subordination to their banker's wishes), one of the best chemists in Europe was studying the apparatus and materials which had been removed from the room which Wilfrid Ralston had occupied in Bell Street in the light of the formula with which Miss Merivale had supplied him.

The agreement which had been negotiated by Mr. Jellipot between his client and her brother had been as satisfactory a document as Sir Reginald had anticipated. Everything went according to plan, and Professor Blinkwell gave no sign of being further interested in the invention which he had advised Vantons to decline to buy.

The police, who continued to give the Professor's movements a fatherly, if not a friendly, oversight, could not observe that he was engaged in any nefarious activity. He was living a leisurely, well-ordered life, spending much of his time in the domesticity of his own flat, with regular visits to his laboratories, and to his secretarial offices on the lower floor: he attended occasional board meetings at Vantons, and at the premises of some other firms in which he was financially interested. But these firms were of good reputation His telephone calls were recorded, and proved to be of a similar innocence. His correspondence was examined, and contained nothing of a suspicious character, either from his pen, or addressed to him.

The secret information which he had supplied had led to the arrest of the heads of an illicit drug organization which had spread its tentacles to the limits of the civilized world, and the seizure of their stocks to an estimated value of nearly two million pounds; but even in the reports of these arrests, and the prosecutions which were following at several foreign capitals, he appeared to have lost interest. He was observed, at a public restaurant at which he dined, to turn indifferently from a report of such proceedings which was a prominent feature of the newspaper which he had requisitioned, to the pages of sporting and financial news.

It seemed that, having abandoned the perilous means by which he had profited in the past, and escaped the fate which had fallen upon so many of his associates by his own secret betrayal, he had made a wise decision to live a quiet, law-respecting life, content with the ample means which he had accumulated and the honourable business activities with which that wealth, and his genuine scientific attainments, had contrived to provide him.

In this peaceful condition of mind it was not surprising that he spent some time with an obsequious tailor when he called to have an overcoat fitted. It was known that he had always been particular about his clothes.

CHAPTER XI.

"I THINK," Evelyn said with decision, "it's rather worse than being in jail."

"If you knew a bit more about jails than you're ever likely to do," Lord Britleigh answered, "you wouldn't say anything quite so silly as that."

"It's rather worse, because it's a jail I needn't be in if I'd got enough sense or enough courage to open the door, but I'm letting myself be cooped up here—"

"Well, you can't blame me for that. I'd have got it patented right away, and there'd have been nothing in your head that the whole world didn't know."

"I didn't say I was blaming you. But I'm not going to stand it any longer for anyone. I've stayed about the house now for nearly three weeks, never moving anywhere without two or three people hanging round, and if I go into the grounds there'll be Mitchell following ten yards behind and P.C. Gunn looking over the hedge. If I go on this way for another week I shall make an elephant look slim."

Lord Britleigh was unmoved by his sister's petulance. His restless energy enabled his natural slimness to remain in friendly concord with the indulgence of a good appetite. He helped himself to another egg as he answered: "I'm glad to hear they haven't dozed off. I thought things might be getting a bit slack. But if you're so keen on getting thin, you'd find a jail's the right place for that too."

"Well, I'm not going to stand it any longer. I'm going to ride over to see the Priestleys tomorrow. I think it's all been a silly farce from the first."

"I don't think I should do that. From what Reggie told me yesterday we're very near the point when we shall know whether it's a washout or not. I dare say another week will see it through."

"I dare say it will, but I'm going out tomorrow whether or not."

Her brother looked his annoyance, but a long experience had told him that he could not turn her when she used that tone. Besides, he did not really think that there could be much danger in such an expedition. The quietude of the last three weeks had not been without its influence on himself also. It did seem that "Much Ado About Nothing" might be the proper title for the elaborate precautions which he had organized for her protection. All the same, it was silly to run a risk. Just Evelyn's usual obstinacy.

"I suppose," he said, "you won't go alone? You'll take Mitchell at least? It wouldn't be quite fair to Crowe not to do that, seeing what he's paying him to keep you in sight."

"Very well," she said, half reluctantly; "if you put it like that, I suppose I'd better take him along."

"And don't tell everyone for ten miles round what you're meaning to do."

"Cyril, I'm not quite such a fool as that."

Evelyn strolled away to practise cannons in the solitude of the billiard-room, and Lord Britleigh hurried out to his car, for he had a board meeting in the City which he would have trouble to reach with his usual punctuality.

After a time Evelyn went out to the stable yard, seeking Mitchell, who appeared with his usual watchful celerity.

"Ted," she said, "I may want Gwen tomorrow. I'm thinking of riding out in the afternoon."

The man looked startled, but did not venture to voice the protest which was in his eyes. "Yes, Miss," he said. "About what time will it be? I suppose you'll want me to come along?"

"I don't think I'll say what time till I'm ready to go.... Yes, you'd better come, though I don't suppose I shall go over a cliff again."

The man said no more, but the next day, as lunch was over and she was getting ready to go, she received a message that Mitchell wanted to speak to her. He said that Gwen had gone lame.

Evelyn descended to discover the truth for herself in a natural scepticism, remembering Mitchell's previous reluctance to saddle the filly for her use. She found a little group from garage and stable-yard surrounding Gwen, and a veterinary surgeon who had been summoned to examine the injury.

It appeared that the horse had been turned out into a paddock during the morning for exercise, with two others of more sedate character, and had received a kick from one of them whose morose musings had been disturbed by her friskiness. There appeared to be no doubt that this was a genuine account. A boy testified that he had seen the event. The vet did not doubt that the injury had been caused in that way. He was emphatic that the animal could not be ridden.

Evelyn said, "Then I'll take the car." A chauffeur went to prepare it.

Ted Mitchell looked worried. "May I come, Miss?" he asked.

Evelyn was about to refuse. She could drive her car without help, and, besides, Mitchell belonged to the stables, not the garage. But she remembered that Sir Reginald was paying for this man to guard her—more, in fact, than he was receiving for the stable duties that he performed. She knew that Reggie felt a concern for her safety probably greater than that of her brother, and with a larger responsibility, because it was he who had supported Mr. Jellipot's arguments for delaying the patent application, from which her danger (if it had any reality) continued. She knew that he would be annoyed, under any circumstances, by the escapade on which she was resolved. She asked, "Do you understand cars?"

"Yes, Miss. Well enough."

"Well, it doesn't matter. I shan't want you to drive. You can come along."

The day was fine. The sun shone in a sky of misty blue. A south wind was soft and warm with the promise of spring. The road ran high over the downs, and then dipped into a long hollow, with a fir wood close and dark along the left-hand side and rough unfenced land rising upon the other. It was a lonely road at this time of year.

Evelyn stayed with her friends, with whom we have no concern, for a couple of hours, being longer than she had meant to do, but the enticements of tea and talk were too powerful to be resisted until she saw that it was becoming dusk without. She had resolved to be back before dark. She rose resolutely, and a few minutes later was driving rapidly home.

The car was the open two-seater in which she had arrived at Saxton a few weeks earlier. Mitchell sat at her side. When they came to the long low dip in the road, where the fir wood was now on their right hand, the sun had set, though the sky was still red over the open land on their left.

At a point where there was a gate that entered the wood, an empty lorry stood across the road, as though waiting to enter. As it stood, there was not sufficient space to pass behind it, and Evelyn slowed and hooted as she approached. The driver backed the lorry, swinging it half round, so that there was room for her to get by.

As they passed, Mitchell gave a casual glance at the driver, whose face was turned from him, and the next moment he became alert and watchful. He half rose in his seat to look back. He saw the lorry resume its position across the road.

"What's the matter, Ted?"

"I'd go careful if I were you, Miss. There's something I don't like, but I may be wrong."

"Fast or slow?"

"Not too fast to see what's ahead."

His hand went to his hip pocket, and Evelyn saw a pistol across his knee. His glance swept the rough rising ground on their left hand. Evelyn's eyes followed his, but there was no sign of life, for which she supposed he had looked.

His sharp exclamation brought her eyes back to the road. Several men stood across it.

Her hand went to the horn, giving a warning blast as her foot pressed the accelerator. She meant to drive through. It seemed the best chance to her.

Mitchell gripped the hand brake without ceremony. "Steady, Miss!" he said sharply. "There's a cable across the road."

So there was; a strong cable, which would have wrecked them, and perhaps cost their lives, had they rushed upon it. But their assailants did not seek to wreck them. Hence the cordon in front of an impediment which was intended to hold them up.

"We'd better try the side, Miss. It's the one chance. There's no going back." As he spoke the men were no great distance away. They saw the car stop, and began to run forward.

"Do you think we could?" she asked. She had never driven a car over such land as that. But she did not wait for an answer. The car swung round as she spoke, and, as she did so, there came a shot, and then another, from the five men who were running up.

"Be quick, Miss. It's not us, it's the tyres they want." He looked as though he would have liked to have the wheel in his own hands, but there was no time to change seats.

The car bumped over a ditch which was not wide enough to detain its wheels. It lurched up the bank. It jerked and tumbled its way over ground as unlevel as the sand dunes of a stormy coast, and with a rougher, harder surface than they. Every moment Evelyn expected to overset the car. It was impossible to make any great speed, or to guess what it might be. Ted Mitchell saw the speedometer needle swinging madly backward and forward around the dial.

The men had left the road when they saw the way by which the car sought to escape. They were running toward them at a slant.

The ground became more level as they advanced, looking to the eye to rise with a gentle smoothness. There was nothing smooth about the way that they bumped and swung and were thrown about as the car put on speed, but they had less fear of being overtaken. Their pursuers were close on their track now, but may also have concluded that there would be little chance of shortening that separating distance if they should continue to rely on their own legs. They stopped, and began to fire again. Louder than the shots there came the sound of a bursting tyre.

"We've got to run for it now, Miss." As he spoke Mitchell stood up in the car. He fired three times, taking deliberate aim. It was a long range for such a weapon as his, but a loud exclamation of pain told that one bullet had found its mark.

They jumped down, and began to run up the slope. But there was no further pursuit. The men appeared to accept defeat and disappeared.

Half a mile of a pace that varied from a quick walk to a run brought them to the main road, where they were soon able to solicit successfully the hospitality of a passing car. But Ted had expressed a confident opinion that the danger was over before that.

"They had to be careful how they shot, Miss. They didn't want to hurt you. They'd have had orders to get you alive. They mightn't think it was good enough when they found I was shooting back. But it wouldn't be only that. When they found we hadn't been caught in the trap, they'd be in a hurry to get clear away. They'll know they won't have much time before the roads'll be watched for that lorry for a long way round. I wish I'd noted the number, but I expect they'll be altering that."

Mitchell had been able to describe the lorry well, and it was easily identified with one which was found next morning abandoned in a coppice ten miles away. It had been bought for cash at an auction in Birmingham a fortnight before, and its transfer had not been registered. A keen-eyed constable observed a bloodstained stone, which confirmed the fact that one of the assailants had received a wound; another picked up the bullet which had punctured the tyre—or it may have been one that had missed its mark. But these clues led to nothing.

The episode was of no final importance, except in the further proof it gave that Ted Mitchell was a man to trust, which had been sufficiently demonstrated previously. Sir Reginald gave him a cheque for one hundred pounds, and was not sure that he had not been rather mean. Ted gave the police a very accurate account of all that had occurred. He said, with truth, that he had not seen any of the men with sufficient clearness to describe them, nor to identify them if they were caught. The light had not been good. He had thought that the lorry driver had deliberately kept his face turned away, as was likely enough.

He sent a similar report to the principal of his own agency, but he added a postscript thereto:

> P.S.—I thought the driver of the lorry was very like Wally Piler, but I may have made a mistake. I always thought he was a man we could trust. I expect I was wrong, but I thought you ought to know. Anyway, I thought of Wally when I saw him, and that'll tell you the kind of man that he was.

Mr. Billington acknowledged the receipt of this report, but about the postscript he made no comment. It does not follow that it was undigested in his own mind.

CHAPTER XII.

"IT looks," Sir Reginald said, "like an audacious effort at compromise."

"It's about the most confounded cheek that I ever heard," Lord Britleigh commented.

Inspector Combridge did not dispute these opinions, but the document interested him in its criminal aspects rather than in those of commerce or manners. He said that it was blackmail, thinly veiled, but of an unmistakable quality.

Mr. Jellipot hesitated to agree. He took up the letter which Sir Reginald had received, and which had brought the four men together at the banker's office, and read it again with a care that weighed the implications of every word:

Dear Sir,

I understand that Lord Britleigh and yourself are now interested in the development of the Ralston invention, which was refused by Vantons, Ltd., on my recommendation, and with Lord Britleigh's approval, we both being members of the board of that company.

It seems reasonable to assume that Lord Britleigh has received later information which has caused him to alter his opinion of the nature or genuineness of the discovery which Wilfrid Ralston claimed to have made, or of the possibilities of its commercial exploitation.

Following my own lines of investigation, I will say, frankly, that I have seen reason to modify my views in the same direction.

I also consider that it is in Miss Merivale's personal interest that the invention should be patented at the earliest possible date.

I am prepared to join forces with Lord Britleigh and yourself to achieve the objects indicated by the expression of my views in the above paragraphs, on the terms that the patents shall be taken out in our joint names, and that I shall own a moiety of such patent rights as we shall acquire. On these terms I am prepared to give you the benefit of my own experiments, and the support of my continued advice and assistance, for which, as you know, I am accustomed to receive very substantial fees.

Should you reject this offer, I would ask you to bear in mind that it has been made, and that it may, or may not, still be open to you in fourteen days from this date.

Yours faithfully,

Elihu Blinkwell

Sir Reginald Crowe, Bt., O.B.E.
London & Northern Bank, Ltd.
Head Offices, E.C.4

"I don't quite see," Mr. Jellipot said cautiously, "how you can call it a blackmailing letter. It was sent quite openly to Sir Reginald. It wasn't even marked private. And it is capable of quite innocent constructions."

"Yes," Sir Reginald replied, "and the other kind. And since Miss Merivale was attacked last week in that dastardly way, and we all know by whose agents—"

"But," Mr. Jellipot reminded him, "we have no proof whatever."

"It's a lie," Lord Britleigh interpolated, "to say that I approved his report. I declined to vote either way. And, besides, I hadn't his responsibility. I hadn't undertaken to investigate and report to the board."

"It certainly goes beyond the fact on that point," Mr. Jellipot agreed, with his usual precision.

"It seems to me, gentlemen," the Inspector said, "that the most important point to consider is the object of sending such a letter.

There's one thing certain. Professor Blinkwell isn't a fool, and, not being a fool, he couldn't have thought that you'd agree."

"You mean," Lord Britleigh suggested, "that he wrote it so that it could be produced, perhaps to clear himself, at a later date?"

"Yes, perhaps. Or it might be that he wanted you to remember it later, when it wouldn't be equally safe to send. He's looking forward to a future position, when he thinks you may be more in a mood to deal, so that you'll know in advance what his terms are, and you'll be going to him, instead of him coming to you, which it might be dangerous to do then without implicating himself."

"That would be such a position as he might anticipate if he were to be successful in kidnapping Miss Merivale at a second attempt?" Sir Reginald asked, his mind being more concerned for Evelyn's safety than for the commercial or criminal aspect of the matter. "You don't think this letter means that he wants to abandon more violent methods and come to a business deal? You read it in an opposite way?"

The Inspector did not reply directly. He said: "We've got to remember that Professor Blinkwell's a very clever and subtle man. He didn't write that letter with the idea that Mr. Jellipot would be sending a draft agreement round for his signature by this time tomorrow."

"I suppose, Cyril," Sir Reginald asked, "you're quite sure that Evelyn's safe now?"

"She was quite safe when you got this letter. She was quite safe when I left Saxton two hours ago. It'll be her own fault if she isn't now."

"You don't think she'll try going out again?"

"No. We made a deal about that. You know Evelyn wants to be present at the demonstration we're to have to prove the success of the invention, which we're expecting to fix for some time next week? Well, I promised her she should come to that if we had to have a regiment lining the road, if she'd promise me she wouldn't leave the house before then. So we fixed that up definitely."

"I expect she's had about enough of going abroad," Sir Reginald suggested. He couldn't easily think that Evelyn would make a bargain of that kind unless it suited herself. Actually, she had as much right to be at the demonstration as any of themselves without asking anyone's leave, so he said.

"It isn't quite like that," Lord Britleigh replied. "She doesn't know anything about where we're experimenting, or when it's likely to be. Mr. Jellipot agreed with me that the less she knew about these matters the better, in case they did get hold of her by any trick, and she agreed that she'd better not know."

"As I, being her legal adviser, was fully informed," Mr. Jellipot began, and Inspector Combridge, who had been listening keenly, broke in rather abruptly to ask, "How many people know about this arrangement?" He knew that the greatest danger was that Miss Merivale should be lured out by some lying tale. But Lord Britleigh was able to reassure him about that.

"No one knows anything except Mitchell, and I've told him confidentially that it won't be till next week, and perhaps not then. Evelyn's promised not to go out without him, and I've told him not to take any written authority, even from myself or one of you. I've told him that he'll hear it from my own mouth, if at all.... And if anyone writes or telephones that she's to come at once because her great-aunt's dying, or any nonsense of that sort, she won't go, she'll let the police know at once.... After failing the way they did, any-one'd have to get up early to kidnap her now.... If you ask me what that letter means, I should say that Blinkwell feels he's been bowled middle-stump, and that's his last squeal. He mayn't have much hope, but a bit's better than none He may think we'll give him a corner so that we can end the strain."

"You certainly seem to have taken all possible precautions," the Inspector agreed. "It isn't easy to see how anyone can get round them. But I'd like a word with Miss Merivale myself, all the same, if you don't mind We mustn't forget that we're dealing with a very clever man."

Sir Reginald gave instructions at once that the telephone operator should get through to Saxton Hall. "Ask for Miss Merivale herself. Say that I—no, just the London and Northern—or say that Mr. Jellipot wants a word with her." He did not wish to alarm her, or whoever might take the message, with the detective's name, and he remembered just in time the condition on which she had returned to Saxton. Would she consider that he had broken it if he should ring her up? He had no intention of exposing himself to such an implication. It was Evelyn's turn to wait for a voice that she would not hear. But, like so many human precautions and ingenuities, it was a wasted wisdom. Christopher answered the call, then Kate, and then Mary, with the same tale that Miss Merivale could not be found. It was only when Christopher's voice answered a second time in response to the urgent impatience of the enquiry that any definite information came through: "Miss Evelyn left, sir, about half an hour ago."

"*Left!* How do you mean? Did she go by car?"

"I don't know, sir. Peters said she'd gone out."

"Did she go alone?"

"I don't know, sir. Shall I find out?"

Sir Reginald paused with the receiver in his hand. "Britleigh," he said, "you'd better take this on. You know your staff best. All I've been able to learn yet is that Evelyn went out half an hour ago; nobody seems to know where or why."

Lord Britleigh took the receiver in an impatient hand. "That you, Christopher? No, of course you wouldn't. Is Kate there? Then she'd better speak." He turned to the room to say: "She's the only one there with any brains, and they'll never burst her head." But as he did so, he heard her voice. It was evident that the servants were grouped round the telephone at the other end.

"Kate," he said, "send Christopher at once to find out how Miss Evelyn left, and whether anyone was with her. In particular, whether Mitchell went, and, if not, whether he knows anything about it. While he's doing that, ring up Hilton police station, and tell them Miss Merivale's gone out, and you don't know where. Tell them you've told us, and Inspector Combridge is with us here, at the head office of the London and Northern Bank. Then, when you've got Christopher's report, ring us up again." Lord Britleigh put down the receiver, after instructing the operator to connect immediately that Saxton came through, and Sir Reginald got the operator again to add that the line was not to be impeded with other calls. "So that," he said, "is what the letter meant."

"Yes," Inspector Combridge answered, "it looks that way. He hasn't lost much time.... Can I get through to the Yard on another line?"

Sir Reginald directed him to a telephone in the next room. The three men who were left sat waiting for the further news that the next minutes must bring.

"I can't believe," Lord Britleigh said irritably, "that Evelyn would break her word. Besides that, she wouldn't be such a fool. Not after the lesson she's had. We agreed that *whatever* message she got she'd treat it as the trap which it would be sure to be.... That trick's too old to catch anyone but a mug.... Not when you're on your guard.... I expect we'll hear it's all right when Kate comes through again."

"Yes," Sir Reginald answered, "I hope we shall." He spoke as one who was engaged with his own thoughts. He remembered how he had rescued Evelyn once before at a moment of deadly peril with no better weapon than a projecting shadow upon the floor. He could not hope that such fortune would come again. Yet, underneath the keenness of his anxiety for the girl he loved, unadmitted to his own mind, an excitement of adventure stirred which was not wholly unpleasant, and a sanguine hope, born rather of his own temperament than the probabilities of the position, that this might be the beginning of such events as would lead him to the end he would....

The Inspector was quickly back, having been able to say all that was needed in a few words. He had a rather grim look on his face as he thought of the possibility that he might yet bring Professor Blinkwell to his natural end. He had learnt that his use to Scotland Yard was a finished thing. He had given all the information that was required or expected from him. And the Yard would keep faith. From his past connection with the drug traffic, from the separate incident of Wilfrid Ralston's murder, he had nothing to fear. The wealth he had won, by whatever means, he could enjoy as he would. The past was a closed book. But if he should err again, the Yard would close the handcuffs upon his waists with a particularly cheerful click.

As Inspector Combridge entered the telephone bell rang again, and Sir Reginald picked it up, only to break out impatiently: "New York coming through? Didn't I tell you...? I don't care what it is. Let Mr. Matthews take it. Yes. Tell him to do what he thinks best. But he's not to disturb me.... Yes, sell or hold as he thinks best.... Anything over forty-five.... It's a Saxton call that I want.... Yes. Put it straight through.... Here you are, Cyril."

Lord Britleigh took the call. Punctuated with his explosive incredulity, the tale came through clearly, simply, bafflingly enough. Half an hour ago—or a bit longer by now—Miss Merivale had gone away in a large saloon car which had come straight into the yard. She had said nothing to anybody, before or at the time, but she must have been prepared to leave, for she had gone out and got into it as it arrived. It had had no occupant but the driver. Ted Mitchell had got in beside him. It had driven away at once, turning west. There was no doubt about that. There were three witnesses.

Mr. Jellipot's brains had not been idle because he had been content to listen and let other men talk. "It looks," he suggested, "as though they've managed to deceive Mitchell into thinking it's we who have sent."

"Yes," the Inspector agreed, "there's not much doubt about that."

"It may look that way to you, but if you build on it you'll go wrong," Lord Britleigh replied obstinately. "Mitchell couldn't make such a mistake. My instructions were too clear. Besides, he knew that it was at Bastover that the experiments are being tried. He knew

THE SECRET OF THE SCREEN, BY S. FOWLER WRIGHT

where he'd have to drive. And I'd told him he'd have to drive himself. He was the only man I should trust. He'd know something was wrong the second they got out of the gate and turned the wrong way. It isn't as though they weren't all on the alert.... No, it's absurd."

"If you'll excuse me, gentlemen...." The Inspector rose, and left without further words.

"We'd better go down to Saxton and see what we can find out," Sir Reginald suggested briskly. "There's no need for us to start the hunt. The Inspector will have done that before we could get into the street."

He glanced down at Professor Blinkwell's letter, which was still before him. "I'd better answer this now." He decided that Blinkwell was not a man to be influenced by anything except fear for his own skin. He was not one with whom to make terms.

He took a sheet of his private notepaper from the rack.

> Sir Reginald Crowe has received Professor Blinkwell's letter, to which there is no reply. He does not desire to communicate with him now, or at any later time.

Underneath these lines he made a rapid sketch of a gallows from which a man hung in a limp way. He could draw with a facile pen.

Such defiance might not be wise. Inspector Combridge might have advised that the letter be left unanswered. But it was by such audacities that Sir Reginald had come to sit where he did.

CHAPTER XIII.

THE events of the fortnight that followed Evelyn's disappearance may be briefly told, being barren of result, however full they may have been of suspense and excitement as the days went by.

The car in which she had left Saxton was traced sufficiently far to disclose that it had not been driven in a direct way, so that there was little clue to its destination. Its make and colour were settled with some approach to certainty. Its number, even, had been taken by an alert and half-suspicious constable, and proved (of course) to be false.

The activities of the police force of the whole county, supported by a populace which had been stimulated with the offer of a reward of one thousand pounds (increased to five thousand at the beginning of the second week), produced nothing but false reports and abortive theories.

Professor Blinkwell may, or may not, have been conscious of the thoroughness of the supervision to which he was subjected, but he gave no sign of disquiet, and no suspicious circumstance could be recorded against him. His correspondence was minutely examined. He was closely and continuously shadowed. He neither received nor issued any letter which was not of a transparently innocent kind. He went out to his usual directors' meetings; he went to his barber's on his usual day. He bought an umbrella. He ordered a new suit for the coming spring. He dined at home. His telephone conversations were few, and of such a character that it was a waste of time to record them. He wrote no more letters to Sir Reginald Crowe. To connect him with Miss Merivale's disappearance under such circumstances appeared to be an impossible thing.

The only person in the United Kingdom who appeared to be unexcited and unalarmed was Mr. Billington, the urbane head of the Agency which had supplied the services of Mitchell to Sir Reginald's order. His confidence in Ted Mitchell was (he said) too great to allow any doubts of Miss Merivale's safety to disturb his mind.

Meanwhile, the demonstration at which Evelyn should have been present was successfully held. A proposal to defer it until she should have been traced was abandoned on Inspector Combridge's advice. He thought that the announcement of that result, and the subsequent patenting of the process, could not be done too promptly, nor be too widely known. It might force Miss Merivale's captors to show their hand. If they had been persecuting her in vain to reveal it, they might even release her, recognizing that it could no longer be of any value to them.

With the taking out of the patents, the whole romantic history of the invention was disclosed to an eager press, and an enormous publicity resulted. It seemed impossible that, under such circumstances, and in face of a reward of such magnitude, any corner of England could continue to conceal her longer.

It was on the tenth day that the whole story was released to the Press. On the fifteenth, after a prolonged consultation at Scotland Yard, Inspector Combridge telephoned to Professor Blinkwell at 11:30 A.M., and announced his intention of calling upon him during the latter part of the afternoon. The message was so worded as to assume that the Professor would make it convenient to keep the appointment. Its vaguely minatory character, and the interval before it would take place, were intended to create the maximum of uncertainty and, perhaps, fear in Professor Blinkwell's mind. If he were guilty in conscience let him have the pleasure of speculating as to what might have been found out.

CHAPTER XIV.

PROFESSOR BLINKWELL received the Inspector with his usual affability, offering him the comfort of a low chair at the fireside of his private study.

Seating himself on the opposite side of the hearth, he opened the conversation without waiting for his visitor to explain the object of his call.

"You know, Inspector Combridge, that I am willing to give the Home Office all the assistance which I undertook, as I have shown already. I might, indeed, as I consider, have done much less, and still left you without cause for complaint. If you have still more to ask you may find that I am prepared to assist you further, but do you think you are treating me quite fairly when you come here in this open way?"

"I haven't called about that matter at all."

"No? Well, of course I'm pleased to hear that, but it doesn't alter the position materially, does it? I mean as to the danger to myself, and the breach—I don't want to put it offensively, but there it is—of the agreement we made. I can't help thinking that unless it be a matter of extreme urgency—"

"But that is just what it is."

"Yes? Well, perhaps I'd better hear about it before I say anything more. But the interval between your letter and the time of this appointment hardly suggested that to my mind."

Inspector Combridge was not easily disconcerted, and he had come with the expectation of a difficult interview, but he felt that it was first blood to the Professor, and that he was scoring in a quite legitimate way.

It had been agreed that the invaluable (if not exactly voluntary) information which the Professor had been supplying, as the price of his own immunity from criminal prosecution, should be communicated with an elaborate obliquity, and that the police should do nothing to direct suspicion upon himself. The Inspector was conscious that this condition would not have been absent from his mind had he actually been engaged upon the pursuit of the drug traffic organization which the Professor's betrayals had enabled them to paralyse, if not to destroy. As it was, it had not been present at all. Yet the danger to the Professor might be the same. He saw the possibility that there might still be powerful interests at liberty which would have both the will and the means to avenge the loss of their comrades' liberty and their own financial disaster if they should guess their betrayer. Suppose that he should hear of the Professor's murder tomorrow, would he be able to acquit himself of a breach of faith and honour which would have led directly to that catastrophe?

Well, anyway, it was too late to regret that now, and inopportune to consider it; he adjusted his mind to open the subject which had brought him there, as the Professor spoke again.

"Being in a very natural error regarding the probable subject of your call upon me, I had thought it best that we should be alone, but Myra my niece, you know—was engaged upon some rather urgent work, and, with your permission...." He waved one hand toward a littered desk at a far corner of the room, and with the other he touched the bell.

"I am not sure that the matter which I have called to discuss may not be one on which you would prefer to be private."

"Not from my niece, Inspector. Apart from that one subject, in which I have always desired that she should be involved as little as possible, I have no secrets from her."

Inspector Combridge, not being a fool, observed a stage management which he was obliged to admire, though he had no doubt of its artificiality. He recalled the part which Myra had played in the banking operations by which the drug traffic receipts of the gang had been directed to their final goal. Innocently? Well, perhaps. Anyway, she was in the room now, displaying the dark opulence of her half-Hebrew beauty, and offering a hand which sparkled with several rings.... She went to her own desk and resumed the correction of the galley proofs of the Professor's forthcoming book on *Some Problems of Atmospheric Pressure, and a Deduction Therefrom*, which had been the recreation of his scanty leisure during the last two years.

"And now, Inspector, tell me what I can do to help you."

Inspector Combridge, determined not to be overridden as to the tone of the interview, answered with an abruptness which he had not previously intended, "You can find Miss Merivale."

The Professor looked mildly startled. "Of course I've heard of her disappearance. Everyone has. But as to finding her for you....

Isn't that a little out of my sphere? Now if she were a trace of arsenic or a volatile gas...." He smiled somewhat, and then adjusted his face to match the Inspector's unresponsive countenance. "But it isn't a matter on which to joke. Myra and I have both been interested, and I may say anxious—at least Myra has. It's been the first subject for which we have searched the papers every morning at breakfast. Personally, I have felt sure you would find her. I have a great confidence in the police force of this country. As a matter of fact, your failure has cost me a diamond ring. I bet Myra that you'd trace her before the end of last week."

"May I suggest, Professor, that it was a bet that you were not sorry to have to pay?"

"Well, I didn't lose any sleep," the Professor admitted readily. "I should have had to buy it sooner or later, anyhow. Myra had set her heart on the ring.... But I wish you'd tell me straight out, Inspector, what your theory of Miss Merivale's disappearance is, and how you think I can help."

Inspector Combridge, conscious of the direct brevity with which he had spoken, and of the sea of words with which he had been submerged, had some difficulty in accepting silently the implication of this request. But he answered as directly as he had done before: "We have no doubt that Miss Merivale has been abducted, nor that it was done with the object of acquiring her knowledge of the Ralston process. That object has obviously failed. The process is now patented, and may be known by all who are sufficiently interested to obtain a copy of the specification. I am offering no bargain—I am making no terms with the criminal concerned—when I mention the fact that, in view of the position which has now been reached, and that that object has failed, if Miss Merivale were returned uninjured and in good health it is possible that little more would be heard of the matter. Apart from that, there is a large reward to be earned."

"Yes, it is a substantial amount. I am not exactly a poor man, Inspector, but I should be pleased to bank it. The question is: how can I help you, however willing I may be?"

Inspector Combridge looked hard at his antagonist's impassive face as he said confidently: "By releasing her, as I have no doubt that you can."

"I do not pretend to misunderstand you. You are accusing me of being responsible for her abduction. If I were guilty, I should obviously make no admission, and it will, therefore, be a waste of words to deny it, as, of course, I do. But don't you think you may be attributing to me rather more power—and perhaps rather more enterprise—than I possess? And am I not entitled to ask on what grounds you bring this accusation against me?"

"You are as much entitled to ask as I am to decline to reply.... I would ask you to consider, Professor, that I am giving you an opportunity which may not recur."

"An opportunity," the Professor pointed out with his usual precision, "which, so far, I have not declined. If you are disposed to value so highly any help that I could render in the search for Miss Merivale that you are prepared to offer a contingent reward of sufficient magnitude to draw me away from the interests and occupations in which I am now absorbed, I should naturally be alert to hear it. But I may say at once that it must be something more than five thousand pounds. On reflection, I find that that would not tempt me at all."

"Perhaps you will say what would."

"I would much prefer that an offer should come from you."

"I have no offer to make beyond the amount which has been already advertised. But I am willing to listen to anything you may suggest."

"Well, Inspector, since you force me to speak, I will tell you how it appears to me.... I will accept your own theory that Miss Merivale's disappearance may arise from her knowledge of the Ralston process. If that be the case, the responsibility for her rescue must belong, primarily, to those who are associated with her in its exploitation. Were I one of those, you could have the benefit of my assistance to the fullest extent and without thought of reward.... That I am not so situated is entirely owing to the attitude of her friends."

"You mean that if you were let into the patent syndicate, you would arrange for Miss Merivale's return?"

"I mean nothing beyond what I have said, and that, if you will excuse me, Inspector, I prefer to say in my own words.... But I will add this. In view of my position in the scientific world, I should not be prepared to join that syndicate on anything less than equal terms. I expect you know that I communicated those terms to Sir Reginald before the present difficulty had arisen, and received a very silly reply."

While this conversation proceeded, the Inspector had been watching the Professor's niece, who was ostensibly engaged upon the correction of the proofs that were directly before her. But he observed that there was a sheet of paper at her right hand over which her pencil would move rapidly at times, and he was sufficiently conversant with the taking of shorthand notes to have little doubt that she had been recording the conversation in which he had been engaged.

The Professor's eyes followed his, and admitted the fact, with his usual boldness and his usual urbanity. "I see you notice that Myra has been taking a few notes. It's a plan I like. I often find that something has been overlooked when I go over a conversation afterwards. Something quite important sometimes. It's a practice you have at the Yard, or so I've been told. And a very good one too. There's a lot we could all learn from your methods there."

Inspector Combridge did not feel concerned to deny this. He went away feeling that he had been baffled and mocked. Yet he retired from the skirmish with an augmented conviction that Miss Merivale was in the Professor's hands. He saw also that, if that were so, he had been told the terms on which she would be released. They were those on which the Professor had resolved from the first: those which had been set out in his letter to Sir Reginald. Doubtless he would have preferred to get the secret into his own hands. It was impossible to guess what methods he might have employed in the endeavour to obtain it before the taking out of the provisional patent had told him that he was too late for that. But his real aim—his more moderate expectation—had been to obtain a half-share of the invention without the payment of a single penny for its acquisition, and perhaps with the further hope that his scientific abilities would enable him to improve upon it, until successive patents would render it substantially his.

The Inspector saw also that, if these surmises were right, Miss Merivale must be alive, and probably unharmed, and surely, if that were so, it would not be beyond human ingenuity, beyond the resources of his department, to discover where she was hidden.... He spent the night hours in wakeful speculations and plans of further enquiry, and went to the Yard next morning with a renewed determination that he would not admit defeat. There would be the usual batch of letters—absurd suggestions, and useless "clues" to be examined, and passed over to those who must waste their time upon them, and then he would set to work again in his own way.... But he had scarcely arrived when he was told that the Assistant-Commissioner was engaged upon the Merivale case, and wished to see him immediately.

CHAPTER XV.

"GOOD morning, Combridge, just look at this," Sir Henry said, with his usual abruptness. "Tell me what you think of that! The infernal cheek—" He ended as though words were inadequate to express the depths of indignation to which the communication stirred him. Sir Reginald Crowe, sitting at the farther side of Sir Henry's desk, allowed himself a smile which the Assistant-Commissioner was not intended to see.

Inspector Combridge took up the letter. Habit caused him to examine its writing, and the paper on which it was written, even before he commenced to read it. He observed a sheet from a writing pad such as is manufactured in wholesale quantities by Messrs. Wetherhed & Cropfell, and which may be purchased from half the stationers in the United Kingdom. "Stephens's Blue-black," he thought to himself, "and one of those cheap Kingfisher fountain pens." Then he read:

Dear Sir,

If you would like to have a letter from Miss Merivale, you can do so by depositing £500 in £1 notes at the back of the cow house door of Tuckitt's Farm, Millersham Heath, any time before 9 P.M. tomorrow, Wednesday, with a written pledge that you will not attempt to arrest or follow the messenger who will come for the money, nor the one who will bring the letter during the following night.

But if you do attempt to arrest or follow the man who will come for the money you will gain nothing, for that is about all he will know, and the letter will be destroyed.

Keep faith yourself and faith will be kept with you. Make no attempt to watch and you will find the lady's letter behind the same door half an hour before the cowman is due to arrive on Friday morning.

From one who DEALS STRAIGHT

"That," Sir Henry said, "ought to lay the impudent scoundrels by the heels before the week's out."

"Yes, sir," the Inspector answered respectfully, but with a note of doubt in his voice. "If we could get a genuine letter from Miss Merivale, it might tell us a good deal if it hadn't been written under compulsion. But we've got to trust him more than a bit."

"Trust him? Trust who? You don't suppose thought of handing over that money, do you, Combridge, to that blackmailing thief?"

"I don't know, sir. It's a big risk. It mayn't take us very far if we don't."

"It ought to get us one of the gang; and after that, if you can't get him to talk—"

"I don't think it might be quite so simple as that, sir. We're dealing with an exceptionally clever man."

"Unless," Sir Reginald interposed, "someone's trying to make a bit on his own."

"Yes," the Inspector admitted, "he'd be worth catching if that were it. He'd probably spill it out if we got him here.... But Miss Merivale's letter is genuine, if it's like that, and even then it might be worth more. It might tell us all that we need to know."

"I don't mind putting up the cash. Even if it were lost it wouldn't mean much to me, which Miss Merivale's safety does."

"Yes, Sir Reginald. But it's a big risk. I shouldn't build over-much on it if I were you."

"No. Of course, I see that. It may be an utter sell. It's quite likely it's the work of a clever scoundrel who wants to make five hundred pounds in a safe way. He goes off with the money, and isn't watched, and he never comes back. He mayn't have any letter, or even know where Miss Merivale is, any more than we do ourselves; and if we watch him—well, we've broken the conditions ourselves, and we've no right to complain if no letter ever comes within sight."

The Assistant-Commissioner, a fussy, foolish man, who had learnt that it was wise to pause when his subordinates respectfully but firmly differed, had become impatiently silent as the conversation proceeded. He had a great respect for Sir Reginald as a formidably successful man, though, had he disclosed the prejudices which flourished in an otherwise somewhat vacuous mind, he would have questioned the respectability of his birth, the soundness of his judgment, and the standard of his social code. But he had the sense to see that he could not prevent Sir Reginald placing five hundred pounds behind a cow house door if he were resolved to do so. It appeared to him to be an obvious sequel that a trap should be laid to catch the man (perhaps the cowman himself) who would be coming to pick them up, but if Inspector Combridge were disposed to support the banker in a different opinion—well, he had learnt before, in other episodes of a similar kind, that he would get the credit if all went well, and have the relief of being able to blame his subordinates if it didn't. Which was much pleasanter than a contrary order of events would be likely to be.

"I can understand, Sir Reginald," he said, "that you are anxious to get Miss Merivale's letter, and that the importance of that may incline you to overlook other aspects of the matter which our duty will not allow us to do.... Yet, as Inspector Combridge has pointed out, the acquisition of the letter may be of primary importance in the present instance. I have great confidence in Inspector Combridge. I always allow considerable latitude of judgment to the officer to whom I entrust a case.... I could not have allowed public money to be used in such a manner. I am sure you will appreciate that.... But if you are willing to expend it in such a way, and to risk that it may bring no return whatever.... I suppose you will see no objection to the arrest of the man after he has deposited the letter?"

The question reduced Sir Reginald to a moment's silence. He could see no objection to getting both letter and man. It had obvious advantages—if it could be attempted without the risk of an empty bag. If the police should be observed to be hanging round, the man might consider them to provide an excellent reason for not depositing the letter at all. The fact that he was not to be arrested until after the episode was complete would be unlikely to satisfy his mind, even if it could be made apparent to him that this delay would occur. Sir Reginald had a very strong objection to parting with the five hundred pounds, and then failing to get the letter because of the untimely intrusion of a policeman's boots.

Besides that, he had a feeling that it would be hardly a sporting thing to do. But he knew that it would be useless to say that. The criminal law has its sporting moments, its sporting moods, and some police officers are of a sporting kind. But Sir Henry was not of that brand. He had neither the experience nor the imagination which his position required. Few men are fit to be magistrates or police-officers unless they have first known hardship, and perhaps been overtempted to steal.

"If you're sure you won't queer the pitch," he said doubtfully. He looked at Inspector Combridge as he added: "If you'll take care not to come on the scene too soon.... I suppose you know what Millersham Heath's like?"

"No, I can't say I do. I know it's somewhere Wiltshire way."

"Well, it happens I do. It's a bare, high country, with no hedges, and the farms in little hollows among the downs. There's only one good road, and a car going along it can be seen four miles away. You can be sure this has been well planned and the place chosen with care. There'll be no secret about what we do, whatever they've contrived on their side.... I'll just call at the bank to pick up the notes and clear one or two things that I can't leave. I'll telephone Stokes to have a suitcase packed which we can pick up as we pass, then I'll call for you here in a couple of hours, and we'll run down together."

Inspector Combridge said that he would be ready by then.

CHAPTER XVI.

"THE district," Sir Reginald observed, "appears to be somewhat more densely populated than I expected to see it from my memory of a previous visit."

His hand went to the speaking tube, as he addressed the next sentence to the chauffeur, "Piper, slow down when you pass the next man on the road."

Sir Reginald's limousine was approaching the vicinity of Tuckitt's Farm. It had been resolved that it would be impossible to visit it in a furtive way, nor would there be any useful purpose in such a method of approach, though the actual depositing of the money might not be a purpose to advertise nor an operation to be publicly performed.

The car, in addition to its owner, represented Miss Merivale's interests in a comprehensive manner, containing Mr. Jellipot, who safeguarded her business interests, Inspector Combridge, who embodied the protection which the law provides for its obedient citizens, and Lord Britleigh, in whom family affection was personified and by no means absent. When we consider the high quality of these protective forces, allied as they were to love and high finance by Sir Reginald's presence, we may wonder that any ingenuity, however unscrupulous, could have prevailed to hold her hidden so long from their united efforts.

It had been decided that this open approach, by which they could be seen so easily both to come and go, would be the method most likely to give the bearer of the letter the needed confidence to complete his part of a lawless bargain, and that Inspector Combridge's presence, if it should be observed, would hold the implication that the police were consenting parties thereto.

The plan was to stop the car at some convenient place at the roadside as near as possible to the cowshed of Tuckitt's Farm, where a picnic meal would be taken, either in the car or at the roadside, as the weather might decide at a season when the late winter hesitated toward an early spring; and then, when the cowman had been observed to leave, the notes could be inconspicuously deposited by a member of the party, who would stroll around for a lazy interval of observation and exercise.

From his previous knowledge of the district and memory of that lonely road, Sir Reginald would not have been surprised had they seen no one upon it as they drove through the early afternoon of a dreary, grey-clouded day, but there was a sprinkling of men, who wandered idly or sat on stone or fence, scattered about the district, which had occasioned the order by which the car slowed to a crawl as it passed a tramp-like figure which had slouched along before them in a bent-backed way, and now stood on one side, staring straight, if somewhat vacuously, at the occupants of the car. The man wore a broken hat, a dirty raincoat, and boots of which one was burst at the toe and the other was laced with string.

"Know him, Inspector?" Sir Reginald asked, as the drab figure passed into the rear.

"No, but I should from now."

"If he were disguised? Or in a different setting? If he were groomed and dressed?"

"Yes, I expect I should. Disguise isn't as easy as people suppose. Not to those who know what to look for. But I don't know that remembering him's going to do us much good. He didn't mind how much he was seen."

"All the same, it isn't natural to have so many men of that sort scattered about."

"No. I understand that. I wish I knew what it means. I suppose we shall in the end."

"We shall have to pull up about here. There's Tuckitt's Farm on the right. That's clear from the map. The farm buildings are a bit farther on, on the other side."

The car drew up on a patch of rough grass at the roadside, against a low stone wall that bounded the yard around which the farm buildings were grouped. They looked upon a wide empty prospect of arable land, but could observe neither cowman nor any cows, nor any pasture on which they could be grazed.

Sir Reginald, who was born amid the green, cattle-covered fields of the pastoral north, looked round in a natural bewilderment.

"We seem," he said, "to have parked on the only patch of grass that the farm possesses, and this wouldn't feed a cow for an hour. If there's a cowman here, he wouldn't need to stay late to finish his job."

"You'll find the cows here all right," Lord Britleigh answered confidently, being more familiar with the methods of some of the southern counties. "Look at that row of churns by the wall."

Deferring the elucidation of this mystery of modern farming, Sir Reginald directed the chauffeur to bring out the provision which he had made for the refreshment of his guests, and, after that, to go up to the farmhouse and bargain for a supply of milk, not so much to demonstrate the existence of the unseen cows, nor for the nourishment of guests, one or two of whom were more addicted to alcoholic refreshment, as to demonstrate the obvious purpose which had caused his limousine to halt in that lonely spot.

Still seated in the car, for a chilly wind from the east emphasized the discomfort of a meal in the open air while the sun declined to the horizon of the western sky, the four protagonists of this singular enterprise discussed a leisurely meal and a number of abstract subjects such as will come to the minds and mouths of men when they meet in a leisurely social way, where a similar gathering of women would be occupied with more personal and concrete things. They watched an authentic cowman come to feed and bed his unseen charges, who demonstrated their existence by lowings, rattling of chains, and the pails of frothy milk which were carried across the yard. The cowman was a heavy, squat-shaped man, with a curiously bovine face. He gave one indifferent stare at the large, luxurious car which had halted beside the gate, and showed no further consciousness of the existence either of it or its occupants, even when one or two of them descended to take short strolls upon the road or the field paths that branched outward over the farm. The time came when he stumped off down the road in the gathering dusk, and as he disappeared from sight Sir Reginald casually raised the latch of the cow house door, and stood a moment, as though prompted by an idle curiosity, looking into the warm cow-scented gloom of the interior of the byre.

The long row of cows—chained up against the wall, unexercised, overfed, and destined to continue there till, one by one, their milk would fail as their bulk increased, and they would be converted into beef of such quality as their age allowed—stirred with a common impulse of curiosity at this unexpected invasion. Sir Reginald, hearing more than he could see, and conscious that there might be a dozen men who watched him from that dark interior, stooped quickly and laid his packet behind the door before he stepped out and closed it again. As he did so he thought he heard a stir of rats in the straw and had a thought of wonder as to what the letter merchant might do if he found his precious parcel had been gnawed and mutilated during the night.

A claim may be made for a one-pound note, however damaged, or even reduced in size, if its distinguishing number remain, but how could such a claim be put forward for that parcel of notes if they should be mutilated in such a way? Even intact he did not think the work of getting rid of them without betraying their holder would be as simple as might be supposed. They were five hundred new notes of consecutive numbering. He had resolved, if the mystery should not be elucidated earlier, that the whole resources of his bank should be employed to watch for the coming of those notes into circulation, and to trace the sources from which they would be derived.... He strolled back to the car, and the next moment it was gliding swiftly and smoothly toward the Salisbury hotel where they were to remain for the more critical expedition of the following morning.

CHAPTER XVII.

IF there had been no good reason for concealing the first visit to the vicinity of Tuckitt's Farm, still less could there be any for concealing the second. Either they were the fools of a clever hoax, or there would be the letter behind the door for which so high a price had been paid, and of which the value must be in doubt even then.

But Sir Reginald did not doubt about that. To him, if it were Evelyn's authentic message, if it brought news, however meagre, or gave a clue, however slight, to her present location, he knew that he would not regret the loss of that bundle of notes which he had dropped behind the cow house door.

Even Piper, taken into a last-minute confidence, when it had become too late to matter who might know the errand on which they came, shared something of the excitement of that suspense. Only once before had he demonstrated without fear of rebuke the high potentiality of the powerful engine that he loved to drive.

The sun was still below the horizon, and the patches of grass at the roadside showed frost-white in the broadening twilight of dawn, as Sir Reginald descended from the car and went quickly, and without pretence of concealment, to the door of the cow house. As he did so, Inspector Combridge followed to the side of the low wall, on which he rested a revolver that pointed toward the door. The idea that the promised letter was no more than a further elaborate kidnapping trap had never been absent from his mind since he had considered the possible implications of the condition that the police should not be seen to be on the watch, and it had become more probable as he had observed the number of tramp-like individuals who were loitering about the roads. He had warned Sir Reginald of this possibility, and he saw with satisfaction that his hand was in the jacket pocket where his pistol lay. Yet what defence could there be in that if he should be ambushed from the dark interior of the cowshed? If he should be covered as he entered by a dozen guns that were pointed from the shadowy stalls? Still—in that open country—

if they could not rescue, they could surely give an alarm that would render such a capture perilous only to those who had committed the lawless act. The stipulation that the police should not interfere had not precluded him from warning every station for ten miles round to be watchful of the event, and alert for any call that might be made upon them. Of the three who remained in the car, only Mr. Jellipot had come unprovided with a weapon, which he would have been inexpert to use....

The Inspector saw Sir Reginald open the cow house door. He appeared to look round it without seeing that which he sought. He went inside. The hinge of the door made a wide gap through which there shone the flicker of a lighted match. He thought Sir Reginald was on his knees. The next moment he came out with a small piece of paper in his hand. "Yes," he said as he reached the gate, "it's a straight deal."

Without further words he got back into the car and unfolded a small single sheet of thin, brown-tinged paper, covered with small, close writing in a hand he knew. "London now, Piper," he said, "unless I tell you to turn." The car slid forward and was soon gliding swiftly and smoothly upon the London road, as Sir Reginald studied the note he had purchased at so high a price, and his companions waited in an impatient silence, recognizing that he had the first right to a knowledge of its contents.

Inspector Combridge was not so impatient to share that knowledge that he ceased to watch for any evidence that the roads might give. He observed the bent-shouldered tramp in the dirty raincoat whom they had encountered on the previous day, now shambling slowly away. Might it be he who had delivered the note, and perhaps had the five hundred pounds concealed among his untidy garments? He determined that he should be stopped and questioned within the next hour. Surely by then the time of truce would be fairly over.

As he made this resolution, Sir Reginald passed him the note: "Well, Inspector, what do you make of that?" He added, for the information of his companions, "Evelyn's in jail, so it seems. She's written that note on the flyleaf she's torn out of a bible that was in her cell. She says they're pretending she's someone else who's got a five-year sentence."

It was an astonishing piece of news, but to Mr. Jellipot's mind at least it brought a feeling of great relief. A jail is a safe place. It is also one into which the Home Office can enter without denial. Whatever audacious cleverness might have trapped her thus, there could be no difficulty, and little delay, in procuring her freedom now. The number of women in English prisons is not so large that she could be lost among them for many hours when once the order for search should be sent out.

Lord Britleigh had much the same thought, but with an indignation that was less prominent in the lawyer's mind. To a lawyer, even to one whose practice is mainly on the civil side, a jail is a familiar place, to which even knights and barons may be required to go if they are indiscreet in the drink they swallow, the boards they join, or the number of the wives they marry. But Lord Britleigh regarded the matter from a different angle. A Merivale in a jail! He had only a vague idea of the conditions that prevail in those abodes of cruelty and abuse. He had vague ideas of the body of the imprisoned person being publicly washed, dressed in the indignity of grimy, repulsive clothes, which would be taken away at night so that she must shiver on a bare plank, of cell-cleaning under penalty of further persecutions if it should fail to please the official mind, of eyes that watched at all hours, and during the most private of human occupations. Evelyn in a jail! The worst that he had feared to hear had not been so bad as that.... He recalled the impatient exclamation of her ennui that a jail would be better than the more voluntary restraint she had endured amid the dignified comforts of Saxton Hall, and his reply that it would be a slimming process to content her mind. How remote from actuality it had seemed then! People do not jest about jails who are conscious of the shadow of their sombre walls.

Inspector Combridge interrupted these indignant thoughts, and his own study of the flimsy note, to say: "You might tell Piper to stop at Pillinger police station. I want to telephone to have a man detained."

"Can you tell what prison she's in?" Sir Reginald asked impatiently. "We might phone the governor at the same time."

"No, I'm not sure enough to do that." The Inspector spoke with an evident reserve. He looked puzzled. He added: "But if she's in jail anywhere in this country we'll soon have her out. You needn't doubt about that.... I suppose you're sure that this is Miss Merivale's handwriting?"

Yes. He was sure of that. So was her brother. So was Mr. Jellipot. Not a good imitation or a clever forgery. It was Evelyn's own hand. They were all sure about that.

The car was in Pillinger High Street now. "I shan't be more than five minutes, Sir Reginald, if you don't mind waiting. It mayn't be time lost in the end.... You might have a look at the note, Mr. Jellipot, while I'm away and see how it strikes you. Perhaps if you read it aloud...."

The last suggestion came from a consciousness of the angry impatience in Lord Britleigh's eyes, which was easy to understand. The Inspector had meant no discourtesy to him, but the points that puzzled him were more likely to be observed, and possibly explained, by a legal mind. He passed over the note with a request that it should be treated with care, handling it as a precious and fragile thing.

He went into the police station and used the telephone there to such result that the tramp was arrested within an hour. But he was released again before the day was over. He was a man known to the local police and the masters of casual wards as a harmless and shiftless character, and he gave an immediate explanation of his presence in the neighbourhood of Tuckitt's Farm. He had been given a ten-shilling note by a man who had met him after dark, and whom he appeared willing to describe as well as he could, with an expectation that he might get another if he remained in the district. Why had it been given? Just the kindness of an eccentric man. So he had supposed. If a few other notes had been distributed in the same way it was easy to see what the result would be. Easy, also, to observe that the actual collector of the bundle of notes and deliverer of the letter would have been under less probable observation under such circumstances than if he had traversed entirely vacant roads.

That, at least, was the interpretation which was placed upon it. Inspector Combridge thought that he could recognize Professor Blinkwell's technique. The unexpected, confusing detail, with less than an adequate apparent object.... And yet, if that were so, what did it make of the delivery of the letter itself but a trick by the Professor himself, which, whatever its object, could not be intended to assist their search. And it was certain that he would not have done it for the sake of five hundred pounds. The Inspector's puzzled doubts concerning the contents and even the authenticity of the document were not relieved by these reflections.

And while the car continued its rapid journey, and Inspector Combridge, weighing the doubts in his mind with an instinctive certainty that there was some truth that he had not reached, was slow to reply to the questions and speculations that his companions raised, Professor Blinkwell was writing another letter which would do nothing to improve his temper when he would receive it that afternoon:

Dear Inspector,

Miss Merivale disappearance.

Following our recent chat on this subject, I have
been giving it a good deal of consideration, and I feel
sure that I could help to a solution if I were to put my
other occupations and business interests aside for that
purpose.

I may say that, had I been associated with the
Ralston process in its present developments, I should
have felt it to be my obvious duty to assist the search,
as I should have regarded the lady as one of ourselves.

Yours faithfully,

Elihu Blinkwell

CHAPTER XVIII.

IT had been in the morning that Ted Mitchell had come to Evelyn and asked to speak to her privately. He said that Lord Britleigh had instructed him that the demonstration was to take place that evening, and that Sir Reginald would send one of his cars for her during the afternoon. Lord Britleigh (he said) had left a message that it would be well to bring a suitcase with her, as she might not be back till the next morning. "But I wouldn't tell anyone that you're coming out, Miss, if I were you. Not beforehand. We can't be too careful, not after what happened last time."

"Shall we have to go far?"

"I don't know that, Miss. I don't know where it is myself. The chauffeur that comes with the car is to drive it part of the way, and then tell me how to take it the rest. Sir Reginald doesn't mean to take any risk this time."

"Very well. Let me know when it arrives, and I'll be ready. I expect I shall see it, and then I'll come out at once."

She said nothing, even to the maids, packing a suitcase herself, and was ready and on the watch when she saw a strange car coming up the drive. It avoided the front of the house, turning toward the garage yard at the side, and, seeing this, she descended at once, and was in it almost as soon as it had halted and turned. At the same time Ted seated himself beside the driver, and with scarcely a word spoken they drove rapidly away.

Evelyn had no premonition of trouble. She had a complete confidence in Mitchell, who had proved his fidelity more than once before, and in the arrangements which had been made for her safety. She had had a moment's wonder or irritation (it would be too much to call it a doubt) when she considered that she had been talking about the coming test with Cyril at breakfast, and that he had given no hint that it was to take place that day. But she reflected that it was consistent with his usual fussiness that he should show such a needless perversity, to keep the secret as long as possible, even from her.

It had been arranged that he should instruct Mitchell personally, and that he appeared to have done. And Sir Reginald was sending a car. What more could be done than that?

There came a time when she leaned forward to say to Mitchell: "Ted, we don't seem to be going anywhere very directly. Are you sure he knows the best way to wherever he wants to get?"

Ted exchanged a few words with the driver which she could not hear, and then replied: "Yes, Miss. It's what he was told to do—not to come straight. We're near Basingstoke now, and I take over from there."

They ran into Basingstoke as the dusk was closing, and there the driver got down and Ted took his place at the wheel.

"Ted," she asked, "is it a long way from here?"

"It's a fairish bit, Miss."

"Well, you needn't make a mystery of it to me. But what I really want to know is whether we're short of time?"

"No, I wouldn't say that, Miss."

"Then we'll stop here. I'm going to have tea at the Lion."

The man looked unwilling for a moment, and then changed his mind. "Very well, Miss. I could do with a drink myself."

They waited half an hour there, and it was dark when they started again.

"Which way now, Ted?"

"It's a bit beyond Newbury."

"That shouldn't take very long." She tried to switch on the light which was in the roof of the car, but it would not light. Sitting in the darkness she became sleepy, and wondered afterwards whether she could have been drugged, and, if so, when. But it may have been no more than a natural thing.

Anyhow, sleep she did, with the result that when she waked she did not know where she was, nor how long they had travelled, till they ran through the lighted street of a country village and she looked at her watch. Eight-fifteen, she read, and doubted that she had seen correctly. But the village street was deserted, its shops were closed.

"Ted," she said, "we've had time to get a long way beyond Newbury before this."

There was a moment's silence before he answered, and then she thought there was a tone of constraint in his voice, or perhaps it was no more than the effect of the worry that his words implied. "No, Miss. There was a car behind after we left Basingstoke. I thought they were following us, and I had to put on speed and dodge up a road that they wouldn't think we should take. We must have gone round more than a bit."

"We're not being followed now?"

"No. I don't think so."

"What was the place we've just passed?"

"I couldn't rightly say that. There's a lot of small places about here."

"No doubt there are. How far are we from Newbury now?"

"We've got a bit too—too west, I should say."

"I hope it's clearer to you than you seem to want to make it to me."

There was no answer to this. It occurred to her that Cyril might have told the man not to give her the location of the place to which they were going, thinking it best that she should not know it, if, in spite of all their precautions, they should be waylaid again and she fall into their opponents' hands. Very silly, of course, but if he had she wouldn't badger the man. She would know soon enough now.

So they ran on in a silence through which she drowsed again for another half-hour, when Mitchell looked round to say: "We're nearly there now, Miss. I think I'd pull the blinds down if you don't mind. It's the safest way."

"Why on earth—?" she began, and then reflected that if the place where the experiments had been conducted should be known to their adversaries (as was likely enough), and they should have any idea that she might be brought to visit it, it would be round the neighbourhood of the place itself that an ambush would most probably be made.

She looked out to a blackness in which she saw only one twinkle of very distant light. Its remoteness suggested a wide solitude of open fields, or down, or moor, which might be empty of human life. Certainly there was no light of street or house for a great distance on that side. Still, it seemed a needless and rather useless precaution to take. But it wasn't worth arguing. She pulled down the blinds.

She could still see something of the road ahead, on which the car lights shone, and was aware, shortly afterwards, that they were descending an abrupt declivity with the lights of houses on either side. She thought they were in the suburbs of a town, and then out of it, almost at once, and in the quiet country again.

The car slowed down as Mitchell blew a series of signal blasts, long and short, on his horn. It swung round into the shadow of a great arch, through gates which had been opened to let it through. As it stopped, Mitchell got quickly out. Evelyn expected that he would open the door for her to alight.

The door was opened promptly enough, but not by him. It was a uniformed woman who confronted her as she stepped down.

"There's a suitcase," Evelyn said, "on the seat." But the woman did not answer, nor make any motion to get it.

Evelyn looked round, and saw two other women similarly attired. She heard the clang of the closing gates, and saw a man, also in uniform, busy with bolt and key. She looked for Ted, but he had disappeared.

CHAPTER XIX.

EVELYN looked at the women, who eyed her in a sinister silence, making no movement to help, and at the closing of the heavy gates she saw that Mitchell had disappeared. It might all be capable of simple explanation, based on elaborate precautions with which the experimental process had been guarded from interference or observation. Instinct rather than reason warned her that there was something wrong, and the same instinct joined with her own pride to conceal her fear.

Anyway, she was not going to leave her suitcase there. If no one offered to take it for her, she was quite capable of carrying it herself. She turned to take it out of the car. As she did so the nearest woman made a movement toward her, and then saw what she was about to do and stopped. When she came out of the car again with the suitcase in her hand the woman turned with the two words "This way," and made a motion for Evelyn to follow.

They went down a short stone corridor, gloomy and cold, and turned left to a longer passage of the same inhospitable aspect. The woman pushed open the first door to which they came, and stood back for Evelyn to enter.

Evelyn stepped forward sufficiently to see that it was no more than a barely furnished cell to which she was guided, and that her friends were not there. She turned with an exclamation of protest, and would have drawn back, but the woman must have been alert in anticipation of her intention, for she gave her a sudden and very vigorous push, and, as she recovered her balance, the door was closed with a sharp pull.

Evelyn turned to see the woman's face through a grid in the door. "You'll have to go before the matron tomorrow morning," she said; "it's too late tonight." And with those words she was gone.

The woman returned to her companions, her hard-featured face almost good-humoured with satisfaction. "Went in just like a dummy," she said; "she was no trouble at all."

Evelyn hat a corresponding consciousness of the ease with which she had been trapped and handled, yet what use would there have been in futile resistance or undignified protest? Trapped she was, and it only remained to consider how she could get free, and resist meanwhile any attempt to force her to disclose the secret which had brought her there.

Apparently the allusion to the "matron" implied that she would be left alone for the night, and her first consideration must be the discovery of what degree of comfort the cell would offer till the morning came.

There was a light in the passage, and the open grid distributed this sufficiently for her to be able to see the contents of the cell, though not clearly. She felt along the walls for a switch, but without result. Evidently that was all the light which supplemented that which the daylight gave. There was no daylight now. The small, high window showed no stars through its narrow bars. It was a moonless night, and the sky was clouded.

Fear became acute as she looked up at the small, barred window. It must be an asylum or else a jail into which they had lured her. With what purpose? How had it been done? What power it showed! Her hand went down the edge of the door in a foolish effort to ascertain that it really would not open, and felt no handle or latch, nor even a keyhole. There was nothing to turn or pull. Prisoners might kick the door if they would: they could not interfere with it in any other way.

Turning to the interior of the cell, she observed a card on the wall such as is often hanged in an hotel bedroom to give information to guests concerning tariffs or routine. But the light was insufficient to enable her to read it.

She found a narrow plank bed, with thin and meagre blankets, which confirmed her fear that it was a jail in which she was now confined. She knew little of the penal routines of the modern prison which replace the old cruelties of neglect with the utmost limit of physical servitude, but she had read somewhere that a deficiency of bed clothing is one of its calculated and deliberate tortures. Well, she could keep on some of her own clothes, which would be a wise precaution, for the separate reason that there was not sufficient light to ascertain that the blankets were clean.

Maddening as it was that she should have allowed herself to be captured in such a trap, she had the sense to take it without violence of emotional reaction. It was evident that there was nothing she could do before morning, and it seemed that nothing was to be done to her for the same period. It would be silly not to make the best of the position in the meantime. She lay down, with some self-congratulation in the foresight which had brought her suitcase, with its toilet necessities and extra clothes. But then she remembered that the foresight had not been hers. It had been suggested in Ted's message (but was it a message?) to her. Whoever had suggested that had foreseen how she would be placed at night. At least, so she supposed. On the other hand, she saw that it might be genuine and given in good faith. Perhaps Ted himself had been outwitted in some clever way and was now a prisoner like herself.

She lay down, but she could not sleep. The hours passed. Soft steps came along the passage. A light shone into the cell. Eyes looked through the grid, and withdrew, apparently contented with what they saw.

The pillow was miserably small, scarcely raising the head from the level of the plank on which it lay. But for that Evelyn felt she could have slept. She saw that if she should lie awake all the night, she would be in poor form for confronting the difficulties that the daylight might be expected to bring. She got up and put the suitcase under the pillow.

After that she slept, even while the light fell again through the grating and someone softly entered the cell; and when she waked she had reason to congratulate herself on the position which the suitcase had occupied, so reducing the natural anger with which she discovered that her clothes had been removed in the night and others substituted which she was reluctant to wear. And yet wear them she did, for she saw that it would be worse to confront whatever might be before her, or whoever she might have to meet, in the undercloth-ing or pyjamas which were all of her own garments that now remained.

Apart from this annoyance, she had waked in surprisingly good spirits, for which youth and health were more largely responsible than any ulterior circumstances. Wouldn't Cyril be wild! And wouldn't Reggie move heaven and earth (and lower regions, if necessary) to discover where she had been trapped! There was pleasure in that thought, and some grounds for confidence also. Grounds for confidence, too, in the thought that Inspector Combridge in particular, and, behind him, all the police force of the country, would be alert to save her.

And yet more dominant than these thoughts was the morning call of a very vigorous appetite. Surely they would bring her food?

A face looked through the grid. A key turned in the lock. The woman who had brought her there the night before entered the cell.

Evelyn saw through the half-open door that another woman was standing outside.

"Will you tell me," she asked, "what this outrage means?"

It was a futile question, as she knew even while she spoke, but a sudden flame of anger had been raised by a look in the woman's eyes. It was the official gaze that the keeper gives to those who are in her power. Looking at her, Evelyn could read "wardress" in every line of figure and face. She could not doubt that, by whatever contrivance, she was within the walls of an English jail. But behind the official stare there was something else which roused a keener resentment. A look of curiosity, of amusement, of speculation. Catching it for a second, Evelyn saw, with a certainty which was more than words, that the woman knew that she was no legitimate prisoner, but one who had been lawlessly trapped into that position.

At the question the woman's eyes became as blank as a slate is wiped by a sponge.

"If you have any complaint to make," she replied tonelessly, as one who repeats a familiar formula, "it must be put into writing, and will be sent up in the usual way."

"Up what?" Evelyn asked, and was amused to see that the woman was momentarily confused by a question that she was too dull-witted to follow. She added: "Up the chimney, I suppose?" And then: "Are you the woman who stole my clothes in the night?"

"They will be returned to you on your discharge.... You must come to the matron now. "

"It might be more suitable if she came to me.... Anyway, you had better bring me some breakfast first. Do you know that I have had nothing to eat since I was trapped here last night?"

"You will have breakfast on your return."

Evelyn considered this, making an effort to think coolly with an angry mind. She was decidedly hungry, her last meal having been the light tea she had eaten in Basingstoke, and if she was to get no breakfast until after this interview, the sooner she got through it the better. Besides, she had no love for that cell, nor desire to stay within its walls. She wanted to learn what she could. If only she were not clothed in this hateful prison garb, which seemed to give reality to the absurd attempt to transform her into a criminal prisoner, as she felt an angry conviction that they were attempting to do! But that must be as a means, not an end. She could not see that it would benefit anyone to continue to confine her in such a way, even though they should have the power which would make it possible that such an outrage could be sustained. Well, she would see what this matron would have to say. She might be no party to the plot.

She might even hear reason, and start the enquiries which would set her free.

"I'll come and see the woman now," she said, in such a tone as she might have used to Mary or Christopher if she had been interviewing an applicant for a charwoman's job. The wardress made no answer, but turned and led the way, her prisoner following in the rear.

CHAPTER XX.

A BARE, cold, dirty-yellow table in a bare, cold room, with dirty-yellow, long-since-distempered walls. At the table a woman sat, with an open, blue-leaved ledger before her. She had a pen in her hand, and there was an inkwell beside the book. Otherwise the table was bare.

The woman was skinny and tall, with high, red cheek bones in a narrow face, and wisps of greying, dirty-yellow hair.

She looked coldly at Evelyn, who stood between the two ward-resses, trying to preserve her dignity, to forget the ugly degradation of the dress she wore, and to remember that if this woman were not a party to the fraud which had trapped her there it was of the first importance that she should make a good impression upon her.

"Number forty-eight," the woman began in a toneless official voice, raising a pair of eyeglasses to consult the ledger before her, and lowering them again as she looked through Evelyn rather than at her, "you are sentenced to five years' penal servitude, subject to the usual remission of sentence should your conduct earn it. For the first four weeks—"

"Pardon me," Evelyn interrupted her, "you are making a very serious mistake. Will you please tell me who I am supposed to be?"

"There is usually a serious mistake about the innocent women who are sent here," the matron answered, her lips curving into some-thing which was almost a smile. "You are *supposed* to be Gladys Thirlman, convicted as an unregistered baby farmer, and of the man-slaughter of two infants who were placed in your care. You appear to be a very fortunate woman to have avoided the rope. But we have nothing to do with that. If your conduct here is satisfactory, you will be transferred in due course to—"

"But I am not Gladys Thirlman. I have not been sentenced to anything. I am the Hon. Evelyn Merivale. I was brought here from Saxton Hall last night by a trick."

Having made this statement, Evelyn became silent. She felt that the matron's response must disclose whether or not she were a party to the fraud of her kidnapping, and so guide her as to the nature of the peril in which she stood.

But she was baffled even in this. The matron heard her protest with attention, but with an expressionless face.

"The statement you make," she answered, "is absurdly improbable, but its truth can be easily tested. I shall record your protest, if you seriously ask me to do so, and I need scarcely tell you that you will do yourself no good if you are unable to sustain it. Do you persist in saying that you are not Gladys Thirlman?"

"Yes, certainly. If you will communicate with my brother, Lord Britleigh, or with——"

"We shall not trouble Lord Britleigh, or anyone else, with so unlikely a tale. Wragge"—(to the wardress)—"you will have this woman's fingerprints taken, and send them to Scotland Yard for verification. You can take her back to her cell."

"Isn't she to be searched?"

"Not for the present. Take her back now." She turned to Evelyn again to add: "You will find instructions for your conduct on the wall of your cell. I must warn you that any breach of discipline while you are here will be dealt with promptly and severely."

She ceased to regard Evelyn further as she said this, adjusting her glasses, and commencing an entry in the ledger.

The wardress put a hand on Evelyn's arm to lead her away. Drawing back from the touch, she turned to the door and made no difficulty about returning to the confinement of the cell. She saw that the test which the matron had offered was really a conclusive one, if it were honestly meant, and, if it were not, then what use would there have been in elaborating the protest she had made?

She went back to a breakfast of thin porridge and thinner tea, and a piece of bread which had been smeared with something that might be butter, or might not. As her brother had done a few hours before, she recalled that rash comparison by which she had complained that her luxurious confinement to the precincts of Saxton Hall was worse than the rigours of prison life.

But the mystery of how she had been trapped and imprisoned thus, or the question of whether she were really believed to be Gladys Thirlman, was beyond solution. She felt that there was something unusual in the treatment she had received, but she was too ignorant of the routine of prison life to judge of such facts or to appreciate their significance. She could only console herself with the assurance that she would soon know; and meanwhile she could read the grimy card on the wall, that instructed her on the polishing of tins from which she must learn to eat, and in the cleaning of her cell. And there was a narrow deal table against the wall, and in this table, a drawer, in which there was a Bible, very dirty and worn. There would be something there at least which would help her to pass the time.

Looking at the soiled pages of the book, she wondered through how many hands more miserable than her own it had already passed. For she did not doubt that she would soon be free of this place. And then she forgot everything else in a sudden anger as she observed that, while she had been absent from the cell, her suitcase had been taken away.

Yet, if she were supposed to be Gladys Thirlman, what better could she expect? And her clothes were marked with her own name! There was hope in that, if there were any around who were not parties to the fraud that had brought her there. But, even so, the fingerprints would be a thousand times the more absolute proof. If they were honest, it could not fail.

As she brooded over these speculations, the wardress entered with the apparatus to take the fingerprints which should set her free. Willingly she pressed her hand on the inky pad.

CHAPTER XXI.

DURING the next ten days Evelyn was increasingly puzzled, and finally frightened, by the placidity in which she was allowed to remain.

She had expected either that her protest would disclose the fact that she was not the woman in whose name she was confined, in which case she must be released, and her foes confounded; or else that she was in the hands of those who already knew the truth, and whose criminal conspiracy against her would be developed into an active persecution, to obtain the information which she supposed it to be their purpose to gain.

But she was not released, nor was she molested in any way. She asked the wardress, Wragge, from time to time, when she brought her meagre meals, whether any communication respecting the fingerprints had been received from Scotland Yard, but the woman was negative in her replies. There was that look in her eyes which Evelyn had seen and resented before. Was it derision? If so, it might equally well mean that the woman mocked her, knowing the truth; or it might be that she thought of her only as Gladys Thirlman, and was amused by the absurdity of the futile claim she had made.

But if there were no news of release, no investigation as to her identity, it was equally true that there was no attempt to obtain information from her, no offer of freedom in exchange for the betrayal of Wilfrid Ralston's secret, no threat of violence or starvation to extract it from her.

As the days passed, it seemed increasingly probable that she had, indeed, by some crafty criminality, been substituted for the convicted baby farmer—perhaps even her fingerprints exchanged in anticipation of that convincing test—so that she was shut away alike from friend and enemy in the strong walls of an English jail.

The days passed, incredulity lessened, and terror grew. It had seemed hard to believe at first, because it seemed so purposeless, so abortive an outrage. But suppose that Professor Blinkwell—and could she doubt, after her previous experiences, that it was he?—suppose that he had given up the expectation of gaining the formula, and had had no thought but revenge?

She could not guess how he should have contrived to place her in such a position, but it was a fact that she was there, and it was useless to consider the improbability of the experience which was hers. Hope, if there were any, lay in the possibility that she might meet with someone who would believe her tale. A chaplain? She had asked for one, but he did not come. She had heard vaguely of visiting justices, to whom prisoners might appeal. She responded restlessly to any sound in the corridor which might mean that a stranger came. But she saw no one but the wardress, Wragge, and two others at times, the names of whom she did not know.

She was not exercised with other prisoners, but was offered the opportunity of walking the corridor in the women's escort, which she declined in a moment of repulsion, after which she would not alter her word.

She saw a faint hope ahead in the fact that (as she supposed) if she were condemned to penal servitude, this could only be a preliminary detention, and at the months end she would be transferred to other conditions, where she might have a better opportunity of making her protests heard.

And then, on the tenth day, the wardress who brought her evening meal loitered a moment, and looked at her with cunning eyes, as she said, in a stage whisper for which there could be no need, for the corridor was empty without: "I suppose there's no letters you wants to send?"

The woman was short and plump, with a fat face, which gave a delusive aspect of kindliness to a superficial observation. She had once been employed by a wholesale poulterer, where she had killed countless thousands of fowls with a bustling good humour very pleasant to see, until they had been fined for plucking birds alive; and though she had not been personally convicted, and her voluble protests that her assistants had acted against her instructions had been impossible to disprove, yet she had been recommended to seek other employment, and had then taken up that of a wardress, for which women with characters as excellent as her own must always be in demand.

"Oh yes, there are," Evelyn replied, a sudden hope overcoming her repulsion to the source from which it came, "if I thought they'd be delivered to the right address."

"I suppose there'd be good pay?"

"Yes. You could be sure of that."

"How's I to know?"

"You won't know unless you try. I can't give you any now. It was all in my bag, which was taken away. You know that well enough. If you could get a letter to Lord Britleigh, or—or to Sir Reginald Crowe, I'm sure he'd give you a good reward."

"It's a big risk. Would it be worth five hundred pounds?"

"I dare say it would."

"Would you put that in the note?"

"Yes. If you'll let me have a pen and some paper I'll do it now."

The woman shook her head. "You'll get no paper from me. He'd want to know how it got into the cell, if it all came out. You'll have to find something here."

"I can't find what I haven't got. And whom do you mean by 'he'?"

"The guv'nor, of course."

As she answered the woman withdrew, leaving Evelyn to consider the conversation and search her cell for writing materials.

The flyleaf of the bible supplied paper, but she could find nothing which would make legible marks upon it. She had read of prisoners using their own blood, but, apart from a little natural reluctance to make the necessary incision, she had a well-founded scepticism as to the amount of legible writing which would result. When she had scrawled the necessary instructions about paying the reward, without which the postal service was not likely to operate, the surface of the paper might well be covered, even if…. She decided that her blood was likely to be more usefully occupied in her own veins.

Then what about a pin? Had she got even that? It appeared not. But, in the end, her ample leisure discovered one sunk beneath an inside edge of the table drawer.

She experimented with this pin on other leaves of the bible, and was not pleased with the results. The thinner leaves simply tore. The flyleaf at the opposite end from that which she had torn out for her final use showed the scratches as a faint roughness, which could doubtless be deciphered with sufficient care, but what assurance was there that such care would be given? How could she be sure that the letter would be so delivered that its importance would be recognized? That it would be recognized as anything but a piece of waste paper, to be thrown aside?

The same objection applied almost equally to writing by pin pricks, which she also tried on the same leaves, with the further disadvantage that the letters must be made very large, and little could therefore be said on a single page.

Before she reconciled herself to such methods she must question the woman further as to the mode of delivery which would be employed, though she felt that she would have little confidence in any assurance she might receive. Still, the woman would want (with probable confederates) to secure the reward. It was absurd to suppose that she would not wish the letter to be so delivered that it would be understood. It was absurd also that she should not help her with proper writing materials if she were to be recommended for such a reward. Evelyn determined to try the effect of some plain speaking at the next opportunity.

It seemed that that opportunity would not come as quickly as she had hoped, for the woman did not appear again till the next evening, and then there was the sound of the voice and steps of a companion who came with her, along the passage, though she did not enter the cell. But the woman's thoughts may have followed the same lines, for though she gave no sign to indicate what she had done, Evelyn found, after she had withdrawn, that there was an inch-long end of thin pencil, such as is commonly attached to dance programmes, or bridge-driven scoring cards, lying in the shadow of the tin bowl of porridge which was her evening meal.

The next time that the woman entered the cell alone there was a tiny folded note on the table, which she picked up silently and secreted in her dress before leaving.

CHAPTER XXII.

INSPECTOR COMBRIDGE returned to the car to find the three gentlemen had discussed the letter to their common satisfaction, and were eagerly awaiting the information which they had no doubt he would be able to give them. Even Lord Britleigh's irritation at the indignity which had fallen upon one of his ancestral name was forgotten in the satisfaction of feeling that her release must be so certain and so near. For they had agreed upon that, and were inclined to foresee a further pleasure in the arrest of her enemies, and their speedy experience of all the hardships which she now endured, and for a much longer period. Even Mr. Jellipot's habitual caution went no further than to remind his companions that the letter might be no more than a cunning forgery, or the work of someone who wished to combine a good profit with a practical joke. But he dismissed the latter theory, even as he proposed it. The opportunity and disposition for so clever a forgery as it certainly was, if it were not a genuine document, were unlikely to be united in anyone not immediately concerned in the abduction.

But against any theory of forgery both her brother and Sir Reginald were definitely decided.

"That's Evelyn's handwriting, a bit altered and cramped because she hadn't much space. I'd know it anywhere."

That was Lord Britleigh's opinion, to which the banker added: "It's just her style too. There can't be many who'd be able to forget that."

"Well, gentlemen," Mr. Jellipot agreed, "if you're right, as I think you are, I've not much doubt that the Inspector'll know where to look to find her."

But the Inspector, when he returned, though he shared their confidence with some reservations, did not answer in quite the expected way. He said, "Let me have another look at the letter."

Sir Reginald handed it to him. "It's a pity," he said, "that she wasn't more certain about the name, but I expect you know who it was, and, anyway, it oughtn't to take more than half an hour to spot that."

Inspector Combridge made no answer. He looked again at the neat, cramped writing, and read:

> I'm in jail, they won't tell me where, in the name of Gladys Thurston, or some name like that, who's been sentenced to five years for farming babies that died. We drove several hours. Basingstoke at tea time. Don't know after that. Ted drove me hours more through these gates, and had disappeared when I got out. Matron promised to send my fingerprints to Scotland Yard, but I have heard no more about that. I am Number 48. Seen no one I know. Been asked nothing, and given no information. Understand only here for month solitary confinement, then penal servitude prison. Get me out, and order a good lunch.
>
> Evelyn

The available space for writing was limited by the fact that one side of the flyleaf was glazed, and would not take the marks of the pencil clearly. It was evident that the writer had first attempted to put an address on that side, and then given up the idea, and folded the sheet so that part of the writable side was exposed, and addressed to Lord Britleigh at Saxton Hall. But space had been left for two briefer notes besides the above letter. One read:

> I have promised that you will pay the postage on this letter, is to be £500. You can charge it to me, if it seems a bit high. I shan't need to overdraw to pay that, though I expect Reggie'd let me if I wanted to at his bank, so don't make trouble about that.

The other note was briefer, along a narrow margin left by the main letter.

> There's a lot of good reading in the Bible, particularly the cursing psalms.

Inspector Combridge considered this note again in a silence which seemed long to his companions, and the puzzled look with which he had first read it was more evident than before.

Sir Reginald spoke at last: "It's a pity she isn't more sure of the name, but that oughtn't to make much difference."

"No. It isn't that."

"The convictions of baby farmers are not so numerous that there ought to be any difficulty in tracing the case," Mr. Jellipot remarked. "I expect Inspector Combridge can make a very good guess, even if the name isn't quite right."

But the Inspector denied this. "I don't remember," he said frankly, "any recent case of the kind. But you mustn't attach much importance to that. You see, most of you read the papers, and get to know just a little about all the hundreds of cases that get reported in the Press, and when we're young at the job we follow them all in the same way, and perhaps talk and think about them a lot more than you would. But when a man's been at it as long as I have he's apt to give his mind to the cases he has on hand, and let the rest go by. They're like a noise that he doesn't hear because it's been going on round him for many years. If this Thurston woman has been convicted at one of the county assizes, I've probably heard nothing about it, and shouldn't remember it if I had. But you're quite right that the name oughtn't to make much difficulty. When we get to the Yard we ought to trace every baby farmer that's under sentence in England within half an hour, and if there's one numbered 48, another half-hour ought to have her out. No, it's not that. It's the puzzle of why Blinkwell let us have the letter. It wasn't for the five hundred pounds, though I dare say it's come in handy somewhere to grease the wheels. The reward we've offered is ten times that amount. You mustn't forget that. No, we're meant to have that letter, and I can't see why."

"We agreed," Sir Reginald said, "while you were away, that the letter is certainly in Miss Merivale's writing."

"Yes. I don't doubt that. It might be less puzzling if we were less sure."

"You don't think it could have been written under compulsion?"

"No. It doesn't read like that. If it has, it's a very clever thing.... of course, we've got to expect some clever moves from the other side. I'm not ruling even that out. But I don't think if she'd been writing under compulsion, and putting down what she was told to say, it would have been quite like it is. It reads too much like a genuine letter."

"Then I don't see," Lord Britleigh argued, "that we've much to trouble about beyond that. If it's a genuine letter, we know well enough where she is to soon have her out."

"It does look that way, and I'm not saying you're wrong. But it's very hard to understand, all the same. It isn't only the question of how the letter comes into our hands. It's how the thing could have been worked. It must have meant the corruption of half a dozen, if not more, and some of them rather high up. And even then.... Besides, there's this matter of the fingerprints. It's certain that they weren't sent up for verification, nor any report that a prisoner claimed to be Miss Merivale. It would have been investigated at once."

"You don't think she's being fooled? That she isn't in a jail at all?" Sir Reginald asked. It seemed to him the only logical deduction from the difficulties that had presented themselves to the Inspector's mind.

"No, I don't think that. It isn't easy to fake a jail. Not to deceive anyone of ordinary intelligence. Besides, Professor Blinkwell may be a clever man, and he has money, we know, but he couldn't do that. It isn't sense, even if we hadn't been shadowing every step he takes, and reading every line he writes, ever since Miss Merivale disappeared."

"You think it isn't him, after all?"

"No, I don't say that. I only say there's something I don't understand."

"Evelyn," Lord Britleigh said definitely, "isn't a fool." It was a certificate of mental ability which he had certainly never bestowed upon his sister previously, but his audience made no sign of dissent. He went on: "She's not such a fool that she can't tell when she's in a jail. If she'd had any doubt about that she'd have given us the straight tip, and we should have known where we were. We're all agreed that it's a genuine letter, and written her own way, and if she says she's in jail you can make a safe bet that that's where she is. And if she's in jail the Inspector'll soon have her out."

"I am inclined," Mr. Jellipot said cautiously, "to the same view. It appears to me that it would be a much easier matter to corrupt a number of prison officials than, in the Inspector's phrase, to fake a jail. It is difficult to place a limit to the power of money if it be used boldly, and in sufficient quantities, and we know that those who have carried out this abduction can think in sufficient figures to disregard the reward of five thousand pounds which has been offered for her release."

The Inspector observed that his companions were unanimous in a conclusion from which he found it difficult to dissent. They were able men, each looking at the subject from a different angle, and they produced arguments the force of which he freely acknowledged. Yet he felt that there was something behind it all which they did not know. Something that they were unable to guess. Was he approaching the time when he would have to admit to his own mind, and perhaps to others, that Sir Henry had been right, and that they should have concentrated upon the arrest of the bearer of the letter?

"Well," he said, "we shall soon know."

There could be no doubt about that, for while he spoke Sir Reginald's car slowed down to a traffic block in Trafalgar Square.

CHAPTER XXIII.

"A FOOL and his money.,.." The familiar proverb passed through Sir Henry's mind, but his respect for the chairman of the London & Northern Bank prevented him from quoting it aloud. What he said was: "We are convinced, Sir Reginald, that the document is a clever forgery. That is our united opinion, with which the Home Secretary fully agrees. We are in doubt as to whether it is no more than a hoax, with the object of relieving you of five hundred pounds, which it has succeeded in doing, or a deliberate attempt by Miss Merivale's abductors to draw a red herring across the trail. In the latter case, it has not only relieved you of the money, but has probably gained them the time they required for the completion of their own plans.

"It is an illustration, if you will allow me to say so, of the advantage of taking the advice of those who are most competent to deal with the matter at issue. As, I may say, I should have taken yours on a point of banking practice or banking law."

"Meaning that we ought to have gone all out to catch the messenger, and let the letter take its chance?"

"That was the course which recommended itself to my own mind, and on which I blame myself that I allowed my judgment to be overruled."

This was after two days of feverish enquiry and intensive search had failed to discover the recent conviction of any female prisoner with a name approximating to that of Gladys Thurston, or any baby farmer of whatever name who was not certainly expiating her crimes in her proper person, or any No. 48 in any of His Majesty's prisons who was not positively identified as the criminal that she was supposed to be.

And when this exhaustive search had proved to be barren of result, an intimation had been made to the prison staffs that the five thousand pounds which was offered for Miss Merivale's rescue could be earned by any of them who could trace her among the prisoners in their charge, and that the Home office would allow them to accept the reward. Prisoners had been paraded and invited to declare that they were Miss Merivale, which several of them very cheerfully did, but it was found, when the light of enquiry was directed upon them, that they were not ladies whom Lord Britleigh would accept as sisters or Sir Reginald Crowe desire to marry. Energetic governors, rendered anxious or angry by the suggestion of possible corruption among their staffs, were not content to leave enquiry to others, but examined every prisoner and every vacant cell.

The result of these efforts was shown in the official conclusion which the Assistant-Commissioner now expressed to a banker who looked very unwilling to accept it. He said: "You may be right that we should have gained more if we'd caught the man who was carrying the letter, though it seems less than certain to me. Whoever planned this thing must have considered that possibility, and seems quite capable of having provided for it successfully. But I agree that we couldn't be much worse off than we are now.

"If I could think that the letter was forged, I shouldn't be as much puzzled as I am. We could just put the whole incident aside, and go on with the search as though it hadn't happened. But my trouble is that I still believe that Miss Merivale wrote it, and not only wrote but composed it. And if so, she says she's in an English jail, and I agree with Lord Britleigh that it isn't a matter about which she'd make a mistake. As to that, I think Inspector Combridge takes the same view."

"Then, Sir Reginald, I can only say that you believe two things that are inconsistent. You can take it from me that Miss Merivale is not in any jail in this country. We are convinced of that, and we therefore draw the only logical conclusion that the letter is forged.... If you are prepared to put forward any plausible theory, based on the assumption that it is genuine, and that Miss Merivale is under some delusion, or is intentionally misleading us when she states that she is imprisoned under a false name, I need scarcely say that it will receive our utmost consideration."

But that was more than Sir Reginald was prepared to do. He could only say "Yes. That's fair enough. I see your point of view. But I can't alter a conviction just because it leads up to something I can't explain. The practical question is what's to be done next.

"I can't think that any serious harm's happened to Miss Merivale, because I can't see that that would be to anyone's benefit. But we're up against the fact that she can't be found, though we may say that all the country's joined in the search. Money's failed. The police have failed—"

"Pardon me, Sir Reginald. We have not yet admitted failure."

"Well, I didn't mean it offensively. You haven't succeeded yet. Neither have I. What I was trying to say was that everything that's been tried so far has failed, and there's nothing left but Blinkwell's letter. Can we make anything of that?"

"If you were prepared to accept the terms he offers, which I understand you are not, or if you could provide any evidence which would justify us in issuing a warrant for his arrest—"

"Yes. I see that. Well, good morning, Sir Henry. I've no doubt you'll go on doing all that you can."

He shook hands, and departed. He had learned that which he came to know. The letter had been officially condemned as a forgery, and no further action would be taken concerning it. He felt that nothing would be gained by prolonging the conversation with the Assistant-Commissioner.

He dismissed his car and walked back to his club. He could always think best when he was walking, as is often the case with those of naturally active habits and insufficient time for the exercise they require. He felt little doubt that the letter, whether in Evelyn's writing or not, had been deliberately allowed to reach his hands, and that it was all part of a single plot, of which Professor Blinkwell's blandly written communications were a complementary part. And he had to own to himself that, so far, the Professor had come out on top.

Were they, then, to admit defeat and surrender to him? He might say to himself that Evelyn's safety came before all, but he was not of a temperament that made surrender easy. To have that rogue as a partner in business interests of such magnitude! It was an intolerable imagination. Yet he had to recognize that the Professor was a welcome member of the boards of other public bodies. His reputation was good. Whatever might be known at Scotland Yard, however much more might be suspected, however nearly he might have escaped a criminal prosecution in recent months, nothing of this was known to the outside world.

More than that, there was no doubt of the high quality of his scientific attainments. He was right when he said that they commanded very large fees. He might actually be of enormous value in the development of Ralston's invention, and there was little doubt in Sir Reginald's mind that he could procure Evelyn's safety and freedom by making the financial bargain that the Professor required. Was it fair to her to continue to refuse after all other means had been exhausted and had failed to find her?

Yet it would be defeat at the best. It might be one for which she herself would reproach him. If she were in no acute discomfort, and conscious of no actual peril, she might feel that they had yielded ignominiously where she had shown a superior fortitude.

But could he be sure that she would be in a continued safety? That she was safe even now? If the object of her abduction had been to force the secret from her, that object had failed now that it had become a patented process. Under such circumstances she might become an encumbrance which could not be indefinitely held, or safely released. It was easy to see how great her peril might become under such circumstances at the hands of desperate and unscrupulous men.

Yet he did not think that the probabilities of the position were in that scale. Still believing her letter to be genuine, and considering the information it gave in the light of those that Professor Blinkwell had written, he was disposed to conclude that there had never been any intention of wresting the secret from her by violent methods or wiles. The intention had been less crude. It was no more or less than to detain her indefinitely till her friends should come to the Professor's terms. Her danger, under such circumstances, would not be acute unless or until enquiries were turned in the right direction, and her jailers might think it necessary to do away with her to render their own identification impossible.

Such a plan involved a great confidence in the security with which she could be held, and, so far, that had been justified. The police had failed, let Sir Henry dislike the word as much as he would. The press had failed. His own money had failed. But had it been tried to its full capacity? Five thousand pounds is a large amount, but it was little compared with that which the Professor aimed to extort. He could, at least, try the effect of doubling the sum. He might also try what he could do with the Professor himself. He did not disparage Inspector Combridge's abilities, and the Inspector had failed. But he had some confidence in his own. Impulsively, as the thought came, he determined to convert it to action. He waved a hand to a crawling taxi, and gave the Professor's address.

CHAPTER XXIV.

PROFESSOR Blinkwell was in. He would see Sir Reginald. He came at once. On this occasion Myra was not present. The Professor did not affect surprise at receiving the call, nor ignorance of its object.

"This," he said, as he entered the room, adroitly avoiding the opening ceremony of handshaking, which Sir Reginald might not have welcomed, as he indicated that another chair might be more comfortable than that which the banker had first selected, "this is an expected pleasure." He offered cigars and cigarettes. He suggested liquid refreshment, and accepted refusal with urbanity.

"I feel confident, Sir Reginald," he went on, "when you come on the scene that business is likely to follow. You have the eye for essentials which has rendered your commercial career so spectacularly successful.

"I had Inspector Combridge here recently. I've no doubt you know that. I should be sorry to disparage the police force of this country. They have watched my movements and interested themselves in my correspondence during the last fortnight with a thoroughness which I am bound to admire. It is a quality which every scientist must recognize with appreciation. It is that by which our best results are obtained, and without which the most, brilliant investigator will come to grief. It is true that they have been fishing an empty pool. But that has not discouraged them in the least. I say they are admirable in their own way. But their methods are crude.

"Now here are Lord Britleigh and yourself wanting to find Miss Merivale, as it's only natural you should when she goes off without leaving any address, as you say she did. And the police want to find her also; it isn't equally clear why, because she's old enough to look after herself; and, if you come to think about it, it isn't very clear what right they've got to butt into the matter at all. But having once taken it up I suppose they think their prestige will fall if they don't show that nobody in the country can go off without being traced.

"Anyhow, that's how it is. And so they come to me and suggest that I could help if I liked, and hint that they'd have me arrested for not doing so, if they had the least idea what they could accuse me of doing that isn't a great deal more legal than the way they've been interfering with me. There was Inspector Combridge here talking as though I were denying any knowledge of Miss Merivale, while I really knew her address. He seemed to forget that I've been saying all along that I thought I could help. I've been quite frank about that. But he wouldn't listen to my terms because he thought he could trade at a cheaper shop. I dare say, Sir Reginald, that you've thought much the same. But you're business man enough to know that the cheapest shop is the one that can deliver the goods.

"They've had more than a fortnight now, and what have they done except talk? I've always said I could help, and if I added that I know where Miss Merivale is now (which I haven't done) there'd be no crime about that. But it's for you to say if you think I can help, and to name the price that you're willing to pay."

The Professor ceased at last, and Sir Reginald did not pause in his reply.

"It's very lucidly put, Professor, and I'm sure we understand each other sufficiently well to ascertain in a few words whether it's possible for us to do business together. I don't mind saying that I've often had to carry through a difficult deal where there's been more implied and less said. I'm sure you won't mind if I come to the point at once.

"You know we've already offered a reward of five thousand pounds for information which would enable us to trace Miss Merivale. I'm proposing to double that tomorrow. There must be a number of people who know where she is. There's nothing surer than that. It's a big bait, and at any time someone may think it worthwhile to come on to the side of the law and pocket the money as well. Today, no one will know of my intention except yourself. You can have that money if you wish. And while I've no strict right to promise anything in Miss Merivale's name, I think you can take my word that neither she nor her brother will make any legal trouble about it if she's back uninjured and in good health at Saxton Hall before the close of this week."

The Professor listened to this offer with an expressionless face. Then he shook his head.

"I'm afraid, Sir Reginald," he said, "I'm not personally interested if you've nothing to offer beyond that. I shouldn't care to put my work aside to join in the search for a merely monetary reward.

106

I've tried to make that clear all along, but I don't seem to have been very successful...of course, I wish you luck."

The last words, and the slight enigmatic smile with which they were said, were too much for Sir Reginald's patience. He sprang to his feet, saying angrily:

"Then you've lost your last chance. You're making the biggest mistake of your life if you think your humbug goes down with me. I've no doubt you know just where Miss Merivale is now, and you think you're cunning enough to keep her hid and patient enough to tire us out. But you may find you're wrong. And I'll tell you this, that if she gets so much as a scratch while she's in your hands, or the least annoyance of any kind, I'll see you pay for it in the right way if I have to break your neck with my own hands."

The Professor listened to this outburst without apparent resentment.

"If you think," he said quietly, "that I am in any way responsible for Miss Merivale's absence, I can understand your rather excited manner, and, perhaps, excuse it. But I think, Sir Reginald, that there is one thing that you overlook. The police do not appear to have been very successful in their enquiries for the missing lady, but there is one point on which they should be able to give really exhaustive evidence. They could establish—even, I should suppose, to your satisfaction—the fact that I have done nothing either directly or indirectly in connection with this matter from the day on which we heard that the lady had left her home."

While he spoke, Sir Reginald regained his self-control with an effort of will, and answered in a voice which was as restrained as that which he had just heard. And with that self-control he regained the skill in verbal fencing which his anger had thrown aside.

"Perhaps," he said, "they have learned something else beside that." At which he went, leaving the Professor to interpret this enigmatic answer as best he could.

He was, in fact, somewhat concerned for the first few moments after Sir Reginald left, as he wondered whether it was anything more than a random repartee. But then he reflected that, if they had really discovered anything of importance, he would not have had the pleasure of refusing an offer of ten thousand pounds a quarter of an hour ago.

"Yes," he said to himself with a smile, "I think I can still wait." But there might be a few additional instructions that it would be well to give, a few extra precautions to take. He decided that, when he went out next morning, he would give his tailor another call.

CHAPTER XXV.

AFTER his usual leisurely breakfast, at which Myra was his only companion (for Mrs. Blinkwell took hers in bed), and during which he expressed himself with an easy confidence regarding the prosperity of his future days, Professor Blinkwell dealt with his correspondence, spent a short time in his laboratory, and then ordered his car.

He paid several visits to his tradespeople, purchasing some reference books of which he had need, and spending half an hour at his tailor's, which cannot be regarded as excessive when we consider that he was always careful about his dress.

But it need scarcely be said that the most part of that time was not spent with the obsequious Simpson, but in the offices of Messrs. Tonbridge and Wilkinson, which the Professor had been somewhat annoyed to find were not occupied by the members of that unobtrusive firm.

He waited a few minutes, idly inspecting such papers as were scattered about the partners' desks, and decided that there would be imprudence in further delay. He then made a rather long telephone call, his conversation being of a character which would have appeared quite innocent to anyone who should be listening in and unaware of the identity of those who spoke, and returned by the usual route to his waiting car.

He felt that he had dealt adequately with the position, and, although his was not a mind in which humour ruled, he allowed himself a faint smile of amusement as he considered the probable developments of the coming week.

He, at least, knew what he meant to do, and the method to be employed, and he felt that his opponents were running round like a collection of headless fowls. Who was likely to come out best at a game which was played in that way?

It was at about the same time that Sir Reginald Crowe was occupied with Inspector Combridge, concerting new plans for the confounding of the Professor, and discussing for the twentieth time the disputed authenticity of Miss Merivale's letter, and the veracity of the information it contained.

The Inspector was not used to pay a greater deference to the opinions of the Assistant-Commissioner than his official position required, but on this occasion he said, definitely, that he was of the same mind. Whatever deduction regarding the genuineness of the letter must follow, he was confident that Miss Merivale was not now within the walls of any of His Majesty's prisons.

"But suppose," Sir Reginald asked, "it had been discovered, or even suspected, that such a letter had been smuggled out, would she not have been moved immediately, and every precaution taken to cover the traces of what had occurred?"

"Yes, of course; we haven't overlooked that possibility. It sounds the most likely solution, and I don't say it's impossible, but the enquiries we've made already don't encourage much hope. We've asked the Governors of every jail to consider and report upon it. We've had them all on the wire, and we've had most of the formal reports sent in. They're all definite so far, and they seem conclusive. Without an incredible amount of collusion among people who must all have changed their characters in a night, such a thing simply couldn't have occurred. There are other practical difficulties in most instances that I need not detail. We have also asked the police in each district to give us their views independently as to this possibility, and they seem equally sure.

"Of course, we know that money may have been spent in substantial amounts, and we know its power. Money, even in small sums, gets tobacco into the jails. It's never been stopped yet, and it never will be. We've got to consider the possibility of corruption on a much larger scale, but essentially of the same kind. But even here there's the difficulty that the money isn't all on one side. We've got to suppose that a number of trusted prison officials have been either blackmailed or bribed to risk, not merely the loss of their jobs, but the certainty of a long term of imprisonment if they are found out, and that not one of them will come forward to gain security from punishment and a reward of five thousand pounds. It's an almost impossible thing."

"It won't be five thousand pounds tomorrow. I'm going to double the amount."

"Well, that ought to do it, if money will."

"If it won't, I shall offer more. I don't mean to leave Miss Merivale in the Professor's hands, and I don't mean him to have the last laugh, if I spend every penny I've got, and I'm a long way from that yet. There's no man I'd rather see get that reward than you, Inspector, and no man who deserves it more. You must use your own judgment, of course, but it's still the best tip I can give you that I believe that letter's genuine. That means I believe Miss Merivale's in an English jail, however unlikely it sounds to you. Or, at least, she was when she wrote. You've got to recognize that something unlikely *has* happened, or the whole country wouldn't have been looking without finding her before now. Not with such a reward to be claimed. I feel sure about that, and I shan't alter my opinion until I'm proved wrong."

"I don't say you are wrong, sir. I don't know what to think. That's the honest truth."

The Inspector walked away from that interview a sorely puzzled man. Sir Reginald's confidence in the letter only confirmed his own opinion, when he considered it on its own merits. It was the difficulty—you might call it the impossibility—of crediting its contents that always brought him back to the same point, that it was no more than a clever forgery, designed to set them on a false track while the conspirators operated in another direction. And this probability was increased by his conviction that the delivery of the letter had been engineered by forces which Miss Merivale, if she were placed as the letter stated, certainly could not have controlled.

Had the time been used to remove her from the country? It would not have been an easy matter, in view of the watch that was being kept, which went beyond that of the official police, for the whole country was now alert, and every hour brought reports of suspicious circumstances or movements which must be investigated, and were always fruitless. To the ordinary criminal the attempt to leave the country is as surely fatal as when a frightened rabbit bolts into a poacher's net. But even in this the power of money transforms the problem enormously. The offshore boat in the night, the private yacht...he knew there were so many ways.

And what to do next was the most difficult problem of all. For what was there which was not done already, or was not being done now? Perhaps a distribution of great wall placards, with Miss Merivale's portrait, and the increased reward in huge figures that none could miss? There might be some who did not read the newspapers—illiterates, tramps, and others, whose eyes would be drawn to enquire—perhaps to ask, if they could not read. Perhaps.

He went on to think of other ingenious methods of publicity, of ways of galvanizing police and public to an increased alertness, but he knew that, at the most, there was not much more that could be done. The machinery was in full motion already. He could do little now but wait for something to result therefrom. And the next day there was a new puzzle, and a new hope.

CHAPTER XXVI.

"THIS," Inspector Combridge announced, "is Mr. Edward Billington."

Sir Reginald shook hands, and asked him to take a seat.

Mr. Edward Billington was the junior partner in Billington's Detective Agency. It was understood that he had an elder brother who had retired from active participation in the business, though the income tax returns of the firm showed that the larger part of the profits (which were substantial) went into his hands. Mr. Edward was a rather tall, rather handsome man, with a pleasant smile which came easily and at the right times. Had he chosen the medical profession, his bedside manner would have brought him fortune. As the acting head of one of the best-known and best-reputed of private detective agencies, he certainly did not starve.

"I don't think we have met before," Sir Reginald said, "though we have done some business together."

This was in Sir Reginald's office, on the second morning after the conversation recorded in the last chapter.

It was Mr. Billington who had supplied Sir Reginald with Ted Mitchell as a guard to Miss Merivale, in which capacity he appeared to have so completely failed. Mr. Billington had seen Sir Reginald's secretary on a previous occasion to express his regret at this issue. He had brought copies of Mitchell's record while in his employment, and of his earlier references, as evidence that he had not used the services of a man whom he had insufficient reason to trust. He had expressed his continued confidence that the sequel would prove that that trust had not been abused, but, in the meantime, he had very honestly offered to return the cheques which he had received for the man's services, which Sir Reginald had declined to consider.

Now it seemed that, though the explanation of Mitchell's conduct might still be lacking, his exoneration was in sight, and Mr. Billington might be excused some complacency of demeanour as he produced the letter which he had received during the previous afternoon.

"Inspector Combridge," he said, "will bear me out that I have never altered in my conviction that Ted Mitchell would be found to have acted honourably when the truth should become known."

"So," Sir Reginald agreed, "I have understood."

He held out his hand for the letter which Mr. Billington had received on the previous afternoon, and of which he had very properly informed the police. Sir Reginald, beneath all his eagerness to welcome anything which offered information or clue, was conscious of some degree of incredulity, if not of actual hostility, toward the form in which this prospect of elucidation came. The last letter had cost him five hundred pounds—not that he considered that—and a week of utter baffling disappointment. But there was no reward required for the production of the present document. It had cost precisely three pence, having been posted without a stamp in the neighbourhood of the London docks.

"You're sure it's Mitchell's handwriting?" he asked, as he took the envelope.

"Yes, the letter's his. There's no doubt about that. The envelope's different, but the letter explains that."

It was a cheap envelope, addressed to Messrs. Billington & Co. in an illiterate hand. The single quarto sheet of paper which it contained was also of common quality, but of a different colour and kind. The address at its head was that of a sailors' lodging house in New York, of the lower sort. It was dated a fortnight back. Sir Reginald read the letter, and re-read it carefully before he spoke:

> Dear Sir,
>
> I don't know what you'll be thinking of me, but I hope it won't be worse than I deserve. We were fairly trapped, and I don't know now what I did wrong. I did just what Withers said, and just after we got through the jail gates and I got down I must have had a knock on the head, for I don't remember anything after that till I found myself in a bunk in the *Boston Trader*, and found I was signed on as a trimmer for the voyage here, or someone'd signed in my name.
>
> I thought I'd better make the best of it, and come back the quickest way that I could, and I got on well enough for the first two days, but after that I got worse. The cut I'd got on the head didn't heal, and I

113

got to being dizzy when I stood up, and had to go into hospital.

I'm a bit better now, but not fit to stand, and I don't know what I should have done but for Jim, who has been a real pal. I haven't got an envelope but he's sailing tomorrow, and he's promised to let you have this as soon as he gets back, which is about the quickest way it could come.

I ought to be able to start by when you get this, and if you will cable me instructions and enough money for the fare I'll come on the first boat I can, or I'll try to work my way back if I don't hear.

Yours faithfully,

Ted Mitchell

Sir Reginald looked up at last, and the expression of his face was one which his employees had learnt to dread. It was a maddening—a damnably maddening letter. It went so near and yet just missed telling them the one thing that they wanted to know.

He looked at Mr. Billington as he asked: "You think this is genuine?"

"Yes, it's Mitchell's writing. There's no doubt about that. Besides, it explains why we haven't heard anything before now."

"It gives one explanation, which may be true, or may not." Sir Reginald felt a great doubt, but he was obliged to remember that others took the same view of Evelyn's letter, in which he still believed. There was the same certainty about the writing on the part of the one who was best able to judge: the same puzzle about the nature of its contents. But it confirmed her letter in one vital particular. It spoke of entering a jail. It made it seem more likely that they were both genuine or both fakes. He asked: "Is it Mitchell's style?"

"Oh, yes. I can assure you, Sir Reginald, that that letter is from Ted. I've no doubt about that."

"You've had other letters from him before?"

"Yes. Dozens. Letters and reports."

"Did he sign 'Yours faithfully'?"

"Yes, I verified that."

"Then, if you felt it necessary to verify that, there must have been a doubt in your own mind when you read it."

"If you will pardon me differing, Sir Reginald, that is an inference which goes somewhat beyond the facts. To take every precaution, to take nothing for granted till it has been subjected to every possible test, is the routine in our office. It does not imply any special suspicion. We have a reputation to maintain. And"—(with a slight smile)—"we have some very queer people and some very queer circumstances with which to deal."

"And after taking all these precautions, and with all the queer experiences of your office in mind, you think Mitchell wrote this?"

Mr. Billington seemed to weigh his words before answering. Then he said deliberately: "Yes. I think I may say that I have no doubt at all."

Sir Reginald did not feel an entire assurance regarding Mr. Billington, in spite of the pleasantness of his manner, that he was one of whom it would be entirely true to say that

> His armour was his honest thought,
> And simple truth his utmost skill.

Perhaps that would be too much to expect of anyone in the peculiar profession which Mr. Billington followed. But on this point Sir Reginald felt that he spoke with sincerity. It was an important fact that Mr. Billington, with all his experience, with his knowledge of Mitchell, and of the circumstances of the case, was prepared to stake his professional reputation that the letter was genuine.

"Well," he said, "I suppose we shall know in a few hours." And then to Inspector Combridge, who had maintained a willing silence during these exchanges: "Of course, you've cabled?"

"Yes, we cabled at once yesterday afternoon. Of course, it would be earlier in the day when it reached New York. We've had this back." He handed a cable form across Sir Reginald's desk. Mr. Billington, being human, may have felt a little natural annoyance that the Inspector had not taken him into an earlier confidence, for they had come up in the lift together. But if he did so he gave no sign.

Sir Reginald read the cable, and looked up at the Inspector to say: "Floored again, aren't we?" He had read this:

> Bodger's doss-house large waterside resort seamen British predominate no one named Mitchell now there nor any record, but unsatisfactory register obviously incomplete stop remittance not claimed stop further report will follow.

It was signed with the cipher of the New York City police.

Inspector Combridge understood Sir Reginald's feeling, which he largely shared, but he had had longer to reconcile his mind to the limitations of this development, and his reply was slightly more hopeful.

"Perhaps it's too early to say that. If the letter is genuine, as Mr. Billington feels sure that it is, it must have I been written about ten days ago. There's been plenty of time for Mitchell to move his lodging, or to start home since then."

"What's this about a remittance not being claimed?"

Mr. Billington answered that, "I cabled funds as soon as I got the letter. I felt sure you'd approve, and, in any case, Mitchell's our man, and we couldn't leave him stranded there."

"Doesn't the fact that he'd asked for such a remittance make it very unlikely that he'd go away without a word?"

"Yes, it certainly looks that way."

Sir Reginald turned to the Inspector again to say: "I wish you'd give me your opinion about it. It looks fishy to me, but I may be wrong."

"It's got some weak points," the Inspector agreed, "and others that are a bit queer."

"There's the fact that it wasn't posted in New York. If it had been faked here in the last forty-eight hours, that's just how it would have had to be done to make it look genuine at all.

"Then there's the fact that he doesn't give the name of the jail, nor any indication of where it is. That's what makes it useless to us; but I'm not sure that it proves anything beyond that. He seems to take for granted that we shall know. We can't tell how natural that may be on his part till we know how he came to drive there at all, or how much of the truth he knows or guesses even now.

"The note's written on American paper that wouldn't be easy to get here, though I don't say it's impossible. And the address isn't faked. It's a real place, and a likely one for him to have been taken to if he was ill and being helped by pals when he went ashore."

"But wouldn't they be sure to have some record of a British sailor having put up there? I thought the regulations in all seaport towns were very strict regarding foreign sailors who land between voyages?"

"Yes. But they are not always observed, and particularly not in New York. As a fact, the reply we've got shows at least one thing. The address of the doss-house was not used with the connivance of the proprietor. The last thing he'd want would be to have the police enquiring in such a way that a fifty-dollar bill wouldn't send them away in the right mood. We may just have dropped on one of those places that are used for smuggling men into the country who haven't got passports to let them through. We don't know what little nest of graft we stirred up when that cable went. The boss may have thought he'd got the police squared for the next three months, and then they come down on him without an hour's notice, and want to go over his registers and comb the whole place out."

"Then you think the letter's a real clue?"

"No, I don't go that far yet. I think it's worth following up. There are several queer points about it. If they put him on a boat that was going no further than New York, they must have known that he'd be liable to get in touch with us almost at once. Then there's this talk about the jail again, which I don't understand. But I'd go this far. I think, if Miss Merivale's letter is genuine, this one is too. And I think that if she was in jail, or wherever she was when she wrote it, they aren't likely to have left her there until now if Mitchell knows where it was."

"Well," Sir Reginald said again, "I suppose we shall soon know. It wouldn't take much to start me off to make enquiries myself on the spot." He felt that any activity would be better than to wait while he was doing nothing to set her free.

But the Inspector said that a good man had been despatched to New York already. He was sailing from Southampton that afternoon. Active steps were also being taken to trace the seaman who must have left New York at such a time that he had landed in London two or three days ago.

For the moment, Sir Reginald realized that no more could be done.

CHAPTER XXVII.

DURING the days which followed that on which she had given her letter into the hands of the wardress, Evelyn felt an increased impatience and irritation at the prolonged confinement she was experiencing. Previously, her greatest fear and her liveliest expectation had been that some violent effort would be made to force her to reveal the secret, the possession of which, she could scarcely doubt, was the cause that had brought her there.

Knowing that her friends must be active to trace and rescue her, she had felt that there was a gain in every hour which passed in solitude. But since that letter had been written her feeling changed to an expectation of rescue, which caused her to listen with hope rather than anxiety for the coming of an unfamiliar footstep.

But no one came, neither friends nor foes. No one except the wardress, Wragge, and the other one who had taken the letter, whom she now knew to bear the name of Jopson. And when she tried to question her concerning it, she was met with blank looks and a curt refusal to admit any memory of that incident. What could it all mean?

She had already decided that the matron who had interviewed her on the first morning must be in league with her enemies. It was incredible that her protest, with those convincing fingerprints, should have been sent to Scotland Yard and no enquiry followed. Equally improbable (it seemed to her) that her letter should have been delivered to the hands of her friends without a speedy rescue resulting. Had the woman ever meant it to do so? Had she been trapped into writing something which was to be used for a different purpose? Had it been no more than a trick to get a specimen of her handwriting, so that it might be forged for some sinister purpose, the nature of which was beyond her guessing?

She could hardly think that. The woman's stipulation about the reward, and an obvious anxiety she had shown as to the wording of the letter on this point, were strong arguments in an opposite scale.

Yet she might have failed. She might have committed the letter to the hands of others, and be herself ignorant of its fate. Her refusal to discuss it now might mean no more than that she would take no risk of being overheard in a conversation which could make no difference to the result. Evelyn did not make the mistake of supposing that the woman had any goodwill toward herself. If her motive had been that which it appeared, and she were not guilty of a double treachery, it had been no better than greed of gold.

Anyway, the days went by and no rescue came. And as the time passed, and the fear of any molestation or coercion lessened, it was replaced by the dread that she was really abandoned to an indefinite imprisonment. And in what manner of jail was she so confined? Even her limited knowledge was sufficient to observe some singular features about the manner and details of her incarceration, and her utter separation from the other inmates of the prison, though she could hear, at times, a sound of many footsteps, and other indications that her isolation was not that of any great physical distance from her fellows.

But that she was caught within the walls of an actual prison she could not doubt. It would be difficult to fake the atmosphere of an English jail. Her brother had been right about that. She did not only recognize it for what it was, she saw that it was what it had been for many previous years. The card on the wall that was worn and soiled, the grimy Bible, the dingy, meagre furniture of the cell, that had the aspect of having been scrubbed in vain for a thousand years—they were as unmistakable as were the women who attended upon her. The individualities of flesh and wall and wood had all become subordinate to the system which they had been chosen to serve.

And if she could be substituted for an actual criminal, and imprisoned thus beyond the rescue of the law, beyond the efforts of her powerful and wealthy friends, how great must be the lawless power which could contrive, and would dare to do it! If it were simply for revenge upon her and them, how great a risk for such an object it had been prepared to take!

But was it merely for revenge? It was hard to think. She did not know that the demonstration which she had thought to attend had been successful, and the process was now the subject of a public patent, but she knew that time was a vital factor, if the knowledge were to be obtained from her before that could be done. Yet there was no attempt either to coerce or persuade her, or to bargain for the freedom that she had lost. Even if she were willing to reveal her secret, there was no evidence that anyone would be interested to hear what she had to say. She saw that her disappearance might be used

119

to blackmail her friends, and, if that were so, she could do nothing to influence what might occur. She even allowed herself a smile as she thought of Cyril parting with his wealth in wholesale quantities to secure her freedom. She did not doubt that he had a reasonable amount of brotherly affection for her, but, all the same, it was hard to imagine that!

Reggie, she thought, might write the cheque with a quicker hand. But even he.... She knew him to be rather of the fighting than the surrendering kind. No, it was hard to think.

Anyway, here she was, and the days passed and no one came. Was it the idea to tire her out till she should *offer* to reveal her knowledge as the price of freedom? She saw a subtlety in that idea such as might be expected from the man who (she had no doubt) had lured her into the trap. He would not come at once, threatening violence or privations which she might stubbornly decide to endure if her anger should rise against him. He would just do nothing, and leave her there to think it over till she got frightened and tired, till she went on her knees for release, and he could make whatever conditions he would. Well, if he were waiting for that, he would have to do so for a long time, so she resolved, in spite of the hateful confinement, the long monotony of the daylight hours, the meagre diet that left her hungrier than when she began. What would she not give for, say, a good plate of lamb and mint sauce, which must be coming into season now! What would she give? Well, not the secret of the screen. In fact, she must not allow herself to think on such lines. She would not give *anything* for such a meal. She would give nothing, even for freedom itself, till she should be clear of these walls.

And while she vexed herself with such thoughts as these, and strengthened her resolution to endure, Professor Blinkwell, enjoying his comfortable, well-cooked breakfast, with Myra on the other side of the small, well-appointed table, was saying, in the meditative, confidential way which he found so pleasant in that secure privacy, and which may have assisted at times to clarify the processes of his own mind: "I should never attempt, my dear Myra, to delude Inspector Combridge with any elaborate falsehood. There are few men for whose abilities I have a greater respect. Besides, I have always made it a rule of life to avoid risks. I might almost say that I have never taken a real risk in the whole course of a most interesting business life. And to economize in effort has been an equally basic principle. The laboratory has taught me that the alteration of a single ingredient, or a single quantity, will be as effectual as several in securing that the expected result will not arrive—and that which does can have been more certainly and more accurately foreseen. Which is why Inspector Combridge is worrying himself, as no doubt he is; and I am at leisure to enjoy this really excellent Wiltshire bacon."

He served himself with another rasher as he continued his reflections, to which Myra listened politely, without allowing them to delay her meal, for she also had a vigorous and discerning appetite.

"To use another illustration, if you want to be sure that a man will add up a row of figures to the wrong total, it's more trouble to remove half a dozen than one, and no more certain in its results. After you've done that, you can leave the truth to mislead, as surely as any error, and much more safely. Now, I expect the Inspector's got a letter from Ted Mitchell, and he's worrying his excellent brain to determine whether it's forged, just as he did about another about a week ago.

"He knows that Ted was devoted to Miss Merivale, and he can't make out how he came to drive her the way he did, so he begins to wonder whether the tale's true, or whether both letters are faked, and all the time the explanation's so simple that he wouldn't guess it if he were to try for a year. So he turns down the wrong road at the start, and, then, the letters must be forged, and—well, it would be waste of time to follow all the ways he has to think out of misleading himself, just because he goes wrong at the start; and meanwhile—yes, I'll take another cup, if you please."

"I suppose," Myra remarked as she poured out the coffee, her mind being more easily occupied with concrete facts than the Professor's logical abstractions, "I suppose Miss Merivale's breakfast's rather different from ours?"

"Speculating upon a matter on which I am absolutely uninformed, I should imagine that there is a difference of a very noticeable kind. What a fortunate young woman she is!"

Myra, used as she was to the paradoxes in which the Professor indulged during his moments of relaxation, and shrewdly aware that she was expected to listen rather than to discuss, yet allowed herself an expression of surprise at that unexpected reflection.

"I don't see how you make that out. I thought you'd got her fixed in about the nastiest way she could be."

"I have, as a matter of fact," the Professor remarked, without resenting this supposition, "taken no active steps in the matter in any way, as Inspector Combridge, or his superior officers, have gone to a good deal of trouble to be able to prove. Indeed, I have no doubt that they would be prepared to swear to more than my natural love of scientific accuracy would allow me to endorse, though an attitude of silence might be the controlling impulse of a prudent mind.

"You may be right in assuming that Miss Merivale may be subject to some vexatious restrictions upon her liberty, and limitations of diet, and to that extent you are justified in the observation that you have made. It is a condition which is unlikely to cause me any sympathetic disturbance of mind when it is giving so little concern to her closest friends that they remain indifferent to my offer to assist their search, though they express a very gratifying confidence in my ability to do so effectually.

"Indeed, these repeated refusals are bringing it very near to a position which must be resolved in a different way. I cannot be expected to continue to write letters which are disregarded, if not contemned. Yet I am constitutionally averse to hasty or violent action, and I think I will write one more.

"But on the point to which you took exception, I see reason to regard Miss Merivale as a very fortunate young woman, as you will agree if you consider the position in which she stands.

"The repository, as she was, of a secret of almost incredible value, and having left her home as she did, might it not have been anticipated that she would fall into the hands of violent and unscrupulous men? Men who would have wrested the secret from her, after such experiences as would have been limited only by the degree of obstinacy which they would have found occasion to overcome?

"When we consider how completely she has disappeared, and the extraordinary—I may say the national—efforts which have been unsuccessfully made to trace her, when we consider how completely she must be in the power of those by whom she is detained, and when we remember (as I had occasion to remark in the course of an earlier episode, which is now closed) that she is a young woman of a pleasant pulchritude, we may observe that even the surrender of her secret knowledge might not have saved her from the familiarities of those who feed her. But, as it is, what has she to fear or to regret beyond the lukewarmness of friends who put their selfish interests before her safety, and reject the help of those who would be active to bring her home?"

Professor Blinkwell put the case with such convincing logic that it is difficult to consider his arguments fairly without a measure of agreement which may be surprising to our own minds, but his next remark may suggest that he contemplated developments which it would be less easy to regard with the same complacency. He said: "Yet it should be evident, even to them, that it is a position which cannot continue indefinitely. I will send them another note."

CHAPTER XXVIII.

INSPECTOR COMBRIDGE called upon Sir Reginald Crowe, having made the appointment by telephone two hours earlier, and given time for Lord Britleigh and Mr. Jellipot to be assembled at the banker's office.

Sir Reginald had received another letter from Professor Blinkwell of a somewhat disquieting character, and the Inspector had information to communicate of uncertain, but possibly decisive value; and wished to take counsel with those who were most concerned as to the methods by which it should be sought to utilise it; or perhaps it would be more accurate to say that he came to persuade them of the advantages of a settled plan, for the matter had been under discussion at Scotland Yard during the previous hour, and the procedure which was to be followed was resolved already.

"That," Sir Reginald said, as soon as the gentlemen were assembled, "is the note I have just had." He handed it to the Inspector, who read it without comment, and passed it round. They read:

Dear Sir,

Re Miss Merivale.

I have already made several offers to assist you in the search for this lady, and have advanced a confident opinion that my aid would be of material value where other agencies have apparently failed.

You have rejected these offers, perhaps thinking that the price I ask is more than the lady is worth.

This is entirely for you to judge, and my only object in writing now is to advise you that after the end of the present week, my offer must be withdrawn.

I should be unable to feel any assurance that Miss Merivale, after so prolonged a detention, would

be returned in a condition to fulfil the terms of the offer which I originally made.

Yours faithfully,

Elihu Blinkwell

Sir Reginald waited till the letter had been read by the three
gentlemen whom he had assembled for what he felt must be a decisive council of war, with Evelyn's safety and health—perhaps even
her life—as the stake with which they played, against their own hu-
miliation and financial loss. Then he said: "Gentlemen, you will see
that the letter is a threat and an ultimatum. Beyond that, its implications are obscure, but are of an evidently sinister kind. It may mean
that Miss Merivale is already ill. It may mean that her captors are
not willing to continue the risk of keeping her, if they decide that we
cannot be blackmailed successfully, and they are then faced with the
fact that it is incompatible with their own safety to let her free.

"I have not spoken of it till now, but I will own that the fear of
this position resulting has been in my mind continually during the
last fortnight. It seemed a logical certainty that it must arrive, but
each day has been a respite, with the constant hope that our efforts
might be successful and the danger end.

"Now, as it is Tuesday morning, we have a bare five days during which the Professor still indicates that he will return Miss
Merivale in safety, if we accept his terms. If we explicitly decline to
do so, or if we have treated his letter with the contempt of silence
when that period ends, he will equally understand that there is no
prospect that he will gain his object by further patience. The question is, can we risk that position arising, or what steps should we
take to avert it during the short time that is still ours? I will say
frankly that, subject to any suggestions you may have to make, my
own mind is made up, but I would rather hear your views before I
say more."

He ended in a silence which neither Lord Britleigh nor Mr. Jellipot was quick to break. To the lawyer's mind, the idea of surrender
to such an ultimatum was difficult to entertain: its illegality seemed
conclusive. If his companions had simply said that it was beyond
discussion, he would have acquiesced in their decision as obvious.

But he could not forget that Miss Merivale was his client, and
his first duty to her. She was in an evident and, possibly, a deadly
peril. If Sir Reginald or her brother were prepared to buy her safety
at such a price, was it for him to object? Only if, or as far as, it

might be proposed that her own fortune should be involved, would any responsibility of decision fall upon himself? That was clearly not a contingency for him to propound. Even if it should be proposed by others, ought he not to say that he had no authority—that anything agreed must be conditional upon her assent when released? On the whole, he felt less disposed to talk than to listen to what others might say.

Lord Britleigh's repugnance to making terms with the Professor was as strong as his, although differently based. It was not the money alone. It was the idea of having the Professor beside him as a future colleague, probably for life, for he did not doubt that he had plans in readiness by which the legal fetters would be securely riveted. And even as to the money, who knew how large a share of the loss Crowe might be prepared to take? Let him talk a bit more.

It may be significant that both these silent gentlemen were inclined to assume that Sir Reginald had decided that they must yield to the Professor's terms, and that that impression had resulted as much from a lack of the usual buoyancy in the banker's manner as from the substance of what he said. Yet they may have misinterpreted that gravity according to the complexions of their own minds. He may have meant no more than that still more strenuous efforts for Evelyn's release should be made during the short time that remained. He may have thought that they would be doing no more than she herself would wish if they should reject the Professor's offer with contempt. He may have felt that the position justified an application for the Professor's arrest. He may even have intended to strangle him with his own hands if he did not yield the secret of where Evelyn was confined. But what he thought will remain unknown for ever, for Inspector Combridge, seeing that the others were in no hurry to speak, thought it might not be inopportune to introduce another factor to the discussion.

"Perhaps, Sir Reginald," he said, "before you decide whether to take any notice of that letter, you ought to know of a development that has just occurred. Unless Inspector Corbett's made a mistake, Mitchell's been found."

"In New York?"

"No, in a lodging in Whitechapel."

"That ought to mean everything."

"It ought to mean a good deal. It's the first bit of real success we've had, if it's true. But we've had a long conference about it at the Yard this morning, and it was decided that it would be best to go slow. I wasn't sure that you'd approve, anyway, and I'll own that that letter might have made a difference. But it may be best still....

125

We thought that just watching him might be the surest way in the end. That is, if Corbett's right that it's really Mitchell, about which he seems sure."

"Who's Corbett? Does he know him?" Lord Britleigh asked.

"Corbett's one of our best men. He never forgets a face, and it's said that he can see through any disguise. He was down at Saxton about that first attempt on Miss Merivale, and questioned Mitchell then. He says he saw him after dark in a street off Whitechapel, and knew him at once. He's sure Mitchell didn't suspect anything. He went into Whitechapel to post a letter at a pillar box there. Corbett would have liked to secure the letter, but he felt it was more important to follow the man.

"Mitchell—if it were he—turned back from the pillar box and went to a house in Easton Street. He's been lodging there for the last two or three weeks under the name of John Terrill, going out very little, saying he's ill and out of work, but paying regularly in advance. When Corbett had found where he lodged, he went back after the letter, but he was too late. The box had been cleared. We couldn't have all the letters examined at the district office."

"Suppose," Sir Reginald suggested, "the man gets suspicious and bolts?"

"He'll be clever if he gets away now."

"Well, we seem to be dealing with clever men. Isn't it rather remarkable that Corbett, who'd happened to see Mitchell at Saxton, should happen to run across him again?"

"Not so much as it sounds. It's not so queer as the fact that it's the first time we *have* got on the scent, when you think that every constable in the country's been on the lookout for weeks past, and the reward that's been advertised. But I don't say it's Mitchell for sure. Mr. Billington's certain it can't be true. He says he'd trust Mitchell to go straight, and he won't hear of anything else."

"Well, he knew the man. If it's true, I don't see how there could be a decent explanation of the way he's behaved. What do you really think? Isn't Billington probably right?"

"No. I'd put my money on Corbett. Corbett says that he's sure."

"Then I can't see why you don't have him detained and questioned at once. If he's Mitchell, he knows where he drove Miss Merivale, and if he tells us that, we're halfway home, if not more. If he won't speak, it's like a confession of guilt. You ought to know how to deal with that."

"Yes, sir. That's how it sounds. But, if you think, you'll see that it's not so simple. We've got no charge against him, and as to his driving Miss Merivale anywhere, we've no evidence except her let-

126

ter, and we don't know whether that's faked. Anyhow, it's not evidence of a legal kind. If he says he's Mitchell, and tells us a tale of another kind that we can't check, we may be no better off, and if he's really in with Blinkwell's gang, we've put them all on their guard. And if he just says that he's not Mitchell at all, it mayn't be easy to prove he is. We should want fingerprints for that, which we haven't got. No, we thought, on the whole, it might be better to watch him quietly for a few days, and see where he goes. If he posts another letter, we may get to know a bit more."

Sir Reginald looked less than convinced, but he said after a pause: "Well, you're experienced men. You ought to know best. Suppose we leave it like that for a couple of days, and if he doesn't do or write anything that gives you a clue by then, I should strongly advise that he should be interviewed, and urged to give what information he can. Meanwhile, we may hear something from New York, though it seems rather less likely now. If Mitchell's really in Whitechapel, he must have faked the letter here, unless it's a forgery, and if he did that, he must be in it up to his neck."

"Yes," the Inspector answered, "and that's what I'm inclined to think that he is. Billington's sure we're wrong, but he's equally sure that the letter's in Mitchell's hand, which just cancels out. It's the puzzle about Miss Merivale's letter and the prison over again."

"Well," Sir Reginald said rather wearily, "then it's agreed we do nothing more for the next two days unless we hear something from you. It seems to be the way we always end up. But there does seem to be a bit more hope this time. I suppose we can trust you that you won't let the man slip through your hands?"

"No, sir," the Inspector answered confidently. "I think you can trust us for that."

CHAPTER XXIX.

LEFT alone to consider the position, Sir Reginald was conscious of an acute dissatisfaction at the decision which had been made. It would have been his method to tackle Mitchell (if it were really he) without a moment's delay, and he would have done this himself with some confidence that persuasion or threats or gold would have won the information by which Evelyn might have been freed—perhaps even in a few hours. It seemed the simple, obvious course to take. Yet his reason told him that the police might be right. If he should simply refuse to speak, whether admitting or denying his own identity, or if he should tell a tale which did not help them at all, but which they could not disprove, it might leave them very much where they were, and it might not be easy to formulate any charge against him. If he were really in the camp of their enemies, the knowledge that he was being detained or questioned might alarm Evelyn's captors into disposing of her, even to the extremity of murder, for their own security, and without waiting till the week should end. Yes, the police might be right. But a further two days of inaction would be hard to endure.

These reflections were broken by the memory that he had a Board Meeting at two P.M., and, seeing that the morning was already gone, he ordered lunch to be brought into his private office, and resolutely turned his mind to the business with which he must be prepared to deal when his fellow directors should assemble.

It was wasted time—as futile as the fear of a further period of inactivity which he was not to experience—for he had scarcely crossed the corridor to the boardroom, and taken his seat at the head of the table there, when there was a sharp ring from the telephone that was near his hand.

"Excuse me a moment, gentlemen." He listened for a few moments, and then said: "You can wait ten minutes? Then I'm coming now."

He rose as he put down the receiver, and looked round at his wondering colleagues. "Gentlemen, you must please excuse me. Portland, you'll take the chair. You'll find the agenda quite clear. Matthews can give you any information you need. I'll approve whatever you do." He turned his head as he disappeared through the door to add: "Sorry, but it's the Merivale matter. It won't wait."

The next moment he was out in the street. He jumped into the nearest taxi, giving the driver a pound note as he did so. "Scotland Yard," he said, "and damn the police."

The driver put on the best speed he could as he considered this singular conjunction of instructions and destination. The next moment he heard the voice of his fare behind him as he slowed down in obedience to a constable's lifted hand: "Never mind the traffic signals. Drive through."

The man looked back, shaking his head. "It might cost me a bit more than a quid, guv'nor, if I did that."

"I don't care if it costs fifty." A ten pound note was passed forward, with Sir Reginald's card. The outraged constable took the number of a taxi that shot perilously between the crossing traffic. Sir Reginald had been informed that there was to be a raid upon a tailor's premises in Oxford Street. Inspector Combridge would not say more than that. But he implied that there was reason to hope. They would wait ten minutes before starting. No more. And Sir Reginald, full of curiosity as to what it might mean, and sick of the inaction of the past days, did not mean to be left behind.

The taxi, leaving a train of indignant constables and cursing drivers in its rear, pulled up at the Yard in time for Sir Reginald to transfer himself to a police car which was in the act of moving away, with Inspector Combridge and three other plain-clothes officers already within it.

As it moved forward, rapidly enough, but in a some what more lawful manner than Sir Reginald's previous conveyance, Inspector Combridge gave a brief explanation of the events which had led to this abrupt descent upon the reputable premises of a firm of old-established tailors in Oxford Street.

It appeared that the policy of keeping an unobtrusive watch upon the supposed Mitchell had borne fruit even while it had been under discussion that morning. At about eleven A.M. he had left his lodgings in Easton Street and walked into an adjoining thoroughfare, where he had paused a moment to look round, and then signalled to a passing taxi.

In the seclusion of this vehicle he had proceeded to Bruton Street, at the corner of which he had alighted and walked to No. 17, being an office building, on the second floor of which he had called upon a firm of turf commission agents, Messrs. Tonbridge & Wilkinson. He had remained there about ten minutes, and on coming out he had paused on the landing to count a little bundle of one pound notes before putting them away in the security of his hip pocket.

He had then descended to the street, walked a short distance, and again called to a passing taxi, in which he had returned to his Easton Street lodgings, but leaving it a street's length from his door.

Inspector Combridge had considered this report, and its first appearance had given him very little satisfaction. The out-of-work invalid, John Terrill, had gone to collect a betting debt, and, because he was an invalid, he had very naturally taken a cab. If he were really Mitchell, the incident did not appear to be helpful, and it actually made it appear slightly less likely that he was.

Yet the Inspector's mind worried round the facts for a time, being unwilling to put them aside until he had reviewed every possibility which they might suggest, and as he did so he observed one little circumstance which encouraged him to further effort. Mr. John Terrill, who did not appear to be in affluent circumstances, could have gone from Easton Street to Bruton Street, almost from door to door, by using a bus at a cost of no more than four pence in each direction. Yet he had preferred to use taxis, which he had hailed in the street, and from which he had alighted a short distance from his destination. Taxis, in return for their higher cost, give speed and privacy. The occasion for speed did not appear to arise. It became a reasonable deduction that Mr. Terrill preferred to be unobserved when he went abroad. He only appeared in the street for the short time which was necessary if the man who drove him were not to be able to say where he was going, or from whence he came.

Encouraged by these reflections, the Inspector next made some enquiries as to the reputation of Messrs. Tonbridge & Wilkinson. But here he drew a blank. Their record appeared to be of a peculiarly blameless kind. Even the C.I.D. Officers who specialized in oversight of the betting fraternity had never heard of them before. One said, with emphasis, that there was no such firm. Yet their name was in the telephone directory, where names and descriptions are not inserted as a practical joke.

The next step had been to ring up some of the largest firms of bookmakers and seek information from them. These firms, when they had got over the first nervousness which a call from Scotland Yard might naturally produce, were willing but unable to help. The name of Tonbridge was unknown to them. There was a Jack Wilkinson, but he was a partner in Young & Stammers, whose offices were in Holborn Viaduct. Everyone knew that.

There was, in fact, a common opinion that there was no such firm. Such a business cannot exist without the knowledge of the trade. Most of them do business together, underwriting each other's risks. It would be as reasonable to suppose that a fire insurance company could carry on business unknown to the insurance world.

Considering the implication of this general ignorance, a detective of far less ability than Inspector Combridge might have gone on to consider whether the name might be no more than a cover for some of Professor Blinkwell's illicit activities. But it was known that during recent weeks he had not entered Bruton Street, neither had he addressed any letters to anyone there.

The Inspector, tenaciously following the Professor's tracks, and declining to be shaken off by the coldness of the scent, suddenly had an inspiration. Bruton Street was at the back of Oxford Street, where the Professor rather frequently shopped. He called for a map of London, which was inconclusive. He called for plans of Oxford Street, back of the premises of Messrs. Burrows & Simpson were contiguous to those of 17 Bruton Street. The Inspector was too old at the game to be easily excited, yet he was conscious of a moment of exultation as he observed this fact on the plan. Patient tenacity was to have its reward, as it so often did. At least, that was what he thought then. Later in the day…. But we must not anticipate.

The records of the Professor's movements, so laboriously and, as it had seemed, so uselessly compiled, were now consulted, with results of a most gratifying character. The frequency of his visits to his tailor, and the length of time that he would remain, that had seemed so ordinary, so natural, before, now assumed a more sinister significance. It seemed remarkable that they had not been regarded with an earlier suspicion. The facts were sufficient for a search warrant to be obtained without difficulty. It remained only to discover what the premises of Messrs. Burrows & Simpson might reveal. Even that Miss Merivale might be confined on its upper floors did not seem an unlikely thing.

CHAPTER XXX.

"I DON'T suppose," Inspector Combridge remarked, as the little group descended from the car a hundred yards away from the shop they sought, "I don't suppose Mr. Simpson (I understand that Burrows has passed away) will be in a hurry to show us his upper floors. But if he has a tendency to delay I don't know that we ought to bustle him. We've got all the afternoon before us."

"You're not afraid," Sir Reginald said, "that he may give the alarm, and the Tonbridge and Wilkinson lot, whoever they are, bolt out to Bruton Street?"

"No. They wouldn't find that easy to do. We didn't send anyone too soon. We didn't want any possible suspicion to be raised before we arrived, but the Bruton Street entrance has been watched now since about ten minutes ago. I'm more hopeful that someone will try ringing up the Professor for instructions, if they get scared first, and then find they've got time. But we can't judge yet. We've got to see how things go."

As he said this, the little party came to the highly respectable double-fronted shop where Mr. Simpson carried on his considerable and distinguished trade. The order of procedure must have been arranged previously, for one of the detectives disappeared up a passage which opened at the side of the shop, another remained at the door, and it was with only one companion besides Sir Reginald that the Inspector entered the premises.

Sir Reginald had a passing thought of admiration for the cool self-confidence of a police which could operate with so little demonstration of force, or even its immediate actuality. He was not armed himself, and he rightly supposed that there were no firearms in his companions' pockets. Yet they were venturing into what, for all they knew, might be the headquarters, behind that innocent exterior, of a gang of very powerful and lawless criminals, with ability and resources which had defied the search of the last three weeks. He saw that it was equally true that they might be following no more than a cold scent or a false alarm. There was nothing formidable, neither was there any aspect of fear, in the eager obsequiousness of the young assistant who came forward to meet them. It was clear that he regarded them in no other light than as potential customers.

"Can I see Mr. Simpson?" the Inspector asked.

"Yes, sir. Certainly, sir. I'll let him know." Without even asking for names, the young man hurried to the glass-panelled office at the rear of the shop, from which Mr. Simpson emerged a moment later, and came forward to enquire, with an habitual suavity, what he might do to serve them.

Inspector Combridge, with the experience of a hundred similar encounters behind him, thought: "This man knows nothing, or, at least, he is unalarmed." That improved the probability of surprise, while making it somewhat less likely that there would be anything worth surprising. He decided that it was a case for direct frontal attack. He would ask a question which would startle Mr. Simpson if he had guilty knowledge, and puzzle him if he had none.

"I am Inspector Combridge, of Scotland Yard. I want you to tell me whether there is any way through from this shop to Bruton Street."

Mr. Simpson certainly looked puzzled. In fact he looked blank. "Bruton Street?" he repeated vaguely. "I'm afraid I don't know where it is. No, there's no way through anywhere here." He went on to explain that the room at the back of the shop, where the assistants had their meals, opened into the side passage only. It was a passage that went no further, bearing little traffic but the transit of the daily dust bin.

The Inspector had a vague feeling of disappointment. He saw an innocent man, or the best actor he had yet met.

The fact was that when he had declared his ignorance of the existence of Bruton Street, Mr. Simpson had spoken no more than the truth. Many Londoners spend a lifetime in its main streets without ever gaining the slightest knowledge of the names or character of the network of streets and alleys that lies between them. It is sometimes an almost incredible ignorance, and for them to enter those regions would be like the exploration of an unknown world. At the first moment of hearing the enquiry, it had not conveyed any menace to him. He had no consciousness of any guilt, and the first vague idea that entered his mind as to the purpose of the Inspector's enquiry was that he was endeavouring to trace the flight of some pickpocket or bag-snatching thief. It was only as he turned to lead the way to the back of his premises, to demonstrate their limitations, that the thought of the secret door that the Professor had had built in the closet of the fitting-room entered his mind. Even so, he knew nothing of what the Professor might do when he went through it, nor where it led. The present enquiry might have nothing to do with it. Anyway, it was not for him to mention. He owed the Professor five thousand pounds.

Inspector Combridge glanced in a perfunctory manner at the rear room and the blank wall at the head of the passage. He did not expect to discover anything on the ground floor. He went back to the shop and asked Mr. Simpson to speak to him alone. They went into the glass partitioned office together.

Mr. Simpson had seen that there was another detective guarding the passage, and his mind was prepared to learn that the matter was more serious than and different from what he had first thought.

"Mr. Simpson," the Inspector said in a more official voice than he had used previously, "we have reason to think that there is a way through these premises into some Bruton Street offices. I have a search warrant, and I shall be unable to leave until I have satisfied myself on this point, We are engaged in a criminal investigation, and while I am not suggesting that you have any guilty participation in anything irregular which may have occurred, it is a position in which it is the duty of every citizen to assist the police. I am inviting you now to assist us voluntarily, if you are able to do so."

"I can only say," Mr. Simpson replied, "that I do not know of any way through these premises to Bruton Street or anywhere else. Actually, I don't think I ever heard of the street till you mentioned it a few minutes ago. But I think my reputation should be good enough for you to know that I should not obstruct the police in any way. You are welcome to search the premises from top to bottom. I will come with you, if you like, or you can go by yourselves."

"I don't think we need trouble you to come with us."

"I shall be obliged if you can manage without me. I was just making up my cash for the bank when you came in, and it's nearly three-thirty now."

Mr. Simpson saw the three men go upstairs, and turned to his cash books. It was a genuine necessity, for the hands of the clock over his desk showed that it was now 3:23, and he had had a telephone call from his banker half an hour earlier asking him to pay in that day. But when he had hurriedly completed his paying-in book, and despatched a clerk at a run, with two minutes in which to reach the corner building two streets away, he turned his thoughts to the detectives who were still upstairs, with some uncertainty as to the course which it would be best for him to take.

Of course, if they should overlook the Professor's door...nothing could be better than that. And he did not think it would be very easy to find. He had not thought of any criminal explanation of the Professor's eccentricity previously. He had not seemed to him to be of a criminal type. He had thought rather of some secret assignation. Of disloyalty to a wife who was understood to be more or less of the invalid type. It wasn't a very good explanation to fit the facts of the case. Perhaps a secret experimental process, so colossal in its possibilities that it must be hidden even from the assistants in his own laboratories. That was a more plausible theory. But, in any case, it was no business of his. As a fact, he had never even seen the Professor go through the door at the back of the closet, though he knew it was there. He locked himself in the closet, and after a time he unlocked it again and came out.

If he were actually engaged in some criminal enterprise, and the police should overlook the door, the position regarding the five thousand pounds would be even better than before—without any purpose forming in his mind which can be described fairly as a plan to blackmail Professor Blinkwell. Mr. Simpson was quite clear about that.

On the other hand, if they should find the door, it would be better that he should have mentioned it to them. He did not even know that Professor Blinkwell would wish that he should attempt to conceal it. It was true that it had been made clear to him that it was to be maintained as an absolute secret, on which the continuance of the friendly patronage of the Professor, and consequently that five thousand pounds, entirely depended. But that might not have been meant as against the police. Suppose that there were some treasure there, some priceless secret, which the Professor's enemies now sought to steal, and that their activities had been observed and misinterpreted by the police? Suppose that they might be breaking down a door which they would respect if they knew it to be that of the highly reputable Professor? Suppose that a word from him would satisfy them, and they would withdraw? And then he would be blamed on both sides for having exercised an untimely reticence.

For all these uncertainties there was one solution. With a rather different object from any which Inspector Combridge had anticipated, Mr. Simpson rang up the Professor. In any case, he had meant to do so, for the summer suit which had been tried on last week was now ready for its final fitting.

Professor Blinkwell had differently numbered telephones in his laboratories and in his secretary's office. Those numbers were known to the world. He had one in his private suite, the number of which was not published and was known to few. Mr. Simpson had the privilege of this number. When he was put through, Myra answered.

The detective who had been stationed in a position appropriate for listening-in to any conversations in which the Professor might indulge now had the benefit of these exchanges.

"Is Professor Blinkwell in?"

"Yes. But he's engaged. Who is it speaking?"

"Mr. Simpson. Burrows and Simpson. Could I speak to him a moment?"

"Can't you give a message for him?"

"I thought he'd like to know that his suit's ready for fitting. But I'd rather speak to him, if he can spare a moment."

"Well, hold on, and I'll see."

The next moment there came the Professor's voice: "That you, Simpson? You'd better book Friday morning, eleven prompt. I'll call in then, if I don't before."

"Thank you, sir. That'll do nicely for me. I meant to ring you up earlier, but I've been hindered. I've got some detectives here from Scotland Yard trying to find if there's any way through my premises to a back street."

There was a moment's silence, so that Mr. Simpson had begun to wonder whether he were cut off, when the Professor's voice came in another tone: "Look here, Simpson, I don't know what trouble you're in now, but it's no use coming to me again. I put up five thousand pounds to get you out of one mess, and I told you that you'd got to go straight in the future or take the consequences." The Professor rang off.

There was little to be gained from that, beyond the knowledge that the Professor was too wary to commit himself on the potential publicity of a telephone wire. That was the detective's conclusion, and Mr. Simpson, though feeling puzzled and rebuffed, was disposed to understand it in much the same way. But he felt instinctively from that moment that Professor Blinkwell's secret was of a criminal kind. Was his silence exposing him to even greater risks than could lie in a demand for five thousand pounds which he could not pay?

"Inspector Combridge wants to know if you can lend him a strong chisel."

It was the voice of the Inspector's companion, Detective Fordyce, which disturbed the current of Mr. Simpson's thoughts, and guessing correctly that they had found the door and were seeking means of breaking it open, he resolved on the best method to save himself from any charge of complicity, if it should not be too late already.

"Yes," he said, "there are some tools at the back. I'll see what I can find."

He went into the back room, and came out with two chisels, a hammer, and an iron wedge. It shouldn't be said that he was reluctant to give his help. He did not offer them to the detective, but led the way up the stairs.

He found, as he had expected, that the Inspector and Sir Reginald were in the closet, where an electric torch shone. The Inspector turned as he approached.

"Mr. Simpson," he said, "there's something very like a door here."

The reply came readily: "Yes, but you mustn't go in there. That's the door of Professor Blinkwell's private room."

"Oh, it is, is it? Perhaps you'll tell me why you didn't mention it before."

"I didn't think you meant that. You asked about a way through into another street."

"Well, what's this?"

"It's the Professor's laboratory, I suppose. I don't really know."

"You mean you don't know what's on the other side?"

"I don't know at all. Professor Blinkwell never lets anyone see in."

"Well, we soon shall."

The two officers were now working vigorously to force the door. Sir Reginald stood back, for there was no room for three at the end of that narrow closet. He thought a few words with Mr. Simpson might not be wasted. He asked: "Does Professor Blinkwell own these premises?"

"No. I don't think so. They're part of the Morgan estate."

"Or the business?"

"No."

The two men looked at each other in a moment of doubtful silence. Mr. Simpson understood clearly enough that he was invited to a fuller confidence than his answers had yet given. The banker's queries were curt but his manner was not unfriendly. Frankness seemed wise, while it might still have a voluntary aspect.

"Professor Blinkwell," he added, answering the unspoken question, "advanced me five thousand pounds when my partner died."

"Might be called up any time, I suppose?"

"Yes. At short notice."

Sir Reginald produced his card. "Don't worry about that," he said easily. "After today the Professor may have other things to engage his mind. If there's any trouble, call there, and ask to see Mr. Matthews."

He felt that it might be worthwhile to purchase Mr. Simpson's goodwill, and that he was going the right way to that end. So he was; and amid the loud splintering of a door which was now yielding to the expertly applied energy of the two detectives, Mr. Simpson confided to him the circumstances under which he had given the Professor permission to construct that secret entrance, and the occasions and periods at which he had been accustomed to use it. Unfortunately, he could tell no more, that being all he knew.

There was a loud crash as the door fell inward into the office of Messrs. Burrows & Wilkinson. The two detectives very promptly followed, with Sir Reginald close behind. They were prepared for anything, but expected little more than they were destined to see. If that office had had any occupants ten minutes ago it was unlikely that they would have remained quiescent while it was being invaded in so violent a manner. They would either have resisted or fled. Inspector Combridge had a comfortable anticipation that they would have left at the first sound of the forcing of the door, and walked into the waiting arms of his colleagues at the end of the passage.

Yet he had learnt from many previous experiences that the unexpected will often happen, and he was prepared alike to face the resistance of cornered and lawless men or to explain his presence to the real or simulated indignation of the lawful occupants of a commission agents' office against whom he had no warrant, nor any more definite charge than that there was a door by which their office could be entered at an unusual side, and that a man believed to be Edward Mitchell had called upon them.

He might have been equal to the situation, as he had proved himself on previous occasions, but he was not faced with either of these difficult alternatives. He looked round on an empty room, which he had regarded as the more probable spectacle. He crossed quickly to the door, turning the handle and finding it to be locked, which was also a likely thing. "Rolfe," he said to his companion, "there's a lock to be opened here."

He turned round to observe that Sir Reginald had picked up an open sheet of paper from a desk which was otherwise bare. The whole room appeared to be singularly vacant of either books or papers. It had a neatness such as can rarely be observed in an office which is in active use. The Inspector had a passing thought that the room might be occupied only by the Professor, and by him only for occasional interviews. If that were so, it might limit the importance of their discovery, but, even then, they would have cut off the means by which he controlled the agents of his illegal activities, and they would have established beyond reasonable doubt that Terrill and Mitchell were the same person, and that he was in the Professor's service. He was human enough to feel a moment's satisfaction in the reflection that, at its best, the discovery would justify the policy which had left Mr. Terrill (or Mitchell) to go his own way.

But these were no more than the passing thoughts of the moment during which Detective Rolfe bent down to examine the lock of the office door, and Sir Reginald, having glanced at the sheet of paper he held, passed it over with the words: "You ought to see this, Inspector. It looks interesting."

The Inspector took it, and read:

Dear Wilk,

Just a line to let you know that I've cleared out. You know I've been fed up for the last month doing nothing here.

Terrill called this morning and I paid him his winnings on Barrymore. That's the last we've got to shell out, and it left me with £6 10s., so I thought it was time to quit.

J. T.

The Inspector read and controlled his temper with difficulty. He heard Detective Fordyce's exclamation of satisfaction as the lock yielded to his expert manipulation and the door came open. "Rolfe," he said, "there's no hurry about that. You'll find it's an empty nest."

"Genuine?" Sir Reginald asked laconically, with his eyes on the open sheet.

"No. Of course not. I wonder who sold us out."

They went down the passage together, turning a bend at which they came upon comrades who had been waiting for rabbits to bolt from an empty burrow. They returned to the office to search it vainly for any clues. But there was nothing there. Not even a piece of used blotting paper, the markings of which might have occupied the ingenuity of the official mind. Mr. J. T. (presumably Tonbridge) had gone. "Dear Wilk" (presumably Wilkinson, if there were such an individual) did not return.

Inspector Combridge wasted no time in assuring himself that there was little more to be gained from that room. He did not believe that John Terrill had called that morning for the collection of a betting debt, nor that J. T. had left as the result of being abandoned to weeks of ennui by a partner who had more engrossing occupations. He had a well-founded conviction that that office had been cleared as the result of a warning which must have reached the Professor, or its actual occupants, within the last few hours. Probably the fact that they had found Mitchell, and had him under observation, had been betrayed, and had caused that instant withdrawal. But betrayed how, and by whom?

It was so short a time—scarcely two hours—since he had observed the contiguity of those offices and the premises of the Professor's tailor in Oxford Street, and the suspicion had stirred in his mind which had led to that instant raid. Who could have betrayed it? How many had known? Had the Professor those who were in his pay even among the trusted officers of the Yard?

He considered the possibility that Mitchell (for he now assumed definitely that it was he) had become suspicious, and had himself conveyed the warning which had caused an instant flight from the room. In many ways it seemed the simplest, most probable solution. He would have accepted it but for one difficulty. He felt a reasonable conviction that that office had not normally been as entirely bare of books, or correspondence, or documents, even of letter paper or the means of blotting, as it now was. The grate was empty of any sign of fire. He felt that there had been a wholesale removal of a thorough, systematic kind.

The building had been under continual observation from the moment of Mitchell's call, but it had not been a very close investment, for it had been considered of the first importance to avoid exciting a premature suspicion. One or more individuals among the many who had been seen to leave or enter the building might have come to or from that room. But the removal of any bulk of books or papers would not have easily escaped observation. That, and the question of the time involved, seemed to point to a probability that there had been warning, probably with the actual removal of office documents, before Mitchell had called.

Two conclusions followed, each of a somewhat disconcerting character, and each urging the necessity of prompt and decisive action. If the warning had not been given by Mitchell himself—if it had reached that office at an earlier hour—he must himself have received it when he called, and must have been alert from that moment, and probably seeking to elude those who watched him in the belief that he was unsuspicious and only seeking to lie close in the hiding place he had chosen. Also, if that office had been so promptly left, and so thoroughly cleared, was it not probable that Miss Merivale's place of detention would be altered also? That if they should obtain the information from Mitchell of where he had driven her—if he should tell all he knew—it might lead them to no more than another abandoned shell?

Briefly, the Inspector expressed these doubts to Sir Reginald. He added: "There's only one thing to do now. That's to run Mitchell in without a second's delay. I'm just going to phone through to headquarters, to let them know how we've got on, and then I'm off to Warden Street. You can come if you like. I don't know whether Sir Henry'll think we can arrest Blinkwell as well on the strength of what we've found here. I don't quite see how we can myself, but it's for him to decide."

He added, another idea having crossed his mind as he spoke: "Of course, this office may have been cleared out by the way we came in. We shall have to look into that."

"I don't think it has," Sir Reginald answered. "I don't think anyone but Blinkwell had the right of way through." He repeated briefly the conversation he had had with Mr. Simpson. He did not think he was holding anything back now.

"I expect you're right. But we can't leave anything to chance. Rolfe, you'd better make a thorough search of the Oxford Street premises. I'll take a couple of men in the car and run Mitchell in."

Delaying only to make a short telephone report to his superior officers, in the course of which he learnt the substance of the conversation which had taken place between Mr. Simpson and the Professor, which did nothing to improve his temper, he returned to the car, which had been left in an adjoining street, and proceeded rapidly on his next mission, which was to "invite" Mr. John Terrill to a friendly talk at the headquarters of the Metropolitan Police.

CHAPTER XXXI.

POSSIBLY for the first time in his life Professor Blinkwell admitted to himself that he was a seriously frightened man.

He had known since the early hours of the morning that Mitchell had been discovered and was under the observation of the police. It was a maddeningly disconcerting, improbable incident to obtrude into his ordered plans. But he had known also that the police were proposing to keep the man under observation for the moment rather than subject him to immediate questioning, and the delay had seemed to be sufficient to enable him to make the fresh disposition that the occasion required.

He was uncertain how much Mitchell was likely to be persuaded to say, but he considered him to be a witness who might easily be discredited if his evidence were unsupported. The trouble was that Mitchell knew where Miss Merivale had been taken, and it had become a vital necessity that she should be moved at once and all traces of her detention obliterated. Mitchell knew of the Tonbridge & Wilkinson office. That also must be cleared, which could fortunately be done with even greater celerity and with advantage to his major plans. But Mitchell did not know of the secret entrance from Mr. Simpson's fitting-room. He did not know that Professor Blinkwell had ever entered the "turf commission agents" office.

The Professor, on his side, did not know that Mitchell would choose that morning—the first on which he was being followed—to visit Bruton Street, which he had been told to do on infrequent occasions, it being considered the safest method of conveying any necessary instructions, and paying him the remuneration which was agreed. Neither could he know that Inspector Combridge would be so prompt to observe the suspicious closeness of the Tonbridge & Wilkinson office to that of the highly respectable firm of tailors on which his patronage was bestowed.

Consequently, when Mr. Simpson telephoned that the police were upon him, it was a complication for which the Professor's mind, already more than sufficiently exercised, was unprepared. As an impromptu effort, we may admit some adroitness in the wording of his reply. He was able to put the receiver down with the satisfaction of feeling that he had given nothing away, if, as he rightly guessed, the conversation was being overheard by those for whom it was not meant.

But he had the sense to see that that reply, however necessary it might have been, was sure to leave the harassed Simpson in a mood of dissatisfaction. He knew the limited extent to which Simpson could betray him. One way or another he felt that Inspector Combridge would probe the secret of that hidden door. He saw that, if Mitchell should also disclose the extent of his own knowledge, that door would become a supporting and confirming evidence of a very sinister kind. It was hard to judge exactly all that it might mean.

Yet all might not be lost; all, indeed, might still be sustained if his plans of the next few hours could be completed with sufficient celerity. He could congratulate himself even now upon the promptitude of his actions in the earlier day. Upon that unsigned, undated letter which Myra had taken out in her muff (what an opportune thing it was that they were just coming into fashion again!) and had handed to a well-paid "friend" in a lift in one of the large shopping stores, by whom it had been sent to 17, Bruton Street in the safe hands of a district messenger. He did not doubt that Jim Tonbridge would have cleared out before the hour at which he now knew that the police had come on the scene.

But, all the same, he was a worried man. Not knowing of Mitchell's call at the Bruton Street office, he could not tell how the suspicions of the police had been aroused concerning it. His prompt action in clearing it might give him satisfaction and some measure of self-confidence now. He had acted on his usual principle that all risk must be eliminated from the details of his illicit activities. But he had not thought the need to be so urgent. It was disconcerting to find that he had so nearly been a day too late. More disconcerting not to be able to understand how the peril had so quickly arisen. Disconcerting, too, that he had no safe means of communicating with Jim Tonbridge, or he with him, at any rate till the later day. There was only his knowledge of the man to assure him that his instructions would have been followed and the premises cleared in time. If not—if Jim and his companions were not on their way to Beckminster now, or perhaps actually there—well it was no use thinking about that.

"Myra," he said, as he enjoyed a leisurely cigar at his study fireside, "if Inspector Combridge or any of his friends should call to see me this afternoon you won't say I'm out. You'll ask them to wait, and keep them kicking their heels here just as long as you can. If they ring up I shall be lying down. I'm not very well, and have given instructions that I'm not to be disturbed on any account till I ring for tea, which, of course, I may do at any time. They can call up again. And again after that. Actually, I'm going over the garden wall, which, I believe, is not a criminal offence in this country if your neighbour doesn't object. I haven't been watched everywhere I've moved for the last month without having had plenty of time to think out how I can get a little solitude if I wish to do so."

"There isn't anything going wrong?"

Myra was sensitive to atmosphere, but her confidence in her uncle's cool, unscrupulous efficiency was too absolute for her to be easily disturbed.

"No. Nothing yet. There might be, if I lost my head or allowed others to do so. I should diagnose it as a condition requiring a more drastic treatment than the slow and gentle methods which I have been hitherto content to apply. It has become necessary to perform the rather difficult military operation of changing front under fire."

"What's the matter, really?"

"Mitchell's let himself be seen."

"Can't you trust him?"

"I don't know. He isn't one of my men."

"He doesn't know much, does he?"

"Nothing about the new organization. Nor the old, for that matter."

"Then I don't see that it matters overmuch."

"I didn't say that it did. But that isn't quite all. Inspector Combridge has been spending the last hour in looking for my private entrance to the Bruton Street office. I've no doubt he's found it before now. He's an intelligent man."

"How did he hear of that?"

"I don't know. That is the point which renders caution so necessary. There's something I haven't learnt yet."

"Will it matter if he gets in?"

"Not if Jim's acted promptly. The note you took this morning was to tell him to clear."

"Then they'll find nothing but an empty room?"

"So I expect. So far as I can now judge, the only real danger lies in what Mitchell may say."

"I shouldn't have thought he could say much, even if they get him to squeal. You told me once that he didn't know you were in it at all."

"I suppose that to be right. I don't suppose he has even heard my name, unless it was from the talk of Miss Merivale or her friends. The point is that he knows Beckminster."

For the first time Myra looked really frightened. The blood receded from a countenance which was naturally too florid to require the aid of any permanent colouring. "But—Beckminster!" she exclaimed. "If he knows that, he knows everything."

"Not exactly. You are going beyond the fact. I mean he knows the way there. Inspector Combridge is looking for Miss Merivale. He isn't thinking about anything else. The point is that if he gets Mitchell to talk he'll take him straight there."

"And, if he does that, it ruins everything?"

"Not at all. That would depend upon what he'd find. There's no law against brass-casting in premises which have been legitimately acquired, nor even in having kept on some of the old hands. It was a very kindly thing to have done. But I think I'd better be going now. You needn't tell your aunt that I'm not in."

"Then you're coming back? She'll have to know if you're not back before long."

"I expect to be in for dinner as usual. If Inspector Combridge finds that I am not here, he will probably think I have gone away, and it will be one of the biggest mistakes that he ever made. I'm simply taking this elaborate but necessary means of making certain that I can give some telephone instructions without being overheard. And, if the Inspector should call while I am away, I am asking you to use the occasion to waste as much of his time as you can contrive to do. I expect he'll waste a few minutes more telling that snuff-coloured ape on the other side of the road what he thinks of him for having let me go off unobserved. Quite unjustly, of course, for it is a most difficult matter to keep alert every moment, week after week, in watching someone who makes no effort to get away."

In spite of the scientific impartiality of this verdict, the tone of the Professor's remark, and the somewhat disparaging description which he applied to the detective in question, appeared to indicate that he was not entirely free from the irritation which may be experienced by lesser men when they are kept under police observation for an extended period. But, if so, it was no more than the trivial annoyance which is felt by one who brushes a persistent fly from his hand. With his usual equanimity, the Professor threw the end of his cigar into the grate, rose quietly, put on his hat and coat, and entered the automatic lift by which he was accustomed to pass from one floor to another of the suite of flats which he occupied.

This lift was capable of descending to the basement, though it rarely did so. From that basement a door opened onto a little space of grass, with a single sycamore at the farther end, dividing its shade between that and a similar enclosure at the back of the adjoining premises.

The Professor walked quietly over the grass, and having gained the shade of the sycamore he got over the wall. He crossed the next rectangle of ground in the same quiet and confident manner. He did not slink along the wall with his neck craning behind and before at many difficult angles, after the manner in which the stage burglar or flying hero advertises to all observers that he doesn't want to be seen. He walked with the unhurried assurance or one who treads on his own ground. Anyone looking out of one of the many back windows that overlooked would have seen nothing to excite suspicion, especially as they could not have seen his transit of the wall, which the tree hid.

Between the next house to his own and the one farther away there was a narrow entry which led to the road. He went confidently down this passage, and turned away when he came out on the road, leaving his own house behind. It might seem, to a superficial view, an elaborate method or contriving to emerge so few yards from his own door. But the issue showed his judgment to be as sound as it usually was. He walked quietly away, neither hurrying nor looking back, and the bored detective who was keeping a weary, eventless watch on his own door did not observe him at all. At the end of the road he got on to a passing bus, and half an hour later, being some distance from his own home, and having taken sufficient precautions to make certain that he was not followed, he went into a public telephone box and did his business with a pleasant certainty that he had freed himself from the curiosities and interference of the police.

When he had completed his dispositions he returned home, in time for dinner, as he had promised to do. He observed that the snuff-coloured ape was still watching his door, and went over to him before entering to offer the courtesy of a cigarette and his condolences on the probability of a wet night. He forgot the puzzled stare of that disconcerted officer when he learnt from Myra that she had not been disturbed during his absence either by call or telephone, about which he felt a vague dissatisfaction, which increased as the evening passed in the same uninterrupted peace.

This feeling had become more acute by the following morning, so that for the first time in her life Myra observed in his words and conduct some of the nervous irritability which is common to lesser mortals at periods of crises deferred.

But he made no allusion to the subject that was in both their thoughts till she asked directly:

"It's getting to look as though Inspector Combridge didn't find anything out after all, isn't it?"

The Professor asked "Why?" in a tone of monosyllabic annoyance for which the question did not appear to give any adequate cause.

"Well, I thought you rather expected that we should be hearing from him before now, if he had."

"It is necessary," the Professor answered, with a deliberate recovery of his self-control, "to prepare for many eventualities which are of no more than a contingent kind. Yet a communication is to be anticipated, and, for Miss Merivale's sake, if it should be much longer delayed, it would be an error of a regrettable magnitude. The young women in the world, even of an equal superficial attraction, are too numerous for the scientific mind to be disturbed by the reduction of a single unit, but I dislike waste of whatever kind. Neither can the matter be regarded as of no more importance than that of a fifty-millionth reduction of the population of the British Isles. She is, as you know, the counter with which I have played—with which I am still playing—for a great stake. Its elimination would therefore alter the whole position in a radical way. I have no reason to anticipate any substantial loss to myself, either in fortune or liberty, nor that our new organization will be molested beyond the possible loss of Beckminster as a future centre of operations. But I will say frankly that, should there be no communication from Inspector Combridge within the next two hours, or perhaps less, I must reconcile my mind to abandoning the expectation of acquiring control of the Ralston process, from which I had anticipated a substantial fortune."

Myra had learnt during many such previous conversations that it was a mistake to interrupt her uncle's elaborately qualified sentences, even though the bulk of his reflections might convey little to her more limited but equally practical mind.

Having no other confidant—for Mrs. Blinkwell professed to regard him, and may actually have done so, as a man in whom scientific brilliance was united to a singularly simple and childlike character, and he had early observed that that was the only footing on which amicable relations could be maintained between them—he was accustomed, at these breakfast-time relaxations, to think aloud rather than to take counsel with one on whose silence and discretion he could rely, but whose intellectual limitations, and lack of initiative, debarred her from more than a subordinate participation in his major activities

On her side, she would subject his conversation to a process of mental filtering, by which the bulk of it was rejected as absolutely as though it had been spoken in a foreign tongue, and the residuum shone with the clarity of this discrimination, like the yellow grains at the bottom of a gold-washer's sieve.

If she interrupted in search of explanation, or to dam a torrent of unmeaning words, the stream was liable to run dry in a manner more provoking even than its previous plenitude. It was better to wait in patience, watching for the grains of gold, and speaking only when there was the pause in its natural flow which invited, if it did not actually expect, her to do so.

Now she said, a note of actual anxiety in her voice, and a shade of apprehension spreading over the selfish good-humour of her normal expression: "You don't mean to say that you've told them to— to get rid of Miss Merivale altogether? Wouldn't it be a bit too dangerous with all the fuss that's going on about her not being found?"

It is fair to observe that Myra was not only a little startled, a little frightened; she was a little shocked also. She had heard previous explanations of the necessity for an occasional homicide in the operations of the gang of international drug-dealers in which the Professor had been head of the English branch, and on the wreck of which he was now building one which he aimed to control entirely. These homicides had usually been of a disciplinary kind, and the occasion for them became apparent when it was considered that large sums of money must pass continually through the hands of men of less than doubtful character, and who could not be subjected to the restraints of the civil law. But a lady—an innocent prisoner— of Miss Merivale's quality...it did seem a bit different.

But the Professor observed her reaction, and was unperturbed. He knew Myra as one who would be moved to a warm and generous indignation if she were told of the tortured miseries of a rabbit in the jaws of a steel trap. But he knew also that if it had been a case of her own dinner being a course short, she would have touched the bell without hesitation and ordered a trap to be set at once. There are occasions when we must all learn to put our weaker feelings aside with a firm hand.

"No," he said, "it is to avoid a possible danger that I came to that decision and gave the necessary instructions yesterday. It has been evident from the first that it would become a necessary course to adopt if neither Sir Reginald nor her brother should think it worth their while to procure her freedom. To release her, except by an agreed and friendly settlement, has become an obvious impossibility. But the developments of yesterday produced a more urgent problem. Prudence compelled me to decide upon the instant abandoning of the Beckminster depot. The stock presented no difficulty. Its bulk, in relation to its value, is comparatively small, as you know. By this time it is probably buried three feet under ground, or within the wall of the canal bridge of which I have told you previously, or—in any of a dozen places which no one would ever find and very few could betray.

"But a living woman, vigorous and intelligent, and doubtless indignant at her detention, cannot be so easily hidden. That is particularly the case when she is one for whom the whole country is looking, with a reward of ten thousand pounds to be earned by her discovery. She was safe in jail, but I know of no other place of an approximately equal security. No, it is a risk which, for more than a few hours, I felt that I simply cannot afford to take. It would be to jeopardize the great business—the certain fortune—that is in my grasp, for the chance of one that I might never gain.

"Yet," he added, after a little pause, as Myra was not quick to reply, "I have not lost hope. I still think it likely that Inspector Combridge may ring the bell before noon. You might let Mullins know that I may want the Bentley at any time."

Myra did not discuss the probability of the Inspector calling, concerning which she had no data on which to form an opinion. She was fascinated by the thought of Miss Merivale's peril. She asked, "What are they going to do with her if they don't hear from you in time to stop it?"

"I haven't the least idea, and I've no intention of enquiring, either now or at any future time. It is not a matter with which a prudent man would associate himself in any way. It is sufficient to be able to feel an entire confidence that the instructions which I telephoned yesterday will be carried out unless I shall personally intervene to stay them. You can let Parker know that I shall be in the laboratories till about ten-thirty, if anyone should call to see me."

"You still think he'll come, more likely than not?"

"I have a fairly confident anticipation." A good breakfast, leisurely consumed, had given a more optimistic tinge to the Professor's really excellent judgment.

As Myra asked the question, she had risen from the table. She passed the window, making her way to the bell. She had asked her uncle several times to have an extension to the table, but he had replied that the exercise did her good. Was it not sometimes all that she would take in a day's length? Now she looked idly down on the street below, with eyes which had not been ruined by study in her younger days.

"You're right again," she said, "there's Inspector Combridge corning along now."

There was a slight anxiety in the Professor's voice as he asked: "Is he alone?"

"No. He's in an open car. There look to be enough with him to fill a bus."

"Do they look like police officers?"

"I can't see now. It's too close under the window. I should say not. They look a mixed lot to me."

"Myra, I'll see the Inspector here, and any others he likes to bring up. You needn't ring to clear away. I dare say they'll be glad of some breakfast, and it'll save time. I shouldn't wonder if they've been up all night."

Two minutes later the Inspector entered the room with Mr. Jellipot at his side. He glanced doubtfully at Myra. "Professor Blinkwell," he said, "may I see you alone?"

"No," the Professor answered, "I don't know that you can. I think my niece will remain."

"As you like. I must ask you to come with me now. I have a warrant for your arrest on a charge of—"

"Never mind what it's about, Inspector. I'm not really interested, and I'm sure you're not going to execute it. It would probably cost Miss Merivale's life, besides making you look a bigger fool than you really are."

Inspector Combridge gave no sign of responding to the almost bantering tone in which he was addressed by his prospective prisoner. He said: "I have to warn you that anything you say may be used in evidence against you."

"Yes, that's the routine, isn't it? I seem to have heard it before. But why not *for* me, Inspector? Isn't that a more likely thing? Do you suppose I'm particularly likely to say anything silly? I tell you that if you execute that warrant now it will probably cost Miss Merivale's life, and if you don't listen, it's for you to explain, when it's too late, in your own way. You know very well that that warrant's no more than a silly bluff, whether or not. You couldn't hold me a week. When you get into court your guesses won't take you far."

"Perhaps if you'd listen to what the charges are...," the Inspector began again, and there was no compromise in his tone, though the Professor thought that he saw evidence of irresolution of a subtler kind.

He interrupted him again to repeat: "But you see, Inspector, I don't care. You'd be a really capable officer if your methods weren't so extremely crude. Now I was just saying to Myra, not five minutes ago, that you'd have been up all night, and some breakfast would do you good and save time in the end. That's why it hasn't been cleared away before now."

At this point Mr. Jellipot interposed. He looked at the Inspector's unyielding face, and said, with an anxiety which sounded almost more than the occasion required: "Perhaps, considering how long it is since we've had a meal—"

The reluctance of the Inspector, whether real or simulated, gave way before this appeal. "Well," he said, "if you put it like that, I suppose half an hour won't make much difference."

"Myra," the Professor said, without showing any surprise or satisfaction at this concession, "you'd better ring for some fresh coffee, and some more plates, and—you'll know what to order best. You'll find the gentlemen will like a good meal. And if Lord Britleigh and Sir Reginald are down below, as I've not much doubt that they are, we'd better have them up too."

Mr. Jellipot, his mind working with its usual precision in a tired body, for he was older than his companions, and less robust of habit, had a thought for the fifth member of their party, who must be as hungry as the rest. He may also have wished to see the effect of his words upon the Professor's exasperating complacency.

"There's Ted Mitchell," he said, "with us as well."

The Professor did not appear to be disconcerted by this information, though it was apparent that his hospitality hesitated. But he overcame whatever reluctance he may have felt to adding the groom to the list of his breakfast guests.

"Well," he said, after a pause, "we're not short of another chair. Whoever he is, I expect he needs something to eat. There's nothing private in what I want to say, if you feel the same."

The Inspector noticed that Professor Blinkwell was careful not to admit any knowledge of the man whom Billington's Agency had supplied. He had good reason to doubt the genuineness of this ignorance, though it was a fact that Mitchell had not come previously into the Professor's presence. But, be that as it might, he was resolved that he would not be manœuvred into any compromising bargain by the bland assurance of one who had succeeded once before in making terms with the civil power when not his liberty alone, but his neck, had seemed to be beyond any insurance premium. A hundred percent loss it had seemed, and then—well, once was enough. And the Inspector's mind was sore over the discoveries of the night. Beckminster, *of course*. The explanation seemed so simple, so obvious now. Well, he wasn't going to be fooled again.

"There's nothing private on our side," he said coldly. "I've told you before that anything you say will be at your own risk."

"Do you mind," the Professor enquired courteously, "sitting with your back to the fire?"

CHAPTER XXXII.

IT was something after four o'clock on the previous after noon when Mr. John Terrill (or Mitchell), having finished an early but substantial tea, stood looking out of the window of the first-floor front which he rented in Easton Street, and observed a rather large car of an open pattern come rapidly up the street and stop immediately beneath him. A man much less alert and intelligent than himself, considering his occupations of the last two months, and having digested the hint which Jim Tonbridge had given him a few hours earlier, would have quickly realized that he was about to receive a visit from the police.

He had hoped that he might avoid this development by remaining in an even more strict retirement than he had done previously. He had no reason to suppose that he had been observed already. He thought the risk had lain in his call at the Bruton Street office, which Jim had told him he had been warned to vacate in haste. He thought (though without certainty) that he had got back unobserved. He was not committing an indiscretion in looking out of the window, for the lace curtain was opaque with dirt. He hoped to avoid trouble, but the warning had prepared his mind for its coming, and the visit lacked the element of surprise on which Inspector Combridge largely relied for its success.

As it was, it is extremely likely that, if he had come alone, the Inspector would either have arrested a man who refused to make any admissions (which might have proved a very barren proceeding) or have gone empty away. But he had taken the precaution, even at the cost of a short delay, of gathering others to whom Mitchell had been previously known, and that gentleman did not now observe the Inspector alone, but (with a much greater annoyance) that Lord Britleigh, Mr. Jellipot, and Sir Reginald Crowe were also getting out of the car. The programme of denying his identity, which he had been previously inclined to favour, suffered an instant modification.

Well, it was no use trying to shirk the position. By certain standards, he had done his duty throughout. His conscience, if not entirely clear, was doing quite as well as could be expected under the somewhat unusual circumstances of the case. When the landlady announced the names of his visitors, he would see them and hear what they had to say. So he resolved, but he found that they did not delay for the formality of being invited upstairs. They just came.

The Inspector stood in the open doorway. He looked back at the three gentlemen in his rear. They looked at Mitchell and nodded affirmatively. There was no doubt of the man.

"Ted Mitchell," the Inspector said, in his more formal official voice, "you have given us a lot of needless trouble by hiding here. You were the last person seen with Miss Evelyn Merivale, who has now been missing for several weeks. I don't say you've done anything wrong yourself, but you've withheld important information we ought to have had long before now. I shall have to ask you to come with me to Scotland Yard, and I hope you'll be able to clear matters up there. But whatever you've done, you'll be a wise man if you give us all the help that you can from now on."

"Perhaps you're running on just a bit too fast," the man answered coolly. "You'd better show me the warrant first, and then we'll discuss who I am."

"I'm not arresting you yet, Mitchell. We wish to give you an opportunity of explaining first."

"Then I think we'll talk where we are, if we talk at all."

"Ted," Sir Reginald interposed. "I paid you to take care of Miss Merivale, and I thought you were a straight man. If you are, you'll give us all the help you can now; and if you're not—well, there's ten thousand pounds for the man who puts us on the right track if we find her safe in the end."

"You oughtn't to say that, Sir Reginald. I never had a penny from you, except the hundred pounds you gave me when I got Miss Merivale clear of the car, and half-a-crown the week before, and I didn't ask you for that."

Lord Britleigh and Sir Reginald spoke at once. "Then you admit you're Mitchell. I paid Billington's Agency, which is the same thing."

The man answered Lord Britleigh first: "I never said I wasn't, did I? Not to those who've a right to know. You don't know what I'm doing here, or what my right name is, for that matter, and it's no business of yours." Then he turned to Sir Reginald to say: "It's not the same thing at all. Billington's paid me, and I took my orders from them. You should talk to Mr. Billington, sir, if you're not satisfied, not to me."

The tone was more deferential than the words, and the argument had a force which his hearers could not deny, though it left much to be said.

The Inspector interposed to ask: "Are you going to tell us, Mitchell, that Mr. Billington told you to help in abducting Miss Merivale?"

"Of course not, sir. I'm only saying that I was employed by Mr. Billington, and if Sir Reginald isn't satisfied he ought to complain to him."

"Perhaps he ought. But, you see, you had disappeared, and Mr. Billington said he had absolute confidence in you, and was sure you would explain everything when you turned up."

There was no answer to this. The man stood in an evident indecision, of which the three who confronted him were quick to take advantage by their different methods. Each of them was an expert negotiator in his own way, and the combination placed a man who was no more than a private enquiry agent of average ability, and fundamentally decent instincts, at a tactical disadvantage by which more expert dialecticians, and with a clearer case than his, might have been overthrown.

"The best thing you can do for your own skin, Mitchell," the Inspector said curtly, "is to tell us just what those instructions were."

"It is not only that I paid Billington's for you to protect Miss Merivale," Sir Reginald said, in a milder and more persuasive manner. "You've got to remember that she trusted you for that reason. I'm not asking you to help us for the sake of the reward, if you think it wouldn't be the right thing to do. But you've got to remember that it was because she trusted you that she went off as she did. Now we think that she may be—even her life may be in an urgent peril unless we can trace her quickly. Don't you think, even if you feel you can't take the reward, that you ought to give us what help you can?"

Before the man could reply, Mr. Jellipot's precise voice took up the argument: "If Mr. Mitchell is, as I understand to be the case, in the employment of Billington's Agency, and if, as he has led us to understand, though he may not have stated it in explicit words, he is under orders from them to remain silent concerning any knowledge or complicity which he may have or have had in connection with Miss Merivale's departure from Saxton Hall, then I would suggest for his consideration the fact that we have been in touch with Mr. Billington during the last few hours, probably more recently than himself, and that that gentleman gave us no reason to doubt that he was desirous of doing everything in his power to assist the search. If, after hearing this, he should still hesitate to give us the information which may be vital to Miss Merivale's safety, I suggest that he should be given an opportunity of communicating with Mr. Billington on the telephone and obtaining further instructions from him."

The man received this proposal with a moment of obvious indecision. He had a genuine regard for Miss Merivale, and would willingly have rendered any assistance that was in his power. Beyond that, he had been confused by the apparently contradictory instructions which he had received from Mr. Billington while at Saxton Hall, and during the subsequent weeks. But he knew, so long as he obeyed intelligently, it was no part of his duty to reconcile or to understand them. He would have adopted Mr. Jellipot's proposal without hesitation had not a doubt entered his mind that it might be a preconcerted plot to entrap his employer. He looked at Inspector Combridge, and observed that he did not look pleased. Reassured by the expression of his face, and seeing that, if he did not accept the suggestion promptly, the Inspector was more likely to veto than to support it, he said: "Yes. That seems fair. I'll do that."

Inspector Combridge did not demur. In fact he looked pleased. The idea which the man had feared had already entered his mind. Telephone conversations can be overheard, and this one seemed likely to be of an interesting kind.

"Very well," he said, "we'll go along to the Yard, and you can phone there."

But Mitchell shook his head, and his mouth set obstinately. "There's a call-box two streets away," he said. "I'll phone from there, if at all, and we'll keep together, gentlemen, if you please, in the meantime."

The Inspector answered with equal decision, and a curter tone: "Oh no, you won't. You'll phone just how and where you're told, if you do it at all." How could they even tell that he would phone to Mr. Billington if they should let him go into the box alone? It was an absurd thing to propose.

He might use the opportunity to call his friends to his rescue, or warn them to further flight.

But Sir Reginald interposed, in a tone which he seldom used, but which his fellow directors knew as the signal that he had determined on a course from which he would not be lightly turned.

"If you please, Inspector, I think we must let Mitchell do this in his own way. We've got to remember that it's Mr. Jellipot's suggestion, not his. A word with Mr. Billington ought to clear the ground so that we can go straight ahead. I always trust a man till I've found him go crooked, but if we've been double-crossed by that—well, I won't say what he'd be if he had—but I'll make him sick of his life before I've done with him if I break every law in the land. You'll find, when Mitchell's had that talk, he'll give us all the help that he can."

The Inspector made no further protest, and the whole party were soon on their way to the telephone booth in the Inspector's car.

Three minutes later Mr. Billington, who was then giving benign advice to a young couple who wished to know how the necessary legal evidence for a change of partners could be most economically and safely faked (an assistance for which we can only condemn him to the extent by which we consider perjury to outweigh adultery as a social evil), was interrupted by the information that someone who would not give a name, but who had supplied the code word used by his agents when they wanted to report privately, was on the telephone, and urgently insisting on being put through to him without delay. Mr. Billington, to whom such interruptions were of the routine of his peculiar activities, asked his clients to excuse him for a moment, and retired to an inner room, to take part in a conversation which Inspector Combridge had been right in thinking that he would have been interested to hear.

"Yes, who's that?"

"Terrill speaking."

"Terr…but you weren't to ring up here at all. You were to receive instructions through the B. Street office. Unless it's something you're bound to report to me, you must ring off at once."

"Well, sir, I didn't forget the instructions. But I can't go there again. I went this morning, and they're clearing out. There's some trouble on there."

"I know all about that. You must stay where you are till you hear from me. You ought to know better than to ring up like this."

"It isn't only that, sir. I'm speaking from a call office, with Inspector Combridge, and Lord Britleigh, and Sir Reginald Crowe waiting outside."

Mr. Billington cursed half audibly. A quick motion of the receiver took it halfway to the hook. Of course, every word was being overheard by the police! What an utter blundering fool the man was!

But he saw, in the next half-second, that if the conversation really was being overheard, he could not escape the difficulty so easily. To ring off would be an action very hard to explain. He might have put his foot in it sufficiently already by his allusion to the "B. Street office." He put the receiver back to his ear as he replied: "Well, I'm engaged now. You'd better come up and report."

157

"I don't know that they'd let me do that, sir. They want me to ask your permission to give them what help I can in tracing Miss Merivale."

"Well, you must come here. I can't give instructions on the phone. I can't hear your voice very well, and I'm not sure enough who I'm speaking to."

"We're not being overheard, sir, if you're thinking of that. Inspector Combridge didn't want me to phone from here, he wanted me to go to the Yard."

"Then why did he give way?"

"Sir Reginald made him."

"Then listen to me, Mitchell, and don't make any mistake. You're to tell the police everything, and say you have my instructions to do so. You'll tell them how you drove Miss Merivale to Basingstoke, and after that to the coast near Hastings, and about the boat in which she was taken off to the ship that was waiting a couple of miles out."

There was a moment's silence. Had they been cut off? Mr. Billington called impatiently: "Are you there, Mitchell? Did you hear what I said?"

"Not very well, sir.... I think I'll resign, if you don't mind."

There was no doubt that they were disconnected now, nor was there any doubt this time as to the audibility of the curse with which Mr. Billington concluded the episode. He went back to his interrupted interview, but he found it unusually difficult to maintain his customary urbanity, or even to direct his mind to the problem on which his young clients desired his help.

CHAPTER XXXIII.

THE mistake which Mr. Billington had made was that of reliance upon a well-tested quality in the character of Ted Mitchell, without appreciating its logical consequence under a strain to which it had not been subjected previously. He knew him as a man of a stubborn loyalty, who could be trusted to carry out any instructions he received with exactness, and with some courage and intelligence also. He knew that he had once been offered a very heavy bribe in the course of an earlier investigation, which he had merely entered without comment on his report of the case. Had he instructed him to maintain a continued silence, it is possible that the united eloquence of a very able banker, and the representatives of law and the legal profession, would have been unable to move him from it, and it is certain that the argument of arrest would not have availed. But a man of Mr. Billington's particular experiences should have seen, even in the urgent stress of that unwelcome telephone call, that it did not follow—was, indeed, of a consequent improbability—that he would be prepared to concoct an utterly mendacious statement as to the destination to which he had conveyed Miss Merivale, making himself an active accessory to the abduction, and to any subsequent criminality which may have occurred.

Without attempting an analysis of his own feelings, or of the ethics of the position, he rejected instantly an instruction which he felt that his employer had no right to give. Seeing the necessity of disobedience, resignation appeared the natural consequence. In an instant the words were spoken, and the conversation cut off. He went out of the booth to rejoin the four men who stood in a group on the pavement by the waiting car.

As he approached they ceased an argument concerning the probable result of the conversation in which he had been engaged, in which the sanguine anticipations of Mr. Jellipot and Sir Reginald had been ineffectual to inoculate the Inspector to an equal optimism.

"Even if Billington's had a big fee from Blinkwell to let us down, which seems the most likely explanation," Sir Reginald was saying, "though you own yourself that he's got as good a reputation as men of his kind can expect to have, I don't see what he could do now but see that the game's up, and that Mitchell has got to tell what he knows. There was Mitchell actually being paid by me to take care of Miss Merivale, and they are known to have gone off together, and you can't make me believe that Billington would ever have the face to tell us that he's instructed him to keep quiet as to what happened, and where they went."

"No," the Inspector admitted, "it sounds all right when you put it like that. But there are quite a lot of other things he might say that we can't hear now. He might tell him to fob us off with a lie—that's about the likeliest thing—or give him the tip that he's to refuse on the ground that he isn't obliged to incriminate himself. He might even persuade him that silence is really best for the sake of his own skin. We can't even judge whether that's true till we know what he really did. And, as I've told you before, it's quite likely he isn't telephoning to Billington's at all."

"Well," Mr. Jellipot observed, as he saw Mitchell put the receiver back, "he's coming out now, and we shall soon know."

"And if looks mean anything, gentlemen, you'll find I've not been far wrong."

There was some reason for this remark, for as Mitchell came out of the booth his face scarcely wore the expression of a man whose perplexities have been lifted from him. But whatever scepticism the Inspector might have expressed to his companions, he did not allow any lack of confidence to appear in voice or manner as he said briskly: "And now you've got Mr. Billington's authority, I suppose we shall be able to get ahead."

"It doesn't matter what Mr. Billington says now. I've thrown up the job."

"You mean you're free now to give us all the help that you can, without reference to him?"

But it appeared that this point was not equally clear to Ted Mitchell's mind. He had thrown up his job rather than accept uncongenial instructions, the motive of which was not disclosed, and was of a dubious and possibly criminal kind. It did not follow that he was free next moment to betray the secrets of his previous employment. So he said, and for some time he resisted the arguments and persuasions of his four opponents, with inferior fluency, but an equal determination.

Finally, they arrived at a suggestion of compromise on the basis of an undertaking being given that Mr. Billington should not be penalized by civil or criminal process as a result of any revelation that he might make. The Inspector gave a guarded and limited assent to this proposition, under Sir Reginald's urgent persuasion, and pointing out that it might be overruled by superior powers. But Mitchell's scruple was not primarily occasioned by any fear that his employer might have rendered himself liable to legal penalty in official eyes. Rightly or wrongly, he believed that the business of Billington's Agency was conducted within the limits of legal regularity, or at least within those of the criminal code. He was more concerned lest any disclosure he might make would betray his employer to the necessity of a difficult explanation to Sir Reginald, and, perhaps, to a civil action for breach of confidence or professional misconduct. He felt that Sir Reginald would be stirred to a natural anger when informed of the instructions on which he had acted, the contradictory nature of which was a mystery to which he was still without any guiding clue. He did not feel that his resignation released him unconditionally from the obligations of reticence regarding the events of his employment, which were of an obviously confidential nature.

But Sir Reginald, however strongly he might have expressed himself half an hour earlier at the thought of possible treachery in Mr. Billington's conduct, had one purpose in mind to which he felt that all other considerations must be subordinated without reserve. He saw in Mitchell—if Mitchell would only speak!—the probable means of affecting Evelyn's speedy rescue, and whatever terms the man might make, whether in gold or less substantial considerations, must be paid without cavil. Billington's immunity, whatever he might have done—and nothing had yet been proved against him—simply did not weigh in that scale.

But having had such assurances as could be given that anything he might disclose should not be used to the detriment of his late employer, Mitchell began to talk at last. He was, in fact, glad to do so, and would doubtless have given a full account of Miss Merivale's abduction, and of his part in the matter, but for the effect of his first utterance upon the Inspector's conduct.

They were still standing on the pavement between the telephone booth and the waiting car. Inspector Combridge had observed that Mitchell would answer Sir Reginald more readily than himself. In such an investigation he was not easily stirred by any personal feeling: he looked only to the end in view. He was quite willing to stand back and leave the questioning in the banker's very capable hands.

But the first answer that came roused him to the necessity of immediate action.

"What we want to know first of all," Sir Reginald began, "is where you took Miss Merivale after you left Saxton Hall, and if you can tell us whether she's there still."

"I can't tell you whether she's there now, sir; nor whether she stopped there at all, but we were driven to Basingstoke, and my orders were to take her from there by a roundabout way to Beckminster Jail, so that we shouldn't arrive till it was quite dark."

The sentence was hardly finished when the Inspector's voice broke in sharply: "Beckminster Jail! Here, jump in all of you. Mitchell, you've got to tell this at the Yard. No, don't look like that. It's nothing, against you. Nothing at all. But there's no time to waste, and we'd better be on the way, instead of standing here. Mitchell, get in with me. Get in behind, gentlemen, if you please. What's it all about, Sir Reginald? Doesn't Beckminster mean anything to you?"

As he said this, he had already bustled his companions into the car, and the steering wheel was between his hands. He looked over his shoulder to add: "I'll tell you what it means to you. It means that if I can have orders put through to Beckminster quickly enough, and the police surround the jail there before they get Miss Merivale moved, she'll probably be safe home in a few hours."

"That's the best news I've heard for some time; but you don't sound over-pleased."

"I've told you what it means to you. What it means to us is that Scotland Yard's going to be the laughing stock of the world if we don't get Miss Merivale safely back, and that won't save us if that letter of hers ever gets known."

"You mean she's been in jail all the time, while you've been saying it isn't possible?"

"No. Of course not. It wasn't possible. We were right there. But a child ought to have guessed the truth. *Beckminster Jail's been closed and sold for the last two years.*"

"You mean she's been shut up in a real jail that's no more than a fake now? Do you know who bought it, and when?"

"No, I don't. But I soon shall." The tone was curt, almost savage, and it was evident that the Inspector was disinclined for further conversation. Indeed, at the pace at which he now drove, he needed both eyes and mind for the immediate task that engaged his hands.

Sir Reginald was content to digest the information he had received. It was better than he could have hoped. He had expected to hear that Evelyn was in some remote or dangerous place, or that

Mitchell had handed her over to others who had taken her he knew not where. But now it was only a question of a sufficiently speedy rescue—and it need not be half an hour, if the telephone were properly used, before the Beckminster police might be around her hiding-place, and every exit barred. He could not be expected to worry himself overmuch that the development might suggest annoying possibilities to the official mind. Nor was he impatient for further details. He recognized, like the Inspector, that they had secured the one central fact which it had been vital for them to know. Only speed mattered now. He answered Lord Britleigh's impatient speculations and exclamations with little interest he gave a polite assenting monosyllable to Mr. Jellipot's solitary remark, after he had reflected upon this surprising development, that Professor Blinkwell must be a very able man.

CHAPTER XXXIV.

THE Superintendent at Beckminster was polite, but incredulous. As he listened, he became serious, and finally half convinced He was to surround and raid the old Beckminster jail? To search it to the last stone? To detain everyone to whom the least possible suspicion could be attached? He enquired whether Scotland Yard would take full responsibility for these proceedings. He said plainly that if a mistake were being made, he wanted it to be their funeral, not his. He covered the mouthpiece for a moment to say to his chief assistant: "Bates, you'd better listen to this." He meant to have all the evidence he could of the definite nature of that verbal pledge.

Finally, he agreed to conduct the operation on the assurance that Inspector Combridge was already on the way, and would take control on his arrival. He was coming by road, it having been found that there was no train that would reach Beckminster in less than three hours. In about an hour he would be on the spot.

Having undertaken to comply with the request of the C.I.D., Superintendent Bracer showed no lack of energy in its execution. He had already ordered that all available men on the spot should be paraded in the station yard, and others urgently summoned, before he found time to compare his own and his assistant's opinions upon the sudden excitement which had descended upon them.

"I thought," he said, "that the old jail was now occupied by Deepfields and Richardson. They're not going to tell me that Billy Richardson's running a kidnapping gang!"

"Sounds a bit loony to me," Bates agreed with the acquiescence which a wise police officer shows to his chief, and the cheerfulness of one who expects to get much less of the responsibility, and a bit more of the fun.

"Any part of it underlet?"

"Not that I know of. Better ask Billy about that."

"Not exactly. The first thing he's to know is that he's being run in, or, at any rate, can't go home to his tea."

164

"Well, it's only till Combridge arrives."

"And I'm glad it'll end there." Had he spoken all that was in his mind he might have added that he hoped so too. It would not be pleasant for it to appear that the old jail had been used for illicit purposes without exciting the suspicion of the local police, nor that the solution of the Merivale mystery had lain within half a mile of his own office. But whatever he thought, he had every exit of the old jail guarded within twenty minutes, and it was only three minutes later that Mr. Richardson, in the act of signing his letters for the evening mail, heard his office door open, and looked up to see Superintendent Bracer enter with Bates and two other officers behind him, and without the formality of having announced his coming.

"What can I do for you, gentlemen?" he asked, with perhaps something less both of surprise and resentment than he might have been expected to show, unless allowance be made for the fact that he was well acquainted with the Superintendent, with whom he had enjoyed many games on the links, and at snooker in his own billiard room, and that he was familiar with the other officers from the angle of one who had a seat on the local magistrates' bench.

"I am sorry, Mr. Richardson," the Superintendent replied, in a tone that was not unfriendly but somewhat more formal than their usual exchanges; "we've got a request from the C.I.D. that we can't ignore. Can you tell me whether your firm occupies the whole of these premises?"

"No, not nearly, if you mean have we got the whole in use. It's too big for our present trade. There's a good portion we haven't even converted from what it was when we bought it two years ago. There are the old cells still there. I don't mind letting you a few, if you're hard up for accommodating some of your guests."

"I didn't exactly mean that. Is there any portion you've under-let?"

"No. There wouldn't be many offers in the state it's in now. We've been adapting it, as our trade's grown. But if you'll tell me what you're driving at I may be able to give you more help."

"Could anything have been going on here for the last two months without your knowledge?"

"Yes, of course. Lots of things do. I've no doubt of that. I can't be everywhere all the time. What kind of things do you mean?"

"You have heard, of course, of the disappearance of Miss Merivale some weeks ago?"

"Yes. Everyone has."

"We have definite information that when she was first abducted she was brought here. We have confirmatory evidence in a letter received from her that she was kept here for several days, if not more. There is strong presumptive evidence that she is here still. I ask your permission to search the premises."

"Yes, of course. Though it sounds utter nonsense to me. I should think someone's been pulling your leg, or performing that operation on your friends at the Yard. But if you take it seriously, you don't really ask my permission. It's your duty to have a thorough search made."

"Yes. I don't deny that. But I'd rather have your consent, which I didn't think you'd refuse."

"Meaning you've got no search warrant?"

"No. They asked us to act at once. The information only came through half an hour ago."

"I see. You did quite right to come straight here. I'll give you one, if you like."

They exchanged smiles at the absurdity of this suggestion. Yet it was a fact that the Superintendent's position would have been more regular if he had had a search warrant signed by a partner in the firm whose premises he invaded.

Mr. Richardson's voice took a more serious tone as he added: "Of course, if Miss Merivale is, or has been, confined on these premises, I shall be only too glad to give you any help that I can, but I tell you frankly that I think it's a mare's nest. I know my staff fairly well, and I don't think it's possible that such a thing could have happened here, either with or without their knowledge." He rose as he spoke, and added "Shall I show you round?"

"No. I'm sorry, but I'm afraid I must ask you to remain here."

"Do you mean me to understand that I am under arrest?" Mr. Richardson asked, in a voice in which indignation and amusement appeared about equally mingled.

"No. Certainly not. But we'd rather do this our own way, if you don't mind. The information on which they're acting at the Yard seems to be of a very definite kind. Inspector Combridge is on the way here now, and he'll be taking charge within the next hour."

As he spoke a clerk entered the room. He looked at the group of police officers who still stood as they had entered, between desk and door, and at his employer, who had also risen as the conversation continued. He seemed to hesitate as to whether he should speak, till Mr. Richardson's rather curt: "Well, what is it now?" brought the reply: "There's the L.M.S. wagon here, sir; and they won't let us load it up."

"Who won't?"

"The police, sir. There are police all round the place."

"Never mind, Jackson. Let the wagon go. It's only a day's delay, and I dare say we can get compensation, if we think it's worthwhile to try. Tell the porter that Superintendent Bracer is going to search the place, with my permission, and he's to let him have any keys that he wants."

"Very well, sir."

The clerk withdrew, and the Superintendent, an experienced man in such judgments, decided that he, at least, was innocent of any guilty knowledge. Indeed, his conviction strengthened that they would draw in an empty net.

He had confirmed this conviction, in the course of a search which he had just completed, when he met Inspector Combridge, with his four companions, at the entrance to the premises scarcely more than half an hour later.

"Found nothing?" the Inspector asked, which was an easy guess from the expression of the man that met him.

"No."

"Nothing suspicious?"

"Not much, if anything. Nothing you'd call suspicious if you weren't looking for it before you began."

"Sure you've examined the whole place?"

"I don't think we've missed much."

"You haven't let anyone leave?"

"No. But I don't see how you can hold them here. There are over forty workpeople, besides the warehouse and office staffs, waiting to go home now. It'll be all over the town as it is."

"I've no doubt it'll go farther than that. Superintendent, we *know* we're right, and we can't afford to fail now. They'll have to kick their heels for a bit longer yet. What have you found that wouldn't be suspicious if we weren't looking for it?"

"Well, it's true that some of the old prison's been left like a prison still; and there are even a few of the old warders and such. There was a skeleton staff kept here after the Government gave up using it, till it was sold, and the firm took some of them over as cleaners and so on. Mr. Richardson acted kindly to them, and he says he's had no cause to regret it. They all had excellent characters, or they wouldn't have been were they were."

"So you think we've been stirring up a mare's nest?"

"I should think you've been hoaxed by someone who knew this place had once been a jail."

"Well, I don't. I'm going over it myself now." He spoke confidently, but he was conscious again of a thought which had been uncomfortably present and suppressed with difficulty during the drive of the last hour. Suppose Mitchell were deliberately leading them on a false scent? Suppose Billington had told him to do so? Or suppose he had not spoken to Billington at all? Had he had instructions from one of the Blinkwell gang (of the existence of which there could be little doubt since the discovery of the secret entrance to the Bruton Street office), after coolly fooling him into allowing that telephone conversation to take place without being overheard?

With this doubt in the rear of his mind he had kept Mitchell beside him, and had questioned him closely as to the instructions he had received from Mr. Billington while at Saxton Hall, by obedience to which he had first gained the confidence of Miss Merivale and her friends, and afterwards used that confidence to her betrayal.

The man's account was simple, and, in itself, credible. He said that he had, from first to last, literally and in good faith, carried out the instructions he had received from the Agency to which alone he was responsible. He had understood at first that his duty was to protect Miss Merivale from the risk of abduction, and these instructions had never been cancelled. He had been required to report fully, which he had done. He had reported that Miss Merivale might be going to a place at some distance, the address of which had not been communicated to him, to attend a demonstration of the invention in which she was interested, and his report had included the arrangement under which instructions for the journey were to be accepted only from Lord Britleigh himself.

After that, he had had a definite and detailed instruction from his employers, under which he was to do exactly what he had, in fact, subsequently done, including a specific order to inform Miss Merivale that those instructions were from Lord Britleigh himself. The confidence established by the fidelity with which he had carried out his previous instructions had rendered this deception easy, and it could be said in his own defence that, however inconsistent or even treacherous his conduct might appear, it had actually been consistent throughout. He owed no obedience to Lord Britleigh. He had, from first to last, loyally and to the best of his ability carried out the instructions of the Agency which employed and paid him.

He went even further than that in his own defence, asserting that he had not, in fact, known that any treachery was intended to Miss Merivale. The instructions, however they reached him, might have been those of Lord Britleigh himself, or of Sir Reginald, in whose interests he had understood that he was employed; the one-time jail, for all he knew, might have been the place where the demonstration would be made.

Even now he did not know why his instructions should have been so given that his mission of protection had been changed to that of betrayal. Such, at least, was the account he had given to Inspector Combridge as he sat beside him on the way to Beckminster, and which, as he heard it, he was disposed to believe; but faced with the barren issue of Superintendent Bracer's search, and seeing the evident scepticism of the man who was in the best position to know the uses to which the old jail had been put, and the characters of those who controlled it, the doubt returned. He turned sharply to Mitchell to ask: "Is this where you brought her in?"

"No, sir. It's not like it at all."

"Then where was it?"

"It was an entrance in Purser Street. It looked like a prison. Not like this." Superintendent Bracer turned his attention to Mitchell as he spoke, and for the first time he believed. It may not have been by any strictly logical process, for a lie may be circumstantially constructed, but the man's voice had the tone of truth, and what he said was a likely thing.

Beckminster Jail, like too many others, had been built with a deliberate ugliness. When the Government decided that it was an uneconomic edifice and should be sold, they were faced with their usual difficulty, from that and other constructional reasons, in finding a buyer.

When the very reputable firm of Deepfields & Richardson came forward with an offer to purchase, they found a Government department which was very willing to deal, and were able to secure the premises on such favourable terms—little more than the value of the land on which the buildings stood—that it was a reasonable set-off to the cost of the alterations which must be made to adapt them to the requirements of their business, and to the fact that they were more extensive than that business needed.

It was a natural thing that they should only undertake the cost of those alterations as, and so far as, the development of their business required, and it was natural also that they should transform the altered building, so far as possible, from the gloomy intentions of its first designer. They had, in fact, commenced their adaptations at the back of the building, and had made fresh entrances, both to offices and works, the large main gateway in Purser Street being rarely, if ever, used.

Now the Superintendent confirmed Mitchell's testimony before Inspector Combridge could cross-examine him further.

"Yes," he said, "that's where the main entrance is. You'd better come through and see for yourself." He led the way through prem-

169

ises, where there was abundant evidence of a busy manufacturing business being carried on, to a door that (he had been assured) was normally kept locked, and then down a long corridor, to cells and warders' rooms and offices which appeared to be still in the condition in which they had been taken over, even some of the original prison furniture having been left undisturbed.

They subjected these parts of the premises to a minute, and by no means fruitless examination, followed by an interrogation of several employees of the firm, including three women who were now engaged in cleaning or warehouse duties, and who had been previously employed by the prison authorities.

The strenuous denials of these women that they had taken part in any lawless activities did not save them from the fate of being sent for detention to the Beckminster police station. However stoutly they might protest, it did not alter Inspector Combridge's conviction that he was on the right track at last, nor that he was likely to come upon more than he had set out to find.

They went back to interview Mr. William Richardson, still confined to his own office, and whose temper that detention had not improved.

As they approached his door Inspector Combridge turned to the Superintendent to ask: "What sort of a man is he? The sort who's likely to be in an illegal racket for a good price? Or the kind of fool who might let things go on round him that he'd never guess?"

"I shouldn't say that he'd come in either category. He's a magistrate of good reputation. Not exactly wealthy, but quite a well-to-do man. But I've been friendly with him—golf, and billiards, and so on. You'd better judge for yourself."

"Very well. Perhaps you'll come in with me, and let me do the talking? And perhaps these gentlemen won't mind waiting? We can't all go in on this errand."

"You're not intending to arrest him?"

"Not if he replies properly. But it's impossible to say in advance."

"Very well. Carry on. I'd much rather you put it to him than I."

"Mr. Richardson," the Inspector began, when the two officers were seated opposite to him, "we've had a look round, and we've satisfied ourselves of two things. One of the cells has been occupied within the last twenty-four hours—I've no doubt by Miss Merivale, though I don't say we've real proof of that yet—the evidences had been very carefully cleared away, but not quite thoroughly enough; and we've found something else that we weren't looking for, though I don't say that I oughtn't to have made a good guess—we've found

170

signs that this place—the portion of it that's not supposed to be used at all—has been used for the storage of drugs, which have also been removed or hidden not many hours ago."

"I can only say, Inspector, that I'm completely surprised, and find it hard to believe."

"You might find it easier if you saw where a packet burst, and they couldn't get up all the powder that lay between the bricks. There are other signs besides that. But what I have to say is that while we're making no accusation against yourself, and I don't want you to take it the wrong way, still, here's the position. These premises are under your control—practically in your own possession—and they've been used for traffic in illicit drugs, and possibly in even worse ways. You're not bound to answer questions unless you wish to do so. I needn't tell you that, you being a magistrate. But we're engaged in a search in which every hour may be of vital importance. Can you give us any help—any information—that may assist us in the pursuit of those who, we have good reason to believe, had Miss Merivale confined here up to a few hours ago?"

Mr. Richardson, hearing the last statement with real or well-simulated surprise, paused slightly in his reply. Then he said: "I've told you already, Inspector, that what you allege is a complete surprise to me, and I find it hard to believe it now. But when I think how little this building has been used, or even entered, on its other side, I don't say it's absolutely impossible.

"You can judge from that ignorance how much, or, rather, how little, I'm likely to be able to help you. But it goes without saying that I'll give you any help that I can. Bracer wouldn't have needed to ask me that. He knows me too well."

"Thank you, Mr. Richardson. It's the reply I expected to hear. Could you tell me whether Professor Blinkwell has any financial interest in this business, or in these premises?"

The sudden question obviously took Mr. Richardson by surprise. A startled expression crossed his face, and was instantly smoothed away. "Do you mean," he asked, "Professor Elihu Blinkwell, the eminent scientist?"

"Yes, of course," the Inspector answered, with a note of impatience in his voice. "I didn't know that there were two of that name."

"Nor do I, but I thought your enquiries would be of a different kind."

The Inspector noticed that the question was still left unanswered. He said: "It's a question that's very much to the point. The Professor knows as much about illicit drugs as any man living."

"You surprise me again—that is, if you intend to imply that he might put his knowledge to any improper use." Mr. Richardson paused again. There was a moment of tense silence before he went on: "If I were to give you no more than a literal reply—if I were not really anxious to give you all the help in my power—I should simply say no. Professor Blinkwell has no holding in this company, nor interest in the premises. But if I answer you with entire frankness, as I wish to do, I must add that a lady who is, I believe, a relative of his wife, has a mortgage of five thousand pounds on these premises." There was a moment's further pause, so short as to be almost imperceptible, before he added: "There is also a shareholder who has a rather large holding—in fact two thousand shares—who, I have some reason to believe, is Professor Blinkwell's nominee."

Inspector Combridge said dryly: "I have no doubt you are right." The fact of these financial holdings might not be legal proof, but they removed the last trace of doubt from the Inspector's mind. Mitchell's tale must be true, and this the place from which Miss Merivale's letter had been written. But where was she now? Was the man who sat before them an innocent tool in the arch-criminal's hands, or an accomplice who could reveal everything if he could be persuaded to do so?

The fact that he had stated the Professor's financial interest in the business so frankly was in his favour, but—that second's pause of hesitation. He used it to realize that the information would be obtained sooner or later from other sources, and that he would be self-condemned if he should fail to divulge it now? It was hard to say, but every effort must be made to enlist his help.

"The information," Inspector Combridge said seriously, "makes it certain—if there were any previous doubt—that we are now on the right track. It becomes of the most urgent importance to discover when Miss Merivale was removed, and in what direction. Mr. Richardson, you know your own people better than we can—you know whom you can trust—whom you should suspect—I am sure you will help us in this as far as you can. Something must have been seen or heard. There may be things known or suspected among your employees, although they have failed to come to your own knowledge."

Mr. Richardson said: "Yes. Yes, of course. Of course I'll do all I can." He appeared to ponder, and then added: "We'd better ask Batson. Yes, we'd better see if he knows anything he can tell us about these matters." But the Inspector was not destined to discover whether this suggestion were of a helpful character, for as it was spoken Sir Reginald Crowe entered the room without ceremony.

"Sorry to interrupt," he said, "but Lord Britleigh's found out something that can't wait, or at least there's a constable who put him on to it, whom we mustn't forget if it leads up the right street." As he spoke, the room was crowded by the further invasion of Lord Britleigh, Mr. Jellipot, two or three constables, and a very seedy individual who looked sufficiently uncomfortable, which may be attributed with about equal probability to the uniforms which surrounded him or the natural diffidence of a modest man.

It appeared that Lord Britleigh, having been politely told to stay outside while Mr. Richardson was interviewed by those who had an official authority to do so, had developed a separate activity, and enquiries among the police who now surrounded the building, supported by Sir Reginald's pocketbook, which was very ready to open, had resulted in one of the constables introducing him to a man whose principal daylight occupation appeared to be that of leaning against a lamp post at a street-corner in Purser Street, by which means he appeared to obtain sufficient remuneration to render him a tolerated, if not welcome, nightly patron of a neighbouring doss-house.

From this favourable position he had observed a Standard saloon car containing several persons leave the main gateway of the old prison early in the afternoon. As to the exact time he was somewhat vague, but his other particulars were of a very definite character. The car was painted dark blue. Its number was DZ 3002. It was not singular that he should remember this. He was a man of leisure. It was a number that could be remembered easily. He had, in fact, seen the car before, though not often.

Leaving the local police to deal with the investigation of the recent uses of Beckminster Jail, and to release its occupants at their own discretion, Inspector Combridge directed his immediate energies to the pursuit of this car. The wires stirred till there could be few members of the police force throughout the country who were on duty at the time and were not alert for its detection. Further local enquiries confirmed the information already received, though with less exactness of observation. It was agreed that the car had turned left at the top of Purser Street. Apparently it was heading south.

Soon there was further information of a most definite character. At four-fifteen P.M. a car of the same description had come to a standstill in Swineham High Street, having some trouble with a wheel, which it had been necessary to replace with a spare, and this had required the borrowing of a jack from a local garage. The village constable had stood by while the work was done. The garage

173

proprietor could almost remember the number of the car. It had been 3000, or something like that.

It seemed clear from the time of this incident that the car had taken a straight road at a rapid pace. It appeared to be making a direct course to the south coast. Inspector Combridge, having first arranged for every police station in that direction to be pressed with further enquiries, and stirred to a fresh alertness, started in swift pursuit. He went in his own car, with the same companions, none of whom was willing to be left behind. Even Mitchell, his mind releasing itself as the hours passed from the feeling that he was a paid servant of Billington's Agency, and substituting, as his thoughts were concentrated upon the pursuit and rescue of Miss Merivale, the memory of a more natural loyalty, was anxious not to be left behind.

The Inspector, realizing that he might have violent and probably formidable resistance to encounter, borrowed a revolver from the Superintendent. He was followed by another car filled with constables, who were armed with such weapons as could be hastily found in the peaceful atmosphere of the police station of Beckminster.

So they pursued through the night. To tell at length of the speed they made, the clues they found, the final moment of half-triumph, half-suspense, when they saw the car they had pursued so long standing idly on the open downs, would be to rouse the false anticipation of a climax which did not come.

They entered the empty car, to find a sheet of open paper on the cushioned seat at the back, on which was written in a small neat hand: "Hoaxed again, Inspector Combridge, hoaxed again!"

Faced with this impudent message, and the empty car, the Inspector did not act as a more competent detective would have been sure to do. He did not find a clue under the cushion, nor apply his microscope to a half-burnt match. He did not even stop to decide whether the note had been written with a Swan pen or a Waterman.

He just got out of the car, and said: "Johnson, bring her along, if you find she'll run. It's London for us. I've had about enough of this sort of thing. I reckon we've got enough evidence now to put Professor Blinkwell where he belongs, and perhaps, when we get him there, we shall hear him alter his tune."

Sending his escort back to Beckminster, for it was evident that they would not be required further, he returned rapidly to London as the morning came, obtained a warrant for Professor Blinkwell's arrest without difficulty, and proceeded to the interview which has been spoken of in an earlier chapter.

CHAPTER XXXV.

PROFESSOR BLINKWELL, though he had finished breakfast, courteously resumed his place at the table, and seconded his niece's efforts to serve the needs of those who had invaded his room with so little friendliness of intention. When their cups were filled and their plates supplied, they continued to gaze upon one another for some time in a pregnant silence.

The Inspector did not relax the uncompromising grimness of expression with which he had entered the room. Lord Britleigh's face showed the alert impatience which was his most frequent attitude to disconcerting rebuffs. He had been even more decided than the Inspector that the right policy was to arrest the Professor and make him talk. Had it rested with him, he would never have agreed to that respite, even for the breakfast he needed, but it had been decided before he came on to the scene. Mr. Jellipot's face bore the inscrutable expression which the law teaches to those who expound and practise its treacherous perils. He had spoken one sentence to a decisive purpose. He might not speak again till there should appear to be an equal occasion. Sir Reginald alone looked in the mood to meet the Professor on his own ground and negotiate with him. Ted Mitchell was content to concentrate upon a really excellent breakfast.

Professor Blinkwell, looking round on his guests with an aspect of leisurely urbanity, concluded that they were in no hurry to open the conversation. It was one of those occasions when the superior intellect should take control. His eyes were upon Sir Reginald as he said: "And now suppose we talk sense?"

The Inspector answered with disconcerting curtness: "Suppose you begin?"

The Professor declined to be disturbed by this unmannerly answer. His eyes were still on Sir Reginald as he went on: "You will appreciate that I should be in a better position to advise if I were more cognisant of the events which have brought you here. If you

175

will inform me how you have spent the night, I will undertake to give you information of at least equal value."

Sir Reginald was quick to reply, before the Inspector could do so. "There's no reason you shouldn't know." He wanted to get the Professor to talk, by whatever means. The Inspector looked at him and remained quiet. He had learnt that Sir Reginald was no fool, and also that he was difficult to turn from his own way.

Briefly, lucidly, he began to narrate the incidents at Beckminster, and of the pursuit in the night. Before he had concluded, the Professor commented upon the narrative as one who foresaw its end. "Obviously," he remarked, "an abortive chase."

"Or we shouldn't be here now?" Sir Reginald suggested.

"No. I wasn't thinking of that. The trouble is that Inspector Combridge reads too much detective fiction, or takes it too seriously. I shouldn't wonder if he actually expected to find Miss Merivale in the car."

"It did cross our minds," Sir Reginald admitted, adroitly adding himself to the defence against the Professor's ridicule.

"And you didn't think that the man on whose information you relied might have had a small tip (I think five shillings should have been enough, or, perhaps, eighteen-pence too much) to tell you about the car?"

"Yes, we've thought of that, too. But too late to do us much good. But would you mind explaining, Professor, why we shouldn't have expected to find Miss Merivale in the car?"

"Because whoever has got her would presumably want to keep her unobserved, and that can't be done except in a crowded place. It's only in books that people are hidden in lonely spots that can be seen for ten miles round, or in little villages where a cat can't cross the road without being seen and remembered for half a year. When you saw the car heading the way it did you ought to have known that it was only meant to draw you off the right track."

"Then," the Inspector interrupted, "Miss Merivale's been taken to another town?"

"So I should presume. But you will understand that I know no more than yourselves. It is a mere guess."

Sir Reginald heard this retort with obvious dissatisfaction. Miss Merivale's present address was the one thing that he sought to know. Had he been fooled again? "Professor," he said, commanding his temper as best he could, "you promised to exchange information of at least equal value. You don't think you've done that when you've only told us that the Inspector reads too much detective fiction?"

"No, of course not. What I will tell you is that Miss Merivale, in my opinion, is in very grave and imminent danger."

"And while that's the case you let us sit talking here—"

"Sir Reginald, there is no occasion for any excitement. Besides, I could not judge the position till you had told me what had occurred already. Also, if I may say so without offence, both you and the other gentlemen present have shown such indifference to her welfare in the past. I might almost say that I have been the only one who has demonstrated any concern to make terms to effect her rescue."

Sir Reginald declined to be drawn aside by this curious proposition. "Why," he asked, "do you say that she is in peril now, if you don't know where she is?"

"Because it is a logical deduction from the premises which we all know. I may have further reason than that. But before I say more it is for you to say that you ask my aid, and for us to make an agreement concerning it. The Inspector's peculiar method of threatening to arrest me because he thinks I could do what he can't do himself may seem brilliant to the official mind, but I am scarcely likely to regard it as a satisfactory basis for any negotiations between us."

"The trouble with you, Professor," Lord Britleigh interposed, "is that you don't see that the game's up. We all know why you kidnapped Miss Merivale, and if any harm comes to her you'll have to answer for it in the dock, on the top of a few other things that were found out at Beckminster yesterday. The best you can do is to tell us just how we can get in touch with her, and how soon, and if she's safe and well you can call it your lucky day, even if you spend your first night in the cells, as you will unless you get bail, as you're not likely to do."

The Professor looked at Sir Reginald with a slight smile, which was the only emotion which this outburst appeared to rouse. "In view of the overwhelming rewards which Lord Britleigh offers for my assistance...," he began, and left the sentence unfinished.

Inspector Combridge felt that no progress was being made, and that it was time to deal with the position in a more orderly way. The claims of appetite were more or less satisfied, and, in any case, they had never had the first place in his mind. The suggestion of that breakfast had not been his.

"If that's all you've got to say," he interposed, "we'd better lose no more time. You can come in your own car if you like. But if you want to do that you'd better order it now." He thought that when he got him at Scotland Yard he might talk in a different way.

"I have already ordered my car," the Professor retorted coolly. "Having had what is evidently considered an exaggerated anxiety for Miss Merivale's safety...." He again left the completion of the sentence to the imaginations of those who heard him.

"Just a minute, Cyril...half a moment, Inspector," Sir Reginald interposed. His method might be right or wrong, but he could not endure the thought that while they skirmished there Evelyn might be in actual, and perhaps increasing, peril. So the Professor had hinted, and it seemed to him that, at whatever cost of compromise, the truth should be ascertained and the final reckoning left for the consideration of a later day. The Inspector might naturally incline to legal methods, might consider legal regularity of procedure to have weight even against the risk of a human life, but to him Evelyn was not "a" human life; she was the girl he loved. It seemed to him that their attitude went some way toward justification of the Professor's sneer, that they held her life to be of small account.

The Professor was quick to see the division of feeling among his foes. "If you would like me to retire," he suggested pleasantly, "while you talk things over among yourselves?"

"No, you don't," Inspector Combridge answered with emphasis. "You won't leave this room alone."

"I suppose it would be useless to tell you that I've no intention of leaving till we have brought these matters to a businesslike settlement? You can retire into the next room if you will, and I will stay here."

"That," Lord Britleigh remarked, "would be open to the same objection."

The Professor made no answer to this beyond a slight lifting of the shoulders. His expression implied that it may be necessary for a wise man to suffer fools patiently. He looked at the clock on the mantelpiece, and then at his niece to ask: "Isn't that a little slow?" The words were doubtless intended to remind them that while they talked, things might be happening elsewhere which it would not be possible to undo.

Sir Reginald understood the significance of the words, and it determined him to bring matters to the issue at which he aimed.

"Professor," he said, "this is between you and me. Tell me plainly on what conditions you'll release Miss Merivale, and I'll give you a prompt yes or no. I tell you straight, I'll go to a good price, and if you don't deal now you can see for yourself that you won't be very comfortably placed. You can't want anything to happen to her. She's the only good card you've got in a wretched pack."

But the Professor shook his head slightly. He looked at Sir Reginald's colleagues, indicating them with a gesture of the hand, as one who asks: "What can you expect, being associated with such madmen as these?"

Then Mr. Jellipot spoke again: "As one who is here to represent Miss Merivale, and is only concerned for her interests, may I suggest that I should have a word with Professor Blinkwell apart, which can be without prejudice on either site?"

Sir Reginald turned quickly to the Inspector. "You're surely willing to agree to that?"

"I don't mind if it's not more than five minutes," Inspector Combridge answered rather grudgingly. He was doubtful himself what was the best way to deal with the deadlock that had arisen, and did not wish to dispute it in their present audience. But you can't play fast and loose with a criminal charge.

Mr. Jellipot looked at Sir Reginald. "May I consider that I represent you also?"

"Yes, Jellipot. I couldn't be in better hands."

Professor Blinkwell made no objection to this proposal, and the two men retired together to the adjoining room.

CHAPTER XXXVI.

MR. JELLIPOT, as a negotiator, had the advantage of being un-swayed by any personal feeling beyond the genuine desire to protect the interests of his client. He was too familiar with all varieties of the criminal world to be conscious of any repulsion as he attempted the first requirement of all successful diplomacy—that of under-standing the mind of his adversary, and the motives that impelled his conduct. He had also, in spite of an occasionally irritating precision of language, for which legal training rather than character was re-sponsible, a habit of going very directly to the core of any matter with which he dealt. Being now anxiously aware that time might be a vital factor in the issue that was before them, he did not wait for the Professor to open the conversation, but put the position at once as he saw it to be, with some force and a commendable brevity.

"I want you to understand, Professor, that I have no interest in this matter apart from that of Miss Merivale's safety, and to protect her financially. When I say that, I speak for Sir Reginald as well as her. Help us to release her now, and I can promise you that no legal action will be taken against you by either of my clients, nor have any support from them. If you will consider, you will see that that promise covers a good deal of ground. Beyond that, if you will name any reasonable figure—even perhaps an unreasonable one—as the price of your present services, it will be paid.

"But if you ask us for that which we cannot give, and Miss Merivale comes to any harm by your delay, your position—whatever it may be now—is much worse, and you have made foes of those who might have been neutral, or even something better than that.

"Inspector Combridge is now aware of your secret office in Bruton Street, and of your financial interest in the Beckminster premises. He knows that those premises have been used for Miss Merivale's detention, and for the storage of illicit drugs. The consequences of that knowledge are beyond our control—probably beyond his.

"If you prefer that he shall arrest you, and leave Miss Merivale to her fate, whatever that may be, I can say no more, but it seems to me that your position will be gravely worse than it is now."

"If that were equally clear to myself...," the Professor began, and paused in an obvious hesitation, which Mr. Jellipot, who knew when to be silent, did not interrupt. He could not tell whether the irritating self-confidence of his opponent had been disturbed by his statement of the extent of the discoveries which had been made, for his expression had not changed as he heard them; but he knew that the moment of decision had come, and that it might be worse than useless to attempt to hurry it. Professor Blinkwell had, in fact, maintained a bold front before inward consciousness that he was on the verge of ruin unless the rapidly passing minutes—they were barely fifteen now—should produce some formula sufficient for his protection which could be accepted on either side. And all through the incredibly unlikely chance that Mitchell, on one of the few occasions when he had left his lodgings, had been recognized in the imperfect lighting of an East London street!

And now the Inspector had discovered the real use to which the Beckminster premises had been put. How had—how far had—Tonbridge failed to remove the stock which he had had such ample time to do? And there were only twelve minutes now!

"Will you tell me," he asked, "what reason the Inspector has for thinking that the Beckminster premises have been used for the storage of drugs?"

"A packet had burst in the course of its removal."

"That is no evidence that it was there with my knowledge; nor of the date when it was placed there. Unless it could be shown that that date was later than that at which the police already know that I was interested in that trade—"

"That," Mr. Jellipot agreed, "is a sound point."

"The trouble is," the Professor went on, in a tone of sincerity which was less than habitual, "that I would accept your terms if I could, but I will tell you frankly that it may be difficult to give you the assistance which I believe Miss Merivale's position requires without laying myself open to a charge which there is no evidence to support, unless I myself provide it."

"I have supposed that to be your difficulty. It appears to me to be a risk which you have become bound to take."

Professor Blinkwell had an inspiration. "Mr. Jellipot," he asked, "will you be my solicitor?"

Mr. Jellipot actually looked surprised, which he seldom was. But he did not hesitate in his reply. "So far as it would not conflict with the interests of my present clients, I shall be pleased to act for you."

"That would be understood. In the capacity of my solicitor I can inform you, in confidence, that a trunk call will come through for me at noon today at a call box about a mile from here. If I am not there to take it, those who have charge of Miss Merivale may understand that it is too dangerous to hold her further."

"And will consequently release her?"

"No."

"Then it is urgently necessary that we should start at once."

The Professor had recovered his serenity. "There is, in fact, plenty of time. It is now nine minutes to twelve. My car will do the distance in much less than five minutes. If you advise me to that effect, Mr. Jellipot, I am prepared to agree to the terms which you offer on behalf of your other clients. That means that I withdraw the condition on which I have always expressed my readiness to cooperate in Miss Merivale's rescue. I no longer stipulate for a half-share in the Ralston process. It is an enormous concession to make, and it is one that, I am well assured, you will use to my advantage in the final settlement. Beyond that, I leave myself in your hands entirely."

"It is a point to which I shall urge my other clients to give full consideration." As Mr. Jellipot replied he was already half way to the door.

Re-entering the dining room, he made straight for Inspector Combridge, who, he feared, might wish to delay for explanations which there was no time to give.

"The Professor will give us the necessary information. We have to go instantly to a call office. Miss Merivale's life is in grave danger if we delay."

"You don't think we're being hoaxed again?"

"No...but there'll be nothing lost if we are. There's no time to explain now.

They heard Professor Blinkwell's voice in a recovered serenity: "Myra, I hope you've been entertaining the gentlemen? You might ring down for my car to be brought round to the front at once. Yes, of course, Inspector, you can come in it, if you prefer. I expect it's a bit faster than yours. No, Myra, I'm not being arrested. I shall be back for lunch. The trouble with you is the same as with so many other women. You take the police seriously."

182

CHAPTER XXXVII.

"I WANT the telephone box on the island at the top of Corlton Street. Can you do it in two minutes?"

"Yes, sir. Under that."

As the chauffeur answered, the powerful car slid from the pavement and down the street at a pace which caused Inspector Combridge to congratulate himself upon the caution which had caused him to stipulate that he should be in the same vehicle. The occupants of his own car had already been informed of their destination, and must follow as best they could.

It was still a minute to twelve by Professor Blinkwell's excellent watch as he crossed the pavement toward the telephone box, with Mr. Jellipot on one side and Inspector Combridge on the other, and as they did so they could hear the insistent ringing of the telephone bell.

There was a moment's pause of altercation at the door of the box, which the Inspector desired to enter, to which Professor Blinkwell objected with emphasis, and while these views contended the bell ceased to sound.

"If you're not careful," the Professor said with more evidence of passion than he often showed, "he'll have rung off."

Inspector Combridge saw the force of that argument. He stepped back, and the Professor closed the door of the box. As he did so the clock of the neighbouring church commenced striking the hour.

The second car had come up by this time, and the Professor was observed by a dozen interested eyes through the glass door of the box. It was evident that conversation was not proceeding smoothly. He was observed to be agitating the hook. After a time it seemed that he spoke shortly after he came out. He was unusually perturbed as he said, in a voice which he controlled with difficulty: "Inspector, perhaps you can get them to say where that call came from. They won't do it for me. The fool had given up and gone off."

Inspector Combridge entered the booth. He was soon out again with the required information. "It came from Gravesend. Can you get them, now you know that?"

Professor Blinkwell appeared to be moved by an extremity of anger which he found it hard to control. "The utter fool!" he said with a grimness of intonation which threatened evil enough to the too-punctual culprit if he should come within the reach of the speaker's wrath. The Inspector was not sure that he had been heard. But the Professor's next remark showed that he had not only heard the question, but formed his own decision as to what its answer must be. "No. Not there. But perhaps we can. Not in your car. Inspector, what would you give to ransack the best hiding place that we've ever had, and catch some men that have been passing the stuff about that you've never even been following at all?"

The Inspector hesitated. "If Miss Merivale is still safe, we might overlook a good deal in the man who would show us that."

"I can't promise you she'll be safe. It's a matter of who's able to get there first, more or less. But I'll make them pay if I can." He added, under his breath: "Dropping the stuff, and then this!" It was evident that he was a very angry man.

Yet even then he may not have lost his self-control so much as he seemed to do. Faced with the fact that he had missed the call, whether by his own fault or the over-anxiety of the man who should have remembered the exactness of the obedience which he required, he may have decided wisely in his own interest, both upon the course he took and in the manner in which it was done.

He had made a bargain through Mr. Jellipot which would at least ensure a substantial monetary reward if Miss Merivale's rescue were still possible. He had added an informal understanding with the Inspector which might protect him from legal danger on other grounds and at the same price.

However much he might be throwing away his ambitious plans and the wealth he dreamed, he would still have ample means and a position of repute in the world. It was much to save.

He stepped back to his car. "Get out, Stoll," he said curtly. "I'll drive myself. You can take the other car back. Come on, gentlemen, as many of you as like, but there's not a second to lose."

He got in as he spoke, with the Inspector again beside him. He looked round to see that Sir Reginald, Lord Britleigh, Mr. Jellipot, and Ted Mitchell were all climbing into the car. Well, the weight wouldn't make much difference to his engine. Numbers might be useful. Who could tell? He lost no time in objecting. "When I mean to let her out to the full," he said, "I feel safer driving myself."

A few minutes later he spoke again: "I suppose you carry a gun?"

"Not often, but I happen to have one now."

"So have I. But there are a few others under the seat. It might do no harm to pass them round at the back."

"Are we likely to need them?"

"You may. I'll tell you more when we're out on a clear road."

"Very well. I suppose you know you're not on the Gravesend road. You're heading too much southeast."

"We're not going to Gravesend. We're for Batley-Fosse."

"Anyone starting at Gravesend would get there before we should."

"I know that. But it won't be much."

"How will they be travelling?"

"Jim Tonbridge usually uses a motorbike."

The Inspector considered these answers. They were not without interest in themselves, but he was most conscious of a change in the Professor's tone and manner. He no longer fenced or jibed, but spoke in a natural way, as to those who were united with him in a common purpose. And the mention of Jim Tonbridge's name brought a bitter anger into his voice, from which the Inspector judged that the determination to punish him had not been least among the complicated motives which had impelled the Professor to the promised disclosure.

And perhaps it would be best this way. A trial of Professor Blinkwell, on whatever charge, would be very difficult to handle so that matters would not be disclosed which were far better kept in the secrecy of the official mind. There was that old bargain by which the Professor had been induced to betray his correspondents, and enable them to break up the most powerful organization of drug-traffickers which had ever come under the notice of the police of the world. It had been justified by its results, and it would be gravely inaccurate to say that it had condoned murder, but it was certainly open to that construction.

Even last night there had been that abortive chase, and the jeering note with which it had ended. Inspector Combridge had a sound instinct that the Professor was not entirely innocent of its instigation, and liked him no better for that probability.

Then there was the way they had been fooled over the implication of Miss Merivale's letter. That he should have let the letter come through.... Practically delivered it with his own hands, as the Inspector rightly suspected. Why had he done that? Simply to make the police look such fools that they would not wish to bring the affair into open court? He was moved to ask this question. There was no harm in getting a little extra information while his companion appeared to be in the mood to give it.

"I wish," he said, "you'd tell me why you let Miss Merivale's letter come into our hands."

"Whoever did that," was the diplomatically worded answer, "it kept you busy looking at the wrong places."

"It was a great risk to take."

"I think not."

"And how did you—was it managed, to give Ted Mitchell the wrong orders?"

Professor Blinkwell turned his eyes from the road that was receding so swiftly behind him, to regard his companion speculatively. Then he appeared to decide that there could be no harm in a further frankness.

"I hold, as you could doubtless ascertain from other sources, if you should take sufficient trouble, a controlling interest in Billington's Agency."

"I see. May I mention another matter that is puzzling me now? You told us this morning that it was foolish to expect that Miss Merivale would have been taken to a solitary place, but we are now heading for what may be the least populated part of Kent. The district of Batley-Fosse—"

"It wasn't by my advice," the Professor retorted, with a return of the savage curtness which the thought of Jim Tonbridge's conduct had produced previously.

"You feel sure we're on the right track now?"

"Yes. If he rang up from Gravesend, it means this."

"And you expected not only that he would have made a longer effort to get you, but that he would have rung up from another part of the country?"

"Yes. Where from? Anywhere but that."

Inspector Combridge perceived that it was still possible to ask too much. He turned his attention to the little arsenal which he had been invited to investigate under the seat. He found several weapons of more modern construction than was the one he had borrowed on the previous evening, which he therefore exchanged. He offered others to his companions in the body of the car, which they accepted, with the exception of Mr. Jellipot, who said frankly that he had no familiarity with such lethal instruments, and would feel much safer without having one in his own pocket.

When this distribution was made, the Inspector ventured to remind Professor Blinkwell of his promise to enlighten them as to what they were to expect at their journey's end. They were on a straight road now, with the hand of the speedometer trembling in the vicinity of sixty-five, and the Professor answered in short, abrupt sentences, without withdrawing his attention from the slower traffic which he was passing continually.

"Know the woods below Batley-Fosse? Well, there are…about fifty acres. There are some old shafts in those woods. Sunk for coal which wasn't found, or not in thick enough seams to be worth working. Yes, I know. But those mines are ten miles away. These are just holes in the ground, fenced round, more or less, in little clearings among the trees. There were two or three bankruptcies over the attempts to find paying coal there, and the property changed hands time after time. Then there was a dispute over a mortgage, and it went into Chancery. No one troubles about it now.

"There's an old hut in those woods, where explosives used to be kept. Of course, it was emptied long ago. But a rusty padlock's still on the door, and the danger sign is still there. No one's very likely to try forcing that lock. Well, that hut's been used for the last seven years. It's had as much as eighty thousand pounds worth of drugs stored in it before now. Landed at Gravesend and taken there by car. Not straight, of course. The padlock's never been taken off. The way in is under the bushes, and some loosened boards at the back of the hut."

Inspector Combridge remembered that the Professor himself had pointed out the difficulty of maintaining secrecy in a thinly populated district. He asked: "Are there never any poachers in those woods? I should have thought—"

"So did we. There's a row of cottages not far from the wood. They're all poachers there. It's pretty well known that they think they can do all the poaching that wood needs. It's a lot healthier for others to poach somewhere else. I suppose they'll have to look out for another job now."

The Inspector observed the implication of this remark without comment. He concluded that Professor Blinkwell, having committed himself to the main disclosure, had become indifferent to the fate of inferior members of the organization, or he may have seen, with a sound judgment, that it would be useless to attempt to screen them.

"Do you mean that we may expect to find Miss Merivale in that hut?"

"Yes. If we're there in time."

The Professor's eyes went to the clock, and then to the speedometer beside it, and the hedges whirled backward faster on either side as he did so. They were in a quieter country road now, with little traffic upon it, but the surface was uneven in places, and the car bumped and swayed perilously as, with little slackening of speed, he took its abrupter bends.

He braked with a suddenness that threw them forward in their seats as a narrower lane came to sight on the left, into which he must make a sharp-angled turn, and then shot down a steep and curving hill, with a water splash at its foot, through which they plunged without pause to inspect its depth.

They struck the water with a force that shot it high overhead on either side, and as they came out, with scarcely diminished speed, and took the hill on the further side the Professor spoke again: "It's not more than two miles now."

"You think there may be an attempt to resist Miss Merivale's rescue?"

"I can't say how many'll be there, or what they'll do. If they think they've been sold—"

"I see. You mean they won't shoot because they see you, but if they happen to recognize me, and think that you've brought me here—"

"Yes. The best chance is that Jim isn't back."

"There's mustn't be any shooting unless they begin."

The Professor looked at his companion with a new doubt. As men of action they were strangers to each other. The course he was taking under the advice of his recently appointed solicitor held risks enough for his welfare. Had it to be added to these, that he was to face a gang of desperate men, who would rightly regard him as their betrayer, in the company of those who would be unprepared for the conditions of such an encounter? Well, it was too late to alter the programme now. He could but trust to his own coolness and skill. But he wished that a weapon were between his hands, instead of the wheel that he must not loose. If they could leave the car unobserved. All he said was, "Jim shoots quick." They ran on at scarcely diminished speed through a narrowing lane over which the trees closed.

Inspector Combridge had been too long in the service to which he belonged, had intervened in too many lawless episodes, to be easily stirred to excitement or by the anxiety of suspense. But as the moment of discovery neared even his mind was disturbed by the doubt of that which they were about to find. The deep blackness of the narrow hole, perhaps the broken edge when the last foothold failed as the victim was thrust over. Would they be searching those shafts tomorrow for a woman's body that must be found at last, broken or drowned? If his own mind felt the strain of this suspense, what must it have been for those others, brother and lover, who sat behind? He roused from those thoughts by the sight of another car which was coming toward them at a pace almost as reckless as theirs.

There was no possible room to pass. Braking abruptly the two cars came to a standstill even as their bumpers collided, the oncoming one having still sufficient impetus to carry them a short distance backward. It was a large open car like their own, crowded with men.

The man at the wheel was small and spare, with a thin nose, like a knife.

"Well, Professor," he said, "I didn't know you were coming here. But we haven't lost any time. It's a clean getaway, and no traces left."

Professor Blinkwell may never have had greater need of the self-control which had enabled him to overcome the previous crises of his lawless activities.

"You left trace enough at Beckminster," he said coldly. "What have you done now?"

"It's all buried so that it wouldn't be found in a hundred years."

"And Miss Merivale?"

"Wrung her neck, and dropped her down a fifty-foot shaft."

As he spoke, Sir Reginald, sitting in the back of the car, had his right hand resting on the cushion beside him. It was covered by a coat which lay on the seat, and also concealed the revolver which it held. As he heard this confession of Evelyn's murder, in a sudden passion of bitter anger, he raised the revolver to fire. It would have been the last moment of Jim Tonbridge's life but for another incident which occurred simultaneously. If Jim did not recognize a member of the C.I.D. in the man who sat at the Professor's side, there was one behind him who was better acquainted with the detective's appearance and had guessed the peril in which they stood. As he heard that fatal confession made, he rose to his feet with a gun pointing from either hand.

"Hands up," he called, "or I'll riddle the lot of you!"

Inspector Combridge heard, but though he hesitated his hands did not rise. His thought was to take the chance of drawing his own gun, and in another second his courage might have cost him his life, but the sound of Sir Reginald's shot burst behind him. Even as the man shouted his threat he sank dead, the bullet entering his throat in a slightly upward direction and penetrating the lower part of his brain.

In the same moment the men leapt right and left from the car, and dashed for the shelter of the trees.

"After them!" Inspector Combridge called out. "You can shoot now if they won't surrender."

Cooler, but no less alert than his companions, Professor Blink-well found time to look round to Sir Reginald to say: "It may be no more than a lie. There's been so little time." He called in a louder voice, as they ran forward: "This way! To the left! They're running back to the hut!"

The next moment flyers and pursuers had disappeared under the trees. The two cars stood with their bumpers locked, blocking the narrow lane. They were useless either for pursuit or flight, for there was no space either to pass or turn, and what speed could a car make in reverse under those crowding trees? Now and then a shot sounded from the wood.

CHAPTER XXXVIII.

IT had been about noon of the previous day when Mr. Richardson received a telephone call from Messrs. Tonbridge & Wilkinson (with whom anyone who had committed the improbable impertinence of listening in would have observed that he appeared to place an occasional bet of discrete proportions) as a result of which he rang up his wife to say that he should not he home for lunch.

Shortly after one, when the works and offices were almost entirely deserted, Jim Tonbridge came up the private stairs and entered Mr. Richardson's office without the formality of calling the attention of any subordinate to the fact of his entrance.

"Well, Jim," Mr. Richardson asked without cordiality, for he disliked the man himself even more than the risk of his intrusion, "what is it now?"

"We've got to clear from here in two hours."

"What's the trouble?"

"The Professor's got the wind up about something. I don't know what, but you know he won't stand for any risk. I cleared the office an hour ago."

"Yes. He's always careful." They agreed about that. During the last three months most of the heads of their organization throughout the world and a hundred subordinates had been arrested. Only the Professor himself, and those who were under his immediate control, had been undisturbed. How could they guess that it was by his treachery, and to save himself, that the others had fallen? Their former confidence in a chief who was as sound as he was audacious, as brilliant as he was unscrupulous, was increased until there could have been few orders which they would not have taken from him without denial.

"Can you do it safely at this time of day?"

"Yes. We've had a plan ready for that."

"Of course, you will be removing Miss Merivale also?"

"Yes. I rather think it is her they're after more than us or the stuff. I want to pass three men in before the works open, and I shall want some women to help."

"We can arrange that. You can have Morris and Wragge. Morris must be back at two, and she's to say that Wragge has gone home unwell. You can pass her out at your gate."

"That'll do for me. Any time after three, if the cops come smelling round, you can let them through."

"Yes. But I don't suppose they will. It's just one of the Professor's precautions more likely than not. Besides, Bracer knows me too well to suspect anything here."

* * * * * * *

It was half an hour later that Evelyn, who had already been roused to an alert curiosity by the tread of heavier steps than she was accustomed to hear, and other unusual sounds outside her cell, realized that, whatever of better or worse might be before her, the present phase of her captivity was over when the woman Wragge entered her cell and laid a bundle of clothes on the table.

"You'd better put those on at once. You're to leave here in an hour."

She had been told from the first that she was only in that prison as a preliminary to being transferred to a more permanent penal establishment. This may have been with no further object than to give verisimilitude to the nature of her first confinement, but she had sense to see that, however that might be, the heap of her own clothes which was now before her would not have been returned for the purpose of such a transit. Had her friends at last become active to help her? Was the nightmare over, and the moment of release at hand?

Anyway, she was glad to get her own clothes again. A certain looseness, of which she was conscious as she put them on, assured her that the anxiety and meagre diet of the last month had supplied a better remedy for the increase of weight which she previously lamented than her own less resolute efforts would have attained.

The subsequent return of her suitcase strengthened the hope that she was nearing the end of her captivity; but the fact was that those who controlled her immediate movements were themselves in doubt as to the ultimate issue of the orders which they had received. The letter which had been sent to Jim Tonbridge that morning through Myra's hands had been in such guarded language that he knew no more than that he was to clear the Beckminster premises, and to get into telephonic communication with Professor Blinkwell for further instructions at noon.

When he entered her cell, his manner was not uncivil, though it wasted no time in any superfluous courtesy.

"You've got to leave here, miss, in ten minutes. I want to know that you'll go quiet."

Evelyn's resumption of her own clothes had given her an increased confidence in herself, together with a sharpened sense of the indignities to which she had been subjected, somewhat confused by a humiliating sense of the deficiencies of her present toilet. She asked curtly: "Why should I? Where to?"

"I don't know, miss, so I can't say. But I suppose you don't want your head in a sack."

She saw that, especially if this were a commencing ritual of her release, her captors might have good reasons for wishing to conceal the place of her detention, and that in such an event it would be worse than useless to make an undignified demonstration which she had not the physical strength to support successfully.

"Very well," she said, in a manner as noncommittal as the words, but which seemed to satisfy him.

"I thought you'd be one to see sense," he replied. "If you call out once, you'll find it'll be the last time. I'll send along when we're ready to start."

He went back to the gateway yard, where two large saloon cars, of the same make and colour, stood waiting to leave. He went to the one that stood nearer the gate and abstracted from it two reserve number plates identical with the ones which it already bore. There is nothing criminal in a car having duplicate plates.

"Put these on," he said to the group of men who were now in the yard, and they proceeded to take off the plates from the rear car and substitute the duplicates, so that the two cars were now identical in numbers as well as general appearance.

While this work proceeded, the rear car was being loaded with a number of parcels, small but heavy, filling the space beside the driver's seat and the body of the car till there was barely space for two people to be seated within it.

"Wilkinson, you'll take the first car out. You know what to do."

The gates opened, and the front car, containing two men only, otherwise empty, innocent, licensed, and bearing number plates to which it was legally entitled, went out, careless of the number of those by whom it might be observed.

As the gates closed Evelyn was led to the remaining car. She got in as best she could among the cargo with which it had been

193

loaded, and a man whom she had not previously seen wedged his unwelcome presence beside her. The blinds were already pulled down, and the inside of the car was in semi-darkness in the gloom of the archway entrance of the jail.

"You'll keep a still tongue if you're wise," he said, to which she gave no answer, and there were no more words as they sat for ten minutes till the gates opened again, and they ran out into the lighter street, taking the same course as the car which had preceded them.

If there should be those who noticed such a car leave the jail—should even be alert enough to take its number—well, they were welcome to do so. The car that had a good right thereto was making itself conspicuous by its stoppages, its enquiries, even by an accident in a village street. It left a trail that would be easy to follow. The second car turned in a quiet road into a sideway that was little more than a cart-track and would have been impassable in wetter weather. Where the track broadened and there was a gateway into a wood on the left it halted under the trees, and the name plates were changed again, those which it had borne with so little right being thrown away among the bracken of the wood.

They stood there for an hour or more till there was the sound of a motor-bicycle approaching, and Jim Tonbridge appeared. He had now received Professor Blinkwell's telephoned instructions, and was better informed of the critical nature of the emergency in which they stood. The Professor's habitual caution had confined the conversation to generalities, apart from symbolic expressions and code words which could have no meaning to anyone by whom the conversation might be overheard, but his instructions had been clearly given.

Jim was to hide Miss Merivale, together with the stock of illicit drugs with which they had loaded the car, at his own discretion. No place had been mentioned. There were several within the knowledge and possession of the gang among which he might choose at his own discretion. The Professor wished neither to mention names on the telephone nor to be aware of the details of the way in which his instructions would be obeyed. But at noon tomorrow, wherever he might be, Jim was to telephone for further orders, and if there should be no answer he would understand that the position had become so urgent and so desperate that the stuff must be hidden and the gang dispersed. In that case, he must take such steps to secure Miss Merivale's silence as the position required, the nature of which was too evident to require specification.

"Boys," he said, "I'm going ahead. You'd better follow to Batley-Fosse. I'll tell you what to do when you meet me there."

There might be other places where Miss Merivale could be kept as securely for the night, but none that would be so convenient if it should become necessary to dispose of her in a prompt and private way.

CHAPTER XXXIX.

THE hut was not large. It was very solidly built of thick oak planks. It had no window, so that, day and night, there was no light within it, unless the oil lamp should be kindled which hung from the roof. It had an oak table in the centre, heavy and rough, and two chairs of the same style. There was a heap of straw on the floor at one side. On the other, shelves had been fitted, on which small, metal-bound boxes were neatly ranged.

Evelyn sat on one of the chairs, watching these boxes being passed out through the opening by which she had entered, where two planks had been removed in the back of the hut. It had been a stooping, crawling approach, through heavy undergrowth and beneath tearing briars, but she had not been unwilling to come, for she had a growing hope that she was being led to some bargained spot where she would be returned to her friends. She thought she had been ransomed at last. Doubtless it was hard to arrange a time and place at which she could be released and the money paid which would seem safe to both sides. Anyway, it was good to be once more in the open air, to meet the spring in the wood.

From an earlier experience, and her knowledge of the character and past occupations of the man to whom she rightly attributed her confinement, she could guess what those boxes held. It was natural that they should be removed from sight if her friends were to come for her here.

But the boxes went, and the men who handled them also, till there was only one left, and a woman with him. He was a man of a different pattern from those who had brought her there. They had been of the underworld of the city. This man, large, unkempt, unshaven, half-poacher, half-gipsy in his looks, was of the underworld of the woods.

He looked at Evelyn without hostility, yet in a way that she did not like. He reminded her of a dog that watches a tempting bone which it dare not touch. The woman busied herself for some time tidying the hut. It seemed to Evelyn that she was in no haste to go. She began to wonder what would be happening next. For what were they waiting now? Was she to be left here all night? With the thought, wonder began to take the colour of fear.

The answer came when the man pointed a thumb at the straw. "You've no call to sit there all night," he said. "There's a place to lie."

She looked at the straw without moving. "I think I'd rather stay as I am, thank you. How long shall we be here?" She hoped that she had succeeded in keeping the fear out of her voice.

"We can't tell that, as we're not told."

"Then they may be back any time?"

The woman answered. "You'd best settle yourself. They'll be gone for the night now."

"Aye," the man agreed. "They'll not be back before dawn." He turned to the woman to say: "You'd better clear now."

She seemed in no hurry to go. Observing this, Evelyn looked at her with more attention than before. A small, black-eyed, weather-beaten woman, probably worn by rough living rather than age. She was not a companion Evelyn would normally have chosen, but she was very willing for her to remain now.

"I dunno as I ought to be going yet, Saul," she said doubtfully. "Jim said as we mustn't risk being seen to...."

The man looked at her, and jerked his thumb toward the hole at the back of the hut. "Clear," he said, and the menacing monosyllable was sufficient to send her off without further words.

Left alone, Evelyn sat half facing her jailer. She realized that she was now utterly alone, and equally in his power, for her strength against his would have been of no more avail than that of a rabbit that he had trapped.

For what seemed to her an endless time they sat thus. She could not tell how long it really was, for her watch had stopped a week ago, and there was no clock in the hut.

The man showed no sign of fatigue. In fact he was more often awake in the night than through the daylight hours. He had been roused from sleep in his cottage three hours ago when Jim Tonbridge had sent Stitson to knock him up. Now he sat looking at Evelyn without motion or word, in a silence which she could not read but of which she had a fear that was hard to hide.

But when he rose it was only to say: "There's no call to sit there all the night." He went over to the straw at the side of the room. He took about half of it in his arms and carried it to the back, laying it against the place where the loose planks gave the only exit from the hut. Here he lay down, and was soon asleep. Evelyn saw that she could use the straw that was left in the same way if she would, but she preferred to stay where she was. Probably she would have been too excited, too restless, to sleep under such unfamiliar conditions, even had she lain down.

She could try to climb over that sleeping body, and force her way through the planks, if she would. It was not a tempting prospect. She imagined herself half through, and he catching her foot, pulling her back...or she was struggling through the brambles hearing him in close pursuit. But she knew that she would not get that far. She could not get through without disturbing him. He looked to be one who slept in a light way.

Yet he had put himself in her power, for there were weapons in the hut. A shotgun was leaning against the wall, and a long, sheathed knife was hanging beside it. There were other things that could do deadly harm to a sleeping man. Had he been debating in his mind in that long silence whether she were one who could be trusted to make no effort for her own freedom if he should go to sleep thus? Well, he had come to the correct decision. She knew that; though she was not sure whether she should consider it to be compliment or contempt.

Perhaps, had the position been more desperate, had she not had the hope that she would hear the voices of her friends on the next day—but that was no more than speculation—she could not tell what she might have been nerved to try. As it was, she knew that he had judged her soundly enough. He slept safe. So the slow hours passed.

He rose at last, so lightly that she could not tell when he had waked. Nor could she tell whether it was day, for there was still no light but that of the hanging lamp, into which he put some more oil. And as he did so there came a series of taps at the back of the hut, and then the planks were moved aside, and the woman came, bringing a rough meal of bread and slices of ham, and a jug of black tea.

Sharing food is a social habit, which inclines even strangers to talk together. Evelyn tried to draw them to speech, but she got little response. The man gave curt, monosyllabic replies. The woman would probably have talked freely enough had she been alone, but he was plainly unwilling that she should do so, and she had no will against his.

But when the meal was over she did not go. "Jim says I'm not to risk going back. He says there's too many about as it is. We're to stay here till he sends word."

The man scowled, but it was clear that Jim had an authority above his own. He only asked how long that was likely to be. She said they would hear soon after noon, if not before that.

After that he went out once or twice, though probably not far. He brought in some dead rabbits, and snares which he settled down to mend.

Evelyn sat and waited. It seemed that the time would never pass. Surely it could not go on much longer thus. Something—*anything*—would be better than this endless idleness hour after hour. Even in her cell she had made some occupations for herself. There had been the old Bible, which contained the history and the thought of a thousand years. You could never feel that you had quite finished the reading of that. She could not tell that every second of passing silence increased the hint, small hope that she would be alive at the coming of the next night.

But something happened at last, as it always must. There came what was obviously a code of knocking on the back of the hut. The woman answered it and went out. Voices could be heard without, though not words.

The woman came back, looking scared. She said: "There's Billy Stitson there. He wants to speak to you outside." She spoke the man's name with a contempt which showed even through her fright. Billy Stitson was of the disposition of which forgers and thieves are made. He had not thought that his downward career of crime would lead him to be the bearer of such a message as he had now brought.

The man went out. Evelyn felt a vague terror, prompted by the woman's condition. She asked: "Is something the matter?" But the woman made no answer, avoiding her eyes.

The man came back. He sent the woman off, and in contrast to the night before she seemed glad to go.

He came up to the table, standing before it. Evelyn, with the feeling that some crisis had come, though she could not guess what it might be, rose and stood facing him at the other side.

He looked at her with a glance at which she felt a sudden terror, hard to conceal, though it was not of a bad humour. He seemed to watch her with an enjoyable anticipation of what was about to come.

Feeling that she must say something, she asked fatuously: "Shall we go now?"

The question changed his face to a cruel smile. "You're not going at all. I've got orders to wring your neck and drop you down the shaft in the wood."

As he spoke he watched her, as though to enjoy the effect which his words would have. He saw the colour go from her face, but she answered with an attempt at courage.

"But—but you'd never do a thing like that...it wouldn't do any good. Besides, I can give you money. You don't know how rich I am. It would be such a silly thing. You'd—you'd get hanged."

"No," he said. "No one knows you're here. No one'd ever look."

"But I can give you any money you ask," she repeated desperately. "You can't get that much from them."

"No," he said. "Maybe, no. But I shouldn't live over long myself if I did that. There's no traitors in our lot." He watched the growing terror in her eyes as she realized that he meant what he said, and that there was no hope of pity from him. She realized that he was only prolonging the scene because he enjoyed watching her fear.

"I've killed a many things," he went on, "but I've never killed a wench before now, not except once, and that was just sudden-like, so that I hardly knew till it was done. It isn't much to mind, when I've once got a good grip. Just a twist of the neck, and it's all done." He began to move round the table, but not as one in any haste, or as supposing that she would attempt escape. That would have been absurd. He had her safe in the hut. He could have reached over the table had he preferred to do so.

She stood for a moment as though fascinated, too frightened to move, and as he approached he looked her up and down, and his face changed. "Not," he said, "that there's any hurry for half an hour."

As he spoke her eyes fell on the jug in which the woman had brought the tea. It stood on the table, empty now, near to her hand. With a movement as sudden as the desperate impulse from which it came, she seized it, and dashed it against his face. It was so unexpected from her previous terror-stricken passivity that he was taken absolutely unprepared. And in the strength of that terror the jug was shattered against his face. He staggered back, half-stunned, blinded with blood, and, as he did so, the woman put her head into the hut. She said: "Saul, there's something wrong. They're clearing off, and we'll be left—" And her voice dropped as the scene met her eyes.

"You she-devil!" he said, wiping the streaming blood from his face with a hairy arm. "You shall pay for this till—" Evelyn could not hear the last words. The one act of instinctive violence had roused her as though from a broken spell. She had crossed the room now, and caught the knife from the wall. She saw that the man was

still half-dazed, and in no condition to do her any immediate violence. She said: "If you come near me again—" and the knife shone
in her hand.

As she spoke, there came, deadened by the thick walls of the
hut, the sound of shots in the wood.

The woman said: "Oh, miss, if you please!" She was trying to
drag the man out of the hut. She said: "Listen to that, Saul. You can
hear them now."

The sound of shots was nearer, louder, by now. Jim Tonbridge
and his gang were retreating through the bushes, with Evelyn's res-
cuers in a close pursuit. They were retiring instinctively upon the hut
they knew. Billy Stitson, hiding in the bushes near, cursed them
from a cowardly heart. Why did they not go in any direction but
where he lay?

Sir Reginald Crowe, looking down ruefully at the empty revolver in his hand, found Mr. Jellipot at his side. "Considering the
probability that your ammunition might become exhausted should
the conflict be prolonged, and having no expertness in the handling
of such weapons," he said, "it occurred to me that it might be of
eventual assistance if I should bring you these." He held out the two
automatics he had taken from the hands of the dead man in the car.

"Thanks, Jellipot. You're a good man," Sir Reginald replied
rather more briefly, and ran forward faster than the lawyer, who was
very much out of breath (though even that had not shortened his sentences), was able to do. As advanced, he saw a man and woman
break from the bushes at the back of the hut and run away. Was the
woman Evelyn? No, she was too small. But the next moment he saw
someone who was more nearly of the right size. He ran on, careless
now of who might be in his way, or who might escape.

"Reggie," she said, "you always seem to come at the right
time."

Billy Stitson, lying under the bushes less than two yards away,
would have seen the age-old spectacle of a man and woman closed
in each other's arms but for the disconcerting circumstance that
Billy Stitson was dead. The only victim of the ill-aimed shooting of
flying and pursuing men, a stray, ironic bullet had hit the man who
crouched unsuspected and unsought. Inspector Combridge, having
found the entrance to the hut, and surveyed its interior with considerable interest, which included some speculation as to the meaning
of the bloodshed and the broken jug, looked round for Professor
Blinkwell, who, he rightly thought, was best qualified to inform him
concerning some, if not all, of the things he saw. But the Professor
was no longer there. Having had a few moments for reflection as he

had run after the men he had betrayed (but not quite so fast as his companions having less incentive to do so, and a strong objection to getting shot), and believing that Evelyn was already dead, he had seen reason to doubt whether there would be any real cordiality among his companions of the last hour sufficient to make it worth his while to remain to enjoy it.

He went back to the Bentley, which he put into reverse till he had backed it to a place at which it when he was able to move at a better pace. It was his own car.

There is another tale about him.

ABOUT THE AUTHOR

SYDNEY FOWLER WRIGHT (1874-1965) penned over seventy volumes of science fiction, fantasy, classic mysteries, historical novels, poetry, and non-fiction, many of them being published by the Borgo Press Imprint of Wildside Press.

www.ingramcontent.com/pod-product-compliance
Lightning Source LLC
Chambersburg PA
CBHW032006240626
47153CB00003B/1138